32 SECONDS

JOHANNA K. PITCAIRN

32 Seconds. Copyright 2014 by Johanna K. Pitcairn, published by The Manicheans.
Edited by Philip Newey at http://philipnewey.com/All-read-E.htm. Any remaining flaws/errors are entirely the author's responsibility.
Cover by Jenny Zemanek, jenny@seedlingsonline.com.

ISBN: 0990770818
ISBN 13: 9780990770817
Library of Congress Control Number: 2014916265
The Manicheans Carlstadt NJ

FOREWORD

Writing this book was tough, but I made it. After a million rewrites (maybe not quite a million, but close), I finally came up with something to be proud of.

A huge thank you to my editor Philip Newey, for guiding me in the right direction.

Hugs to Minnie Lahongrais, my dear writer friend, with whom I've shared sweet and bitter moments; and she still has a smile on her face!

Thank you Chris K. Without your wisdom I wouldn't have made it very far.

Thank you Jenny, for the amazing cover.

Waves to my writer pals, all over the United States and across the pond. Thanks to all of you. You are my inspiration.

A heartfelt thank you to Mom and Dad.

Thank you God.

And last but not least, thank you Nick for your love and support. You are a treasure I cherish every day.

To thine own self be true.

J.K.P.

*To you, all of you, who keep me sane
one day at a time.*

I

A clean slate was all I asked for.

My fingers tightly wrapped around the steering wheel of my Bubble—a name I cherished as a toddler—I cruised on the highway at a speed over the legal limit.

Leaving everything behind felt like the most natural thing in the world. Almost too natural. Adrenaline rushed through my veins as the high of my escape increased with every mile that separated me from the life I knew and the one I longed to live.

Glancing in the rearview mirror, I watched the city of Los Angeles disappear, the downtown skyline melting like ice cream in the sun against the pale blue ceiling. I took a deep breath. Air filled my lungs, releasing some of the pressure that had settled in earlier and, as my thoughts drifted, tears welled in my eyes.

I refused to look tired and puffy, but the dam had to be broken. Better now, when no one could witness my angry meltdown. I didn't like to cry in public. Showing even the slightest weakness made me feel like a loser.

A sudden shower pelted my windshield, reducing the visibility to almost nothing, but I maintained my speed. The black asphalt licked the bottom of my tires, striking every inch of the rubber, hungry to swallow me whole and transport me to my next destination. And at this point, I could go anywhere. Eager to get out, I didn't even care whether I died in a car crash. After what had happened between Mark and me earlier today, it truly was my way or the highway.

Planning my escape wisely hadn't crossed my mind when I ignited the V8 turbo engine and dashed out of the school parking lot like a hoodlum in panic of being chased and caught by a platoon of law enforcement officials, after an unsuccessful bank heist. Like I said, I wanted out. And whatever I wanted, I achieved by any means necessary.

Running away brought me closer to freedom. No consequences for my actions. No guilt. No pain.

As my foot pressed harder on the gas pedal, I listened to the roar of the engine, which threatened to remind me of the overbearing loneliness I continued to ignore. My hand reached for the radio and I turned the volume to high. My head needed that noise to over-write any internal monologues. Relentless, like waves on the shore, my thoughts wouldn't stop crashing inside my brain, giving rise to a series of hot and cold sweats, while my inner self kept screaming the same question.

Why did I always have to run?

Tears streamed down my face, leaving a thin layer of salt on my skin, which started to itch. Yet the pressure inside my chest didn't subside completely. I thought crying was supposed to make this friggin' ache go away. Useless measures in desperate times. The slight release I sensed had been a mirage, a glam glitz trick, just like my whole existence.

I exhaled slowly, my worries still bottled up inside like a cheap cola beverage knockoff. These darn feelings wouldn't stall me. Safely sheltered from the outside world in my Bubble, I clenched my jaw and focused on the road.

The blasting music kept me distracted. The treble crawled up the skin of my leg as I pressed my knee against the speaker encased in the door. I felt one with my Bubble, protected like a dozing child in a warm quilted blanket knitted just for me by my mom. I scoffed. Mom had never handmade anything for me.

The muscles of my arms tensed up when a light began flashing on my dashboard. What was coming my way now?

I squinted as the rain gradually eased, no longer cascading down my windshield like a waterfall. The fuel level was low. I knew the V8 turbo engine had a drinking problem, especially when cruising at ninety-five.

Where was the nearest gas station around there?

I grabbed my phone and pushed the main menu button.

Blip blip.

"What can I do for you?" Didi, my multipurpose software, asked with her friendly, although computer-generated, female voice.

I lowered the volume of the music before speaking. Didi was a bit deaf at times, especially when background noise distorted my words. Once she ran a web search for the nearest tattoo parlor instead of finding me a dough-nut shop. Maybe doughnut was a code word for hot and heavy business in Didi's language, and I had missed the latest upgrade memo.

"I need gas."

"Let me research the nearest location for you," Didi said.

I nodded. It took Didi a few seconds to work her magic.

"There's a gas station 0.7 miles away. Would you like directions?"

No, I'd use my Christopher Columbus compass to find it.

"Yes," I replied.

"One moment, please."

Right. Whoever engineered this software could have skipped a few steps, honestly.

"Starting route."

As I listened to Didi's instructions, my mind drifted again.

Dad would be furious at me for running away for the x-millionth time.

No matter the circumstances, my movie tycoon of a father always made it all better. He sat a phone call away from his attorney, and his tribe of assistants and second-ary and tertiary minions at the movie studios—not to mention my mother, who also served as back-up help every once in a while. To be fair, she played her house-wife of Hollywood role with much decorum but, since he won the movie lottery two years ago, she cursed my dad to the grave every time he asked her to cook him dinner. Two years during which our life went on full spin, from vanilla, middle-class suburban pace to high-traffic celebrity gossip columns, and I morphed from the nerd with short hair and thick glasses no one was interested in, into the troublemaking babe I am today. The same hottie people wanted to befriend, not because she became cool overnight, but because her daddy was rich and powerful. No one liked my sense of humor, although, I must confess, for my own self-indulgent ego boost, I am pretty funny.

My beloved daddy didn't care for my sick sense of humor either. But he did care about his mighty reputation. So of course he'd make it all better. There was no doubt in my mind about that. Did I want him to intervene though? Not a chance.

The light of the hungry gas tank kept flashing like a blazing dot on crack, reminding me how little my freedom meant based on practical considerations. Upon reflection, I wished I had stolen Dad's helicopter; then again, I hadn't planned my escape very wisely.

Impulsive decisions rarely produced successful outcomes. I would still try to beat the odds. Call me stupid. I preferred "willful".

"Arrived at destination," Didi said.

So there I was, one full tank away from that heck of a Sin City of Angels.

I parked near the pump and switched off the engine. Gathering my belongings, a Gucci patent leather wallet and my Dolce & Gabbana shades, I stepped outside and browsed my surroundings. The station stood like a post abandoned after the battle ended centuries ago, waiting to be rediscovered by a wandering traveler—in this case myself—in search of a few sustaining supplies. How could anyone work, even less live, in that camp of doom?

I never found answers to such existential questions about the mysteries of human nature.

As I selected my fuel and gunned the pump into the tank, I noticed, from the corner of my eye, the clerk staring at me from the window of the minuscule convenience store. The rain had done nothing to cool the air, and condensation clouded my lenses. I repositioned my shades on my nose after cleaning the foggy lenses with the fabric of my tank top, and my breath caught in my throat.

I didn't like people staring at me, especially when they thought they knew who I was. Maybe they had seen me on the latest edition of *Entertainment Tonight*. I had to be cautious, at least for the first five hundred miles.

The guy kept staring and I looked away, focusing my undivided attention on the pump. It finally clicked, indicating the tank was full.

I sighed with relief. I wouldn't have to stick around that middle-of-nowhere gas station for much longer.

I locked the car and paced to the convenience store.

The guy staring at me from behind his dirt-covered, microscopic pane was much less scary face to face. I smiled at the young, harmless fellow and handed him my credit card.

"Thank you," I said, before wandering through the aisles of the tiny store to check if there might be something else I needed.

I browsed the shelves, collected crackers, chips, pretzels, and water. Stepping back to the counter, I dropped the contents of my treasure hunt and smiled again at the clerk, like I had just won an award.

The guy continued to stare at me, looking disenchanted, probably because he worked in a hellhole; and there I stood before him, with my expensive outfit, awesome hairdo and perfectly manicured nails. Envious, much?

Steady breathing in place, I gave him a stare full of love and understanding. Yes, I'd also feel like doodoo if I worked there. Would he smile in return?

Nope. As stern as a rock.

"Your card has been declined, Miss," he said, and I sensed condescension in his tone.

"Declined?" My eyes widened, and my eyebrows shot up to my hairline. "That's not possible. Here, take this one."

I gave him another card from my wallet, one of the fifteen rectangles of plastic I proudly owned, and waited for him to swipe it through.

He shook his head. "Also declined."

Gosh almighty, what the fly was going on here? I didn't max out all the limits on the cards. There must have been some mistake.

"Impossible," I stated, as he swiped the remaining cards, one by one, until none were left to burn through the machine.

My level of frustration increased a hundredfold. Palms sweating against the counter, I struggled to contain the agitation rippling under my skin from head to toe, turning me into a hot, bubbling, angry mess.

The clerk's hand subtly slid toward the bottom of his cash drawer, where I suspected he hid a gun; and as he prepared to blow my brains out, because I couldn't pay for my pretzels and gas, I pulled cash from my wallet and handed it to him.

"Here."

The kid glared at me like I had lost my mind, then gave me the "why didn't you give me the cash earlier, moron" smile, and nodded.

"Have a good day," he said, and gave me my bag of goodies.

I immediately split, before getting trapped, like a mouse in a room filled with cheese death-traps.

Outside I shook like a leaf. The whole experience felt like something from a bad horror flick. After regaining my composure a little, I strode back to the Bubble. Still shaking as I closed the door, I started the engine and let it run for a while. The radio came on, and a stupid song blasted inside the car.

I closed my eyes. Breathe in, breathe out.

I was in control.

But tears, these tears drowning me in a puddle of deep resentment, against those who had put me in this awful and precarious declined-credit-card situation... These tears wouldn't stop falling.

I heaved and panted, my nose filling with snot, which I sniffled away, until I became too tired to even sniffle; then cried and cried some more. Glancing in the rearview mirror, I noticed my mouth had adopted a lopsided grimace of a grin. Not a pretty picture, overall.

A strong vibration erupted from my smartphone. A text message from my beloved father.

"All your cards are dry. See you home, Julie."

I threw the phone on the passenger seat and screamed, pounding the steering wheel with my fists. Tears burned my skin, and I didn't stop cursing until I was out of known or made-up curse words. My guts twisted in knots a well-seasoned sailor couldn't disentangle. My heart pulsed beneath my ribcage, like the beat of the music on the radio.

Dad could wrap his text message in gold and do cartwheels for all I cared. His strong-arm strategy wouldn't make me budge. Who did he think he was?

I was seventeen for banana's sake!

I didn't need him to save me. I could save myself.

Except, when I checked the cash left in my wallet, I counted exactly seventy-five dollars and twenty-seven cents.

Crapola. Seventy-five dollars wouldn't take me far. I needed food, and money for gas. I could always sleep in the Bubble to save on motels. But the rest?

I'd find a way out of this mess. After maxing out the volume on the radio, I put the car in drive and pressed the gas pedal, while another meaningless song played, almost making my eardrums bleed.

I looked too wealthy to beg. Finding a job as a waitress was a hundred miles out of my ballpark. But stealing? I could steal. Granted, small stuff, but petty theft would be a piece of cake. A guilt-free cake, at that.

Okay. That seemed like a good plan for now. I'd figure out the rest once completely broke.

2

Valentine's Day. Sitting at my vanity, I slowly traced a broken heart on the mirror with a tube of pink lipstick. In my head, I repeated word for word my dumb exchange with Mark over the phone less than an hour ago.

"Hey, baby."

Every time he called, I felt like a kid on Christmas morning. Mark, Mark, Mark... My obsession with him was unbearable.

"We need to talk..." But those words translated me into a reality I associated with another couple, another girlfriend. Not me. Every girl was eating her heart out because I was dating the Mark Wilson from the Wilson Family, worth billions of dollars according to last year's Forbes magazine. I must have misheard him. He didn't mean the talk.

"Yes?" Yet my voice was trembling. With shaky hands holding the cell phone, I stared at the wall, my heart dancing the flamenco inside my chest.

"Baby, you know how much I love you?" His words didn't sound right. I should have said I was busy, but couldn't bring myself to hang up on him now.

"Yes, I know you love me very much," I said.

"That's my girl." Listening to his breathing on the other end of the line, I wondered when the bad news would finally hit me. "Listen, I thought about something."

"W-What?"

"We should, uh, take a break. I feel the connection isn't as good as it used to be."

My whole world collapsed. A sharp pain bloomed in my chest and tears welled in my eyes. Cringing, I shut my eyelids and breathed in deeply. He wasn't serious. "Are you breaking up with me?"

"Baby! You know I love you, right? How much do I love you? Tell me—"

"Just say it!" I fired back, and prayed that the call was only a figment of my imagination.

"Baby, I think we need to see where we stand, a'ight? Taking a break doesn't mean I don't care about you. Because I do. A lot. I just think you need to work on some things... You know, like your anger."

What was wrong with him? I didn't have an anger problem. As I tried to hold back more tears, someone else's voice popped into the background. A girl.

"Who's with you?" My tone morphed into an animal grunt. I clenched my fist into a ball and my nails dug deep into my palm.

"Baby—"

"WHO'S WITH YOU?" The fury inside me was unleashed. Tears flowed like a torrent. I punched the wall above my headboard, right next to the poster of Leonardo DiCaprio on the Titanic. I had just hit an iceberg, and I was sinking in misery. Mark, why!

"You answer me right now or I hang up!" I screamed so loud my throat ached.

"Baby! Calm down. It's only you and me, you know that," he continued in the same mellow tone of voice.

"Don't tell me to calm down!" I punched the wall harder. "You're a lying piece of crap. A toolbag. A loser. A freaking cheater!" I stared at the bloodstain my knuckles left on the wall and sniffled.

This conversation wasn't happening. How could he do this to me? No one dumped me. I had never done anything to annoy him. On the contrary. Everything I did, I did it for him. And I compromised all the time! We were meant to be together. Who was the new girl? She couldn't be better than me.

Love was so cruel. I listened to his breathing. Silence invaded the exchange and lingered forever. Mark, tell me you were only joking.

"I'll call you later, okay? I can't talk to you when you're like this," he finally said.

"When I'm like what?"

"Your anger is too much for me, Julie. I don't know what to tell you when you're crazy like this."

Crazy.

Mark, my handsome and filthy rich boyfriend with the bright, hazel eyes, dark, curly hair, olive complexion, pearl-white smile, six-pack abs and impeccable pectoral muscles, neatly packaged in a five-feet-eleven-inch body that I wanted to devour every time I saw him, had just called me crazy.

All the memories of him smiling at me, hugging me tightly against him and wrapping his strong arms around my shoulders, while the scent of his cologne invaded my mind, instantly shattered to be replaced by rage. Blind rage.

Holding onto the phone like a lifeline, my fingers squeezed the device hard enough to break it. Tears continued to fall, but the pain I was experiencing wasn't just from the heartache. I felt cheated and misunderstood. How dare he call me crazy? Who did he think he was? Mr. Perfect? I had accepted him as is, and expected the same in return. But guys... I knew they acted like jerks, and always felt the need to tell girls how to behave. I thought Mark was different. What a lie.

Oh how much I hated him. How much I wanted to hurt him like he hurt me.

"I don't know who you are anymore. Have fun with your new piece because I'm done with you," I finally mumbled, and threw the phone to the other end of the room, where it hit the wall and exploded into pieces.

Just like that, we had closed a chapter that had lasted exactly eight months, five days, two hours, twenty-six minutes and forty-five seconds. But who was counting? Or waiting for her flowers and chocolates, and a dementedly happy teddy bear, holding a heart that said, "Forever yours"? Why didn't he dump me after Valentine's Day was over, huh?

Mark wasn't in the picture anymore. And I had made darn sure to show him how I felt today!

I went to school and did everything in my power to avoid thinking of him, but wherever I stood something screamed his name: his black Mercedes coupe in the parking lot, his locker next to mine and—the last straw—him in the hallway with his new girlfriend, Melissa. I should have been the adult in the relationship and let it slide. Right!

"Hey," I said. Mark had his back to me while Melissa watched me coming. The girl was very pretty. She wore a pair of tight black jeans and an off-white silk blouse, but with her curly blonde mane, high stiletto, patent leather heels, fake eyelashes, and red-painted lips, she still looked like a cheap version of my old self. I should've been the one standing next to him. Not her.

She smiled but kept her mouth shut. She was definitely dumber than she looked.

Mark turned around.

"Hey, babe, how are you?" He took a step forward.

I leaned back and sneered. "In fact, I'm happy you're asking that question." My uncontrollable anger was building like lava inside a volcano about to erupt. "Not so well," I replied.

Mark didn't say anything else, but it was Melissa's stupid smirk that ignited my fuse. As my vision narrowed, I lunged at her and my fist landed right on the bridge of her nose.

"Are you crazy?! What's wrong with you?" She shrieked, and brought her hands to her bleeding face. Slabs of mascara dripped down her cheeks. She looked like a raccoon. Her lipstick was smudged. Her expensive blouse was stained with tiny drops of blood. Scuttling away, she disappeared into the nearest ladies' room. All I could think was how good it felt to see her so miserable. Now it was Mark's turn.

"Proud of what you did to me?" I spat on the ground and waited for a response from him. But he just stood there. Silent.

"You're a loser," I hissed. Boiling inside, I clenched my fists as hard as I could and prepared to punch him in the nose too.

The bastard had broken my heart and he deserved punishment.

Intense heat invaded my body, and my vision blurred. Oh how ready I was to show him what I was made of.

Mark stared at me, a look of pure fright painted on his face.

Students gathered around us, and I overheard the voice of a teacher in the hallway.

My inner voice told me to leave. He wasn't worth the fight. I'd never get him back. He didn't love me anymore.

More students gathered around us.

I wanted so hard to show him how hurt I felt.

He stared at me like a deer caught in the headlights. And I clenched my fists tighter.

Now or never.

The voice of the teacher drew closer. With all those eyewitnesses, I would never have a chance to explain myself.

So taking what was left of the high road, I ran away to my car.

As I cruised through the next town, my eyes spotted a one-dollar store. Bingo.

Upon entering, I didn't detect any security cameras and, if there were any, it'd be too easy to remain in their blind spot. It wasn't my first time stealing, after all. I nonchalantly wandered among the aisles, picking items and stuffing them inside my huge Gucci bag. No one would ever suspect me of dishonest intentions. I just didn't fit the profile. I looked the part of a very nice girl in need of a few cheap things—like a toothbrush, and maybe some extra pairs of socks.

As I stole my goods, my heart felt lighter. Despite freezing all my accounts and credit cards, my father wouldn't have the last word in this battle. A confident smile creased my cheeks when I peeked at my reflection in a pocket mirror I also proceeded to take. This was easy peasy.

After my deed was done, I exited the store and walked to the Bubble, parked on the street behind the loading dock.

"What the heck?" Nervousness made me quicken my stride.

There was an old woman waiting for me, right next to the Bubble. She was dressed in rags and looked like a homeless person, which gave me a bad gut feeling. I hoped for her sake she wasn't leaning against the Bubble. I didn't have time for beggars, especially when I had just become a thief myself in order to survive.

My initial reaction was to tell her to beat it, but when she smiled at me and exposed a toothless mouth, I restrained my tongue.

"May I help you?"

"Lovely lady," the woman said, waving her hand like she was saying hello to someone standing way behind me; except we were alone in that one-way street. If she decided to mug me, no one would come to my rescue. It hadn't been such a good idea to park so far away from the main street and the crowd, but I didn't want to be noticed.

Anxiety tugged at my heart, and my eyes narrowed as she scuttled closer to me, like a squirrel ready to latch onto a fresh nut.

My instinct instructed me to recoil, but I stood still.

If she made a bad move, I'd punch her unconscious. I knew a few karate tricks, after all.

"You are in pain. So much pain," the woman continued, her voice broken; from years of smoking, I assumed. "Let me help."

She tried to grab my hand and I pulled back.

"I don't know what you want, but I'm not interested," I said, holding my car keys and sliding a key between each finger, ready to pop the rest of her teeth down her throat if she approached again.

The woman didn't seem scared and kept moving closer to me. When her lazy eye met my glare, she gasped.

"So lovely, yet so lost," she said. "I can help you."

I rolled my eyes.

"Leave me alone," I ordered. "I have no money for you."

"No, no. No need for money," she said. The stench of her dirty clothes made me retch.

What did I need to do to make her disappear?

"I don't need help. I'm fine. Now please leave me alone." I tried to reach the lock of the driver's door but she strategically positioned herself between the Bubble and me.

"You're hiding from the truth."

I cocked my head to the side.

"What truth?"

"Who you truly are," she replied, with a smile that made me think she was seeing things I wasn't privy to, and had no desire to figure out.

I suspected her words were those of a potential heroin-meth-crack-whatever-else-junkies-cook-these-days-to-get-high addict. A lump formed in my throat and my breathing assumed a staccato rhythm.

"Listen, I don't know what you want, but I've got no time for this." I couldn't stare into her lazy eye any longer. She gave me the creeps.

She went for my hand again, and this time I wasn't fast enough. My fingers pressed against her rugged skin, and she proceeded to study the lines of my palm.

"You're living in so much denial. You must listen..."

I pulled my hand away again, and exhaled like an enraged bull.

"I don't know what you want, but this isn't funny. Now leave me alone."

Shoving her away from my Bubble with my shoulder, I struggled to insert the key into the lock. The woman came back at me.

"I can show you your true nature. Don't you want to know?"

Honestly, not my main priority. I already knew my father had practically disowned me, so all I wanted right then was to get the heck outta there.

"Leave me alone," I repeated, pressing the set of car keys against my stomach.

"I know about your anger." She grinned like a kid in front of an ice-cream truck. Her eyes burned with excitement, and my frustration fired up.

"You do what, now?"

The blow with the car keys would happen in one... two...

"If you don't stop running now, you'll never find peace."

Her face didn't even twitch a little as she said that. I laughed.

"Go get high and leave me alone!"

"Your anger can be fixed."

"Really? And how so?"

She smiled again. "I can show you if you let me."

She wouldn't leave until I gave her what she wanted, so I played along. Was it worth jabbing her in the jaw just because she was delusional? Nah. It would take much worse to make me punch her. She didn't deserve a demonstration of my fighting skills just for saying a bunch of stupid lies that didn't make any sense.

"I told you, I don't have any money."

She shook her head. "No money. I'll do it for free if you eat a chocolate."

"Are you for real?"

No way she'd poison me, on top of being a real pain in the butt.

"Give me your hand," she ordered.

"Why?"

"Stop fighting and give me your hand. I want to help."

This whole charade had lasted long enough. Would she leave if I took the chocolate? I didn't have to eat it right away. I could pretend I would and she'd bounce. Meanwhile, I'd drive off.

"Fix my anger, huh? And you're not trying to poison me and sell my organs on the black market?" I asked.

"You only have to eat the chocolate," she replied.

Her eyes were drilling holes into my head. I didn't want to talk to her anymore.

"Fine, give me the darn chocolate," I said, just to get it over with.

As she dug into one of her pockets, I wondered if it wouldn't have been easier to knock her teeth out and flee. But I had caused enough problems with Mark today already; and after what Dad did to me out of left field, my plate felt full. Adding another collateral casualty to my long list appeared totally pointless.

She handed me a small dark ball.

"Eat," she said.

Hold on. I didn't want to eat this thing now.

"It's alright, I'll eat it later. Thanks for it. Very helpful indeed." I looked away.

She moved her hand to the side of my face and redirected my attention to her lazy-eyed stare.

"Eat now."

I really didn't like this.

"Will you promise to leave me alone once I eat this stupid thing?"

She smiled. "Eat and you'll see how much this chocolate will help you."

I sighed. So what if the chocolate was poisoned? Then I'd die and all my problems would go away. After everything that had gone down today, I was tired of running.

Who would benefit from all the stuff I stole at the one-dollar store? Well, this old lady just might. Not a huge loss then.

Sweeping the chocolate from her hand to my mouth, I swallowed the thing.

"Here, happy?" I asked. But before I could hear an answer, my whole world turned black.

B

My butt hit the pavement. As I opened my eyes, and tried to figure out where I had landed, an explosion popped right next to me. I ducked flat on the ground.

From the corner of one eye, I saw columns of blackish smoke in the distance, and the ruins of a town I didn't recognize. The air had turned into a toxic mess, making my eyes water. To add to the pleasant experience, a violent cough proceeded to shake my core.

The explosions continued and were deafening. My mind told me to run, but my body remained stuck in place.

I rubbed my eyes to make sure this wasn't a dream. It didn't feel like a dream. Maybe the old witch I met by the one-dollar store did poison me with her chocolate, and I had landed in hell?

My body trembled from head to toe. From the little I could take in, the area looked like a war zone. I needed to find shelter before figuring things out. Struggling up on my wobbly legs, I turned in a circle, trying to find an escape route. I strove to regulate my breathing. My lungs burned. I wanted to get angry, to scream and pound my fists at something or someone, but I felt so weak. The same question looped inside my mind. Where the heck had I been transported to, against my will?

Asking Didi for directions was out of the question, since I had been robbed of my phone too. It was clearly my lucky day.

A shape moved ahead of me. I thought it was smoke, or an optical illusion. After a few seconds, I realized the shape was coming in my direction. Shizznit. Was it an animal? The thing ran quickly toward me. Soon I realized that something was actually someone, and that someone looked like a boy.

The muscles of my legs gave up and I fell to the ground. The cough was killing me. My heart was beating at a hundred miles per hour, my quickened breath jamming inside my throat as I stared at the approaching stranger. He opened his mouth and said something, but I didn't understand a word through the ruckus of the incessant explosions. Through my watery eyes, I took in the sight of him. The dark-haired boy wore black jeans and a t-shirt, and his skin was covered in grayish dust.

He yelled something. It sounded like "un."

Not sure what to say in response, I waved at him.

When he finally reached me, I noticed his eyes were glowing green.

"Hey..." I slurred between coughs. To my shock, he leapt like a jaguar and grabbed my arm in the process.

"Run!" he yelled, and propelled me off the ground like I weighed nothing.

Caught in his grip, I had no choice but to follow.

My hand in the boy's hand, we ran like torpedoes through the streets. Buildings in ruins bordered the way. A thick rain of ash showered upon us. Fire blazed through cracked windows, and black smoke filled the empty space, preventing any natural light from piercing the thick cloak. Running didn't distract me from the cough destroying my lungs, but I couldn't catch my breath, as the boy pulled me along faster and faster.

We dodged abandoned cars and ran among fallen debris: torn fabric, plastic containers, and other trash, scattered throughout a mutilated town that stretched onward. I was out of stamina. The muscles of my legs still cooperated—but for how much longer?

The boy finally stopped by an opening in the ground—a sewer entrance.

"Get in!" he ordered, pushing me down.

Grabbing the bars of a ladder, I carefully positioned my feet on the first step and descended into the darkness. The boy followed, shutting the lid after him.

I could barely see below me. The tunnel smelled horrendously of mildew, and felt cold and humid.

I was dying to ask questions, but had to focus on not breaking my neck first. Moving down the ladder, I finally reached the ground. My hand felt a wall nearby and I leaned against it, panting.

"Okay, I think we're safe for now," the boy said.

I looked at him and my jaw dropped.

His eyes glowed so much brighter in the dark, like two flashlights.

He laughed. "Are you okay?"

"What the heck is going on?" was all I could say back. The green halo projected by his almond-shaped, laser eyes accentuated his perfect features: high cheekbones, strong square jaw, and a small dimple on his left cheek. He looked like something made from my imagination. Apart from all the dust on his skin.

"Alright, I guess I owe you a little explanation," he said. "Where should I begin?"

I coughed. "Who are you? And where am I?"

"I'm Evan. And this is the Underworld."

My heart did a somersault inside my aching chest. "The what?"

He laughed again. "The Underworld. After eating the chocolate, you arrived here. The Mighty Listener didn't have much time to explain everything to you, as you were showing resistance—which was expected—so the quicker she could get you in, the better. And she succeeded."

"Who's the what? You mean the old witch who poisoned me outside the one-dollar store?" I tried to wrap my head around what Evan had just said.

He nodded. "Yes. She was looking for you. Just like a private investigator."

I raised an eyebrow. "Um, okay. Why? Why was she looking for me?"

He exhaled deeply. "Darkness has taken control of you and prevents you from accepting your true nature. This darkness inside is fueled by a powerful mental obsession that jumpstarts your anger every time you feel you're not in control of what's happening to you. And the more obsessed you get, the more powerful the darkness becomes. If you let anger dominate every part of your existence, you will end up doing things you'll deeply regret. Things that will ruin your life. You've already done some pretty awful things you aren't proud of. In a nutshell, that's why you're here."

"Okay, wait." My voice broke. "What is this Underworld?"

"The Underworld is your mind, Julie."

I took a deep breath. These words didn't make any sense.

"How do you know my name? Last thing I remember, I didn't live in any Underworld. I left Los Angeles. And I got kidnapped. So where did you take me?" I shouted, before coughing again.

Evan moved closer and grabbed me by the shoulders.

"Julie Jones, I know what I'm saying sounds completely ridiculous."

I energetically nodded. "Yes. Yes, it does."

He smiled. "I know, but you need to deal with your past and change your present, so you can have a future. Things, bad things, happened because of your reckless behavior, and you've been repressing these memories for way too long. You have a problem. You act out and cause others to suffer. Today, you punched someone in the face and broke their nose. Why? Because you cannot deal with your life in any other way. Because your anger is the only feeling you know and you are deeply attached to it. Your mental obsession is driving you further into depression and to the brink of insanity. Running away doesn't take away the pain, or your loneliness. You always feel like you don't belong anywhere, am I wrong? Like everyone is against you?"

I lost myself in his bright green eyes.

"Mark cheated on me." I winced, struggling to catch my breath.

He scoffed. "You justify your anger so you can hurt someone? Physically harm them? Don't you think someone else would have reacted in a less self-centered fashion?"

"I'm not someone else!" I felt tears coming. "And you haven't answered my question."

"What question?"

"How do you know my name?"

"I'm part of your mind, and I'm simply trying to help you."

"I don't need help! I'm fine the way I am!"

His eyes widened. "Really?"

I hit a lump in my throat. Tears started falling and I remained silent.

"Being here is the only chance you have to turn things around and become a better person. Because as much as you want to convince yourself you're not"—he pointed at my heart—"you are hurting bad."

"I'm fine," I replied with a trembling voice. "I want to go home."

Evan pulled me toward him to hug me, and I didn't resist. When my body pressed against his, more tears flowed and I wept on his shoulder like a child.

"There's a part of you that seeks forgiveness, Julie. And I'm going to help you find it. Despite the state of denial you're in."

I wasn't sure why Evan made me feel so vulnerable, but as I kept crying the tension I had been feeling all day lifted a little. I wasn't proud of what I had done to Melissa. But how could I fix her broken nose? By now, I was pretty sure charges would be pressed against me. And Dad's earlier reaction proved I was on my own this time.

Darn it, I didn't want to go to jail!

Evan gently released his embrace and looked at me.

"I'd like you to meet some people who will also help you here. You're not alone anymore. Everything will be okay. I promise."

I nodded, wiping tears from my face with the sleeve of my jacket.

He pointed ahead into the darkness of the tunnel. "We need to walk down that way so I can introduce you to them, okay?"

I nodded again.

He patted my shoulder. "This darkness of yours is really dominating you. But hopefully you'll understand everything soon enough."

I sniffled and frowned.

"Come on," he said.

He took my hand in his and pulled me forward.

As the horrible cough subsided, I suffered now from a migraine. Part of me remained convinced I was stuck in a bad dream. The other part tried to understand what the heck this Underworld place was.

"It won't be too long now," Evan said, as we reached a fork in the tunnel. We continued to the left.

"How do you know where you're going?" I shuffled behind him.

"I've been through these tunnels a lot."

I huffed. "Will I be able to relax once we arrive?"

"Time is of the essence. Your condition will improve. Just have faith."

I stomped my feet on the ground. "Dude, this is too much to take in right now!"

He turned around and looked at me. "Here, here. Calm down."

"I don't want to calm down!" I yelled.

"Julie, please."

I snorted. "Why should I trust you? I don't know you. Maybe you drugged me so you could ask for ransom and kill me afterwards."

He moved closer and stared at me.

"You will stop behaving like this," he said.

My vision instantly fogged and my eyelids fluttered shut, as my thoughts narrowed to complete blankness.

Half a second later I managed to reopen my eyes— the headache was gone. What the heck?

"Dude, what did you do to me?"

"Are you feeling better?" He smiled.

His voice echoed down the tunnel and gave me the chills.

"I-I, yes, yes. But what did you do to me?"

"I told you. I'm here to help you," he replied.

I took a deep breath. "I don't understand. I'm not a good person, okay?"

"Let's keep going, alright? Stop worrying." He resumed walking.

"How did you take away my headache?"

"I have tricks. I helped you with your cough too. So you don't suffer so much and can focus on the important things."

"Do you do that with your eyes? Is that why they glow?"

"Uh huh."

"How did you come here?" My curiosity had been piqued.

"I belong to your memories."

"But how come I don't remember you?"

"Because... you blocked the past," he said.

"How?"

My line of questioning stopped as the tunnel came to an end and we entered a wider space, lit with a series of torches affixed to the walls. The room was in the shape of a dome. Many other tunnel entrances were visible from where we stood, indicating that this area served as a hub of some sort. I wondered where all those tunnels led. Maybe I'd get to figure it out soon. It was still hard to believe I had traveled inside my mind, because if I really had, my mind looked pretty darn unwelcoming.

A group of people waited for us. A girl with short bright red hair and glowing pink eyes came forward and hugged Evan.

"Good to see you. Happy you didn't get killed up there," she said, before looking at me. "Hi, Julie."

I didn't remember her either. On the chubby side, she was wearing black from head to toe, and her heavy makeup, jewelry and the piercings all over her face indicated she was Goth. I had never been friends with this chick. Goth didn't belong in my sphere of experience.

"Hi," I said back.

She chuckled. "I'm Susan. Has Evan told you why you're here?"

I nodded. "Yes. Apparently I'm inside my mind. And it's quite a lot to take in."

"I know," she said.

She waved at a petite Asian girl who immediately approached. Her eyes glowed neon blue. Her face looked familiar, although I was unable to situate her either.

"This is Miko," Susan said. "And you probably don't remember her."

I shook my head. The Asian girl with long, yellow, braided hair smiled at me. She wore a black blazer with a plaid skirt and knee-high white socks. Her shoes were pink Converses.

"Miko doesn't speak much. Her English is a bit broken. But she's a heck of a fighter," Susan continued.

I looked at Miko, then Susan, then back to Miko. "What is she fighting exactly?"

Susan grabbed my hand. "Your darkness wants control, and is destroying every bit of good left in you. Even if you don't remember any of us, that doesn't mean we don't exist. And we fight for survival. So we can help you find the true Julie again. Not this angry, cheap version of yourself."

"I'm not a good person," I said again.

Susan squeezed my fingers. "Yes, deep inside you are. Come on. Let's begin the journey."

4

Back on the street there was an explosion next to us, and I wanted to hide inside a hole.

"Why are we here?" I asked Susan.

"We're taking you back to where everything started," she replied. Evan and Miko stood right behind us.

"It's risky to stay in the open," Evan said, moving ahead.

Susan nodded. "Okay."

"Let's go."

"Where are we going?" I asked.

"You'll recognize the place. We have to keep moving. Quick!" he said.

"Why?"

His glowing green eyes briefly met mine, and a shudder traveled along my spine.

"Your darkness will catch up to us if we stay put for too long," he replied.

"What does my darkness even look like?"

"It comes in many shapes and forms."

"Like what?"

He cringed. "Like 'who' would be more accurate."

"Okay, then who is coming after me?"

"Your best friend, Kara."

The explosions continued and I covered my head.

"K-Kara?"

"Yes. And we're going to further trigger your memory," he said.

"Hold on a second. This doesn't make any sense."

"Just wait..."

Evan grabbed my hand before I could utter another word, and the four of us began our run to gosh knew where. We passed a series of torn buildings, made abrupt turns, entered alleyways, and took shortcuts through stairways and apartments, half hanging in the air, while explosions continued at a consistent rate and within deafening range. I kept my eyes on the ground to make sure it didn't give way beneath my feet. I couldn't hear much of anything at this point, not even my own breathing.

We finally slowed down in a zone where buildings were more spread out and posed less threat of collapsing on our heads. The explosions also diminished, although each one still startled me.

"Why would Kara be after me?" I ventured, my eyes browsing the desolated area from left to right. "And what is this place?"

"Oceanside," Evan replied.

My stomach tied in a knot. "Shizzle! This is not the town where I used to live."

He glanced at me and nodded. "Yes, it is. Oceanside looks exactly that way in your mind."

My heart sank.

"This is horrible."

"Quite a spectacle, isn't it?"

"I don't know what to say." Pressure settled inside my chest. "W-What happened to me?" I asked, my voice trembling.

"You don't remember anything, do you? Kara, Dan, Mike. These names... These people... You don't know what you did to them?"

I shook my head. "No. I-I don't know!"

"Oceanside died in your mind two years ago. You killed it."

I sniffled back tears. "Why? Why all the explosions?"

"The explosions are a result of the darkness destroying every piece of the puzzle that is your mind," Susan answered. "The more you destroy, the less you remember and, therefore, the less chance you have to move on. You're basically auto-destroying yourself by blocking your past—and all the memories you consider painful and unworthy of your attention. You think you're protecting yourself but, in reality, you're only causing more damage."

"Two years ago you suffered greatly," Evan continued. "You unleashed your anger onto the world you lived in, and shut yourself down completely. You thought moving to Los Angeles would give you a fresh start, but you took the ugliness with you. Changing geographics didn't change you. Your darkness grew and became uncontrollable. You tried to fabricate this new version of yourself, slimmer, cuter, more fashionable, but the true you never evolved. Your mental obsession latched onto you like a leech, and misery took over. You saw everyone as the enemy, and were unable to maintain any kind of relationships with your friends and family. Everything quickly fell apart. We had to find you and make you realize what you were doing before it was too late."

"What... What was too late?" My heart slammed against the inside of my ribcage like a caged animal.

"Before you drove yourself so mad, you'd contemplate death as your ultimate escape," Susan replied.

An explosion popped in the distance and I jumped. "Death? What? I don't want to die!"

"Are you sure about that?" Evan stared at me, setting me on edge.

I shook my head and looked away. "I-I don't want to talk about it." I took a deep breath. "Why is Kara after me, then?"

"Because you hurt her, and she's the main reason your mental obsession has become so strong, especially for the past few months. And you know the phrase, 'misery loves company'?" he asked.

I nodded. "Yeah, but I still don't—"

"There you have it," Susan cut me off. "Your darkness will remain powerful as long as you allow your mental obsession to control you."

"I-I don't understand what you mean when you say mental obsession. What did I do to Kara to deserve to land in such a hellhole?"

My question hung in the air as we approached a rectangular, low-rise, brick building. The inscription on the side of the wrought iron gates read "Oceanside High School."

"This is the first step in your recovery. Rediscover the place where your memories started collapsing. You remember your former high school, don't you?" Susan asked.

We crossed the gates and walked across the empty parking lot.

"I do," I said, feeling my chest constrict a little more.

Kara and I had been best friends since she taught me how to surf at twelve years old. I remembered facing the water, my board lying on the sand next to me. I didn't have a clue how to tame the waves. But I told myself it could not be that difficult. And, of course, I didn't ask anyone to show me how. Too stubborn for my own good, I had decided to teach myself something new that day. Surfing was all about good balance and decent swimming skills. And I certainly was a fine swimmer.

Kara happened to be one year older than me, and also my next-door neighbor. Of a shy nature, I had never talked to her. She scared me, to be honest. She seemed so confident, when all I wanted was to hide, like a little mouse.

When she saw me by the water, she must have sensed I needed help, even if I didn't ask for it.

The butterflies had been going hog-wild all morning in the pit of my belly, but the look in her bright, blue eyes changed everything.

"Listen to your instincts. I have faith in you," she shouted, as I entered the water.

My twelve-year-old body ready to engage the elements, I paddled away until a wave reared up like a lion stalking its prey. Swelling with my every breath, the watery mouth looked ready to guzzle me alive, and I fought the urge to swim back to shore.

"Go for it, Julie! Come on!" Kara cheered. The girl could talk. She had been surfing since she could walk! I stared at the mountain of water. "You can do this!" she screamed.

Gripping the board tightly, I set my eyes on the target. Three, two, one... I bent my knees, just like Kara told me to, and spread my arms as if getting ready to fly.

"Go, girl!" When I glanced in her direction for half a millisecond, she gave me both thumbs up.

"Banza-banana!" I screamed back. The wave smacked me hard in the face and I toppled off my board. Tasting the salt of the water, I felt a sharp pain burrow into my right knee. My arms battled to keep me afloat, but I still choked.

Back on solid ground, Kara took over.

"Hey, you're okay. You'll be fine." Her hand pressed on my chest as I slowly came back to what was left of my senses. "You surfed like a champion out there." Her fingers brushed the side of my face. "I'm proud of you," she said. Meanwhile, all I wanted to do was cry.

"Why would I hurt Kara?" I asked, as Evan pushed open the doors leading to the main hallway of the building.

"Because you let the darkness take control of your feelings," he replied. "And because your love for her was stronger than anything—once the friendship died, a part of you died with it. But you never truly mourned that loss."

"I don't remember why our friendship died." My heartbeat quickened as I set foot on old grounds. Like the rest of Oceanside, the school of my past had also been reduced to mere ruin. Paint was peeling off the walls, dust and trash covered the floors. The row of lockers looked like it would fall apart with a single breath.

Evan, Susan and Miko let me take the lead, and I ventured further into the hallway. I remembered the school when it was crowded and full of life. I would always stare at the ground, never looking people straight in the eye, too afraid of what they might think of me. I didn't feel comfortable in my own skin. My short hair and glasses made me look like a nerd. I hid under plain clothes and a heavy back pack, roaming the hallways and going to class, all the time asking myself what I was doing there.

I stopped in front of the locker where I used to stash my books. My fingers brushed the cold, rusted metal, then I opened the door and looked inside, to find nothing but ashes of old papers.

"What happened to me?" I asked with teary eyes, while searching for Evan's reassuring glow.

5

Ruffling through the contents of my locker, I was looking for my Spanish class syllabus. I needed a one-on-one to organize my crap a bit more efficiently. Since no one had volunteered to teach me that basic life lesson, I struggled to find the darn syllabus.

And gosh knew how much I hated Spanish.

As I started losing my cool—and losing my cool meant ruffling through the locker while tearing apart half the shizzle that was in there—I heard a voice.

"Yeah, man, that was a decent play, but look at Griggs, how he tackled that SOB. That, my man, was priceless."

Distracted from my locker rage, I froze and held my breath. Slowly peeking around the edge of the half-open locker door, my heart went on a full roller coaster ride as I studied the owner of the voice as discretely as possible.

His wet, blonde hair stuck to the back of his neck, his skin glistening from the shower he had just taken. The scent of his deodorant reached my nostrils—peppermint!

He was chatting with two other guys whose names I didn't know. My sixth sense told me these three belonged to the football team. When my eyes locked with those of the owner of the voice, butterflies ran havoc inside my stomach and broke the cocoon between my legs. Embarrassed, I blushed and muttered inaudible insults at myself.

"What's up, nerd?" the cute guy fired, obviously amused by my reaction.

I jumped and swallowed my words. "Um, um nothing. All done here." I didn't care about the syllabus anymore. Slamming the door of my locker, I fought with the lock while the three guys watched me, giggling. Where was the next space shuttle to the farthest end of the universe? I'd sell my soul to jump in and fly the heck out of there.

"See ya later, nerd!" the owner of the voice said, as I scooted away as fast as my legs allowed, and found shelter a few minutes later in the ladies' room.

Crapola! How could my lower parts explode in such a fashion just by glancing at him? Of course, this wasn't the first time my lady butterfly decided to take a hike and surprise me with delightful wetness in my underpants, but never had I been the victim of such deviousness when in eye contact with a real guy! My sexual discovery had been restricted to hot scenes in books, or in the movies I watched online at night.

"Hey!"

I jumped. In the mirror I saw a girl with heavy, black makeup and the outfit of a vampire-turned-grunge-queen-overnight, standing behind me. Heart pounding out of control inside my chest, I turned around.

"Hey," I said back, not to be rude. What the heck did this chick want? Embarrass me more?

"We're in math and Spanish together. Susan," the girl said.

Distracted by her nose ring, I made a face. She probably misunderstood my expression for confusion, but I stayed cool and brushed an invisible hair off my jacket sleeve. Why was she talking to me? Now was really not a good time.

I cleared my throat. "Yeah, I know who you are," I answered, and swallowed, only to hit a huge lump in my throat.

She smiled and stepped closer to the mirror to check her makeup.

"Mind if I give you a little piece of advice?" she asked.

I stared at her in disbelief. Okay, this little surprise encounter seriously deserved an explanation.

"What kind of advice?" I asked back, while repositioning my heavy back pack on my shoulder. What was I carrying in there? A whole artillery of machine guns?

"Stay away from losers like Dan Goldberg," Susan said.

My jaw dropped. So his name was Dan. Good to know. Wait. "How on earth do you—"

"Listen." She turned around to face me. "People aren't deaf or blind. I saw what happened by the lockers."

My palms started sweating profusely, and I choked. "No, sorry, uh... I feel a bit sick. I should go to the bathroom. I'll see you in class?" I said, while trying to ignore her raccoon-eye stare.

"Not digesting your Wheaties ?" she continued.

I shook my head. "I'm good. I don't know why you think you should talk to me about Dan, but this is really none of your business."

She chuckled. "Oh yeah. I hear ya." She pulled her cell phone. "We have a few minutes to spare until class."

I frowned and found shelter in one of the stalls.

While locked inside, I took a series of deep breaths. Gosh, I didn't need this chick to give me any kind of advice. She had to go. I waited until the last minute to exit and, when I did, made room for a clique of girls invading the stalls. Rushing to the sink, I busied myself with the faucet and, after taking off my glasses, proceeded to splash cold water over my face.

Susan was still standing there, leaning against the wall near the stalls. She wasn't looking at me, too interested in playing with her cell phone. I glanced at her reflection in the mirror. Susan, from math and Spanish class. Taller than me by a few inches, and also on the chubby side, she always dressed in black. Her hair was dyed bright red, and she painted her eyelids purple and black, colors that contrasted dramatically with the ghostly white of her skin. The last touch to the emo look was the black lipstick, and a ton of piercings all over her ears, in her eyebrows, her lower lip and across the bridge of her nose.

After putting her cell phone away, she approached the sink again and pulled the tube of lipstick out of her purse, adding more black to the already copious amount smearing her mouth.

When done, she smiled at me.

I exhaled loudly. Splashing more cold water on my face and neck, I listened to the toilets flush.

"You don't look that good," she said. "It must have been a really bad breakfast."

I drew in a deep breath. "I really don't know why you're talking to me right now."

She scooted closer to me, her hand resting on the ceramic sink.

"Well, allow me to share my thoughts with you," she replied.

Throwing a paper towel into the wastebasket, I put my glasses back on and scowled. "What?"

"You look worried," she said. "Scared even."

"Right." I huffed. "What do you want, Susan?" I recoiled and peeked at my reflection. "I do look a bit tired, that's all."

She moved closer until her shoulder touched mine, her steel blue eyes staring at me. As the knot inside my stomach tightened, she put her hand on top of mine. "I know Dan is cute. But every girl in this school worships him like a god and, really, besides football and his good looks, he doesn't have much more going for him. Stay away unless you want trouble."

Woah. My breath caught inside my throat.

"Why are you telling me this?" I dared ask, after taking a few more deep breaths to lift the weight from my chest.

She chuckled. "So many things happen. And they happen quickly too. One day you don't know this guy exists. The next, you're doing his homework, and are so madly in love with him you think he'll go out with you. Don't be distracted. I am giving you some friendly advice. Take it or leave it. You've been warned."

I had no idea why she was telling me those things. Pulling my hand away from hers, I grabbed my back pack off the floor and placed it on my shoulder.

"Okay. Thanks, I guess," I said, while moving away from the sink.

She followed my lead. "I know what I'm talking about."

I glanced at her once more before heading to the bathroom door.

"How?"

"Experience."

I nodded. "Okay, then I'll watch my back. Although I'm pretty sure there's nothing to worry about."

She laughed. "Don't be so sure."

The clique of girls that had entered earlier swarmed around the sinks like bees around honey, and I pushed the door open, completely unsettled by Susan's last words.

I decided after that day to avoid Dan, because apparently he had "mega problem" written all over him. Especially when I didn't have a change of undies handy in my already over-stuffed back pack.

Yep... Susan's advice poofed into thin air once I realized he attended the same math class, and asked me on some random day if I could help him with his homework.

"Dan Goldberg..." I whispered.

Evan put his hand on my shoulder, as I became overwhelmed with tears.

"This is good, Julie. You're doing great," he said.

How angry I felt! I slammed my locker door shut and kicked it with all my strength.

"What the heck is going on?" I screamed.

"Here, here." Evan pulled me toward him for another comforting hug. "You're making progress. It's normal to feel this way."

But I didn't want to feel this way. This way was horrible. Like my insides were all torn, and melted into one big pile of organ goo.

"I can't do this," I mumbled, pushing him away.

"Julie, wait," he said, as I paced down the hallway, tears streaming down my face. I didn't even bother to wipe them off.

"Julie!" Evan shouted.

My pace increased into a sprint through the hallways of the high school of my past, and this horrible feeling of dread amplified with every step I took. I felt imprisoned within my mind, with thoughts of hatred screaming from left and right. "You're a bad person!" the thoughts said. "You should stop running and accept your fate! You're only a liar, and all you do is hurt others. Why do you even care to live after all the crap you've done?"

These words poured in, drowning me as I ran as fast as I could through the abandoned building.

There was too much anger boiling inside. I opened my mouth to let out my frustration.

"Make it stop!" I shouted. "Make the horrible voices stop!"

My breath jammed in my throat as I crossed a curtain of cobwebs and arrived in an empty classroom.

The blackboard read: "I hate you."

A few seconds later the words disappeared like smoke, and more tears welled in my eyes. I fell to the ground, burying my head in my hands.

"Why?" I asked out loud. "Why is this happening to me?"

When I thought there weren't any more tears to cry, my body found a way to make me weep like a baby.

"Absolutely touching," a female voice piped up.

Had I heard right? Was someone else with me in the room?

I lifted my head. A girl with long blonde hair leaned against the teacher's desk. She wore a white cotton dress, pretty much like a nightgown. It looked very familiar. It was the exact same dress she had been wearing during her confirmation.

I gasped. "K-Kara?"

Her eyes glowed purple, and her face expressed no emotion, like it had been carved from marble. A dainty string of pearls with a tiny, silver crucifix pendant dangled around her neck.

"Why are you here?" I continued. "What did I do to you?"

She took a step forward. "My, oh my, what have you done to yourself?"

"I...I...I don't know what you're talking about."

The purple glow in her eyes intensified as she moved closer.

"Aren't you happy to see me?" she asked. "After all this time?"

I was petrified.

"I guess not," she said, before snatching my arm and squeezing it between her ice-cold fingers. I shrieked.

"Let her go!" Evan shouted from behind us.

Kara looked at him, and started laughing.

"You think you can beat me, tough boy?"

Evan grabbed me by the shoulder and lifted me off the ground. Kara's nails, buried in my skin, left behind bloody scratch marks. As I remained lost in confusion, Evan stared at me and his eyes glowed like fire, his face as stern as a rock.

"Find shelter," he ordered, pushing me backwards.

I stumbled until I found the wall and crawled to a corner, before grabbing my knees and pressing them hard against my chest to stop my body from shaking.

"You have no business being here," he said to Kara.

"Oh, really? My apologies, but I'm pretty sure I was invited."

"We'll see about that."

Green laser beams poured from Evan's eyes. In response, Kara released purple beams. They cast powerful jets of green and purple light at each other—the whole showdown felt like a Jedi battle, except their swords were their own eyeballs.

Shizzle, this was getting serious.

I watched them fight—while my lower nether region gave way in my pants. A wet puddle formed beneath me, trickling towards my feet.

Kara and Evan cast their laser beams at each other, moving from one side of the room to the other, burning chairs and desks on the way, leaping and climbing the walls like Spiderman. I absorbed the spectacle like I had been transported to a high-budget movie set, and was waiting for someone to shout "cut" anytime now.

That was until I felt a hand on my arm. I was startled to the point that I was ready to pee myself, had I not already done so, and my eyes locked with Miko's glowing neon-blue eyeballs.

"We go now," she said, while pulling me off my pee puddle.

"And E-Evan?" I asked.

"He be fine," she replied.

As we ran away, I worried about him, wondering what would happen if Kara burned him to the ground.

Susan met us outside the classroom.

She came up to me. "Are you alright?" she asked, while checking whether I was missing a limb.

"I-I am fine," I said, still shaking from head to toe.

I didn't want to stare into her pink eyeballs. All this eye-glowing business made me feel dizzy.

"Okay, we need to regroup in the stadium locker room. Evan will meet us there," she added.

"Will he be okay?" I asked, as we started running again.

She smiled. "It isn't the first time he's done this. We'll see him soon."

I was too shaken by seeing Kara, and peeing myself out of pure terror, to ask more questions, so I followed her.

The old football stadium looked like it had been swept by a hurricane. The ground, formerly a field of beautiful grass, was now a pool of mud, covered in various debris, including bleachers and shredded pieces of metal ramps. The goal posts lay flat at the end of the field, last remnant of a memory I had destroyed because Oceanside didn't deserve to be part of my life anymore.

Appalled by the state of complete destruction of the place where I used to watch Dan practice, immense sadness washed over me.

Dan Goldberg, the guy every chick had a dying crush on, like Susan said.

Even me.

Never thought in a million years I'd ever have a shot at being with him. I was fine with that. The nerd with the high school quarterback—that sounded clichéd enough.

I didn't have many friends—good ones—except Kara. Everyone else either considered me a freak or a waste of space. I never really understood why I wasn't cool enough, despite my father working in the movie industry. But Hollywood felt light-years away from us.

I hated high school so much. Despised all my nagging schoolmates. Kara was the only one who liked me for me, despite my awkward short hair and glasses, my slender, curveless figure and my non-existent sense of style.

Kara called the shots with all the guys. She looked cuter, with her doll face, golden locks and bright aqua eyes. She was confident about her stunning physique. She could have been an SI swimsuit model, except she only stood at five feet five inches. At fourteen, I was already five eight, but looked nothing like a centerfold.

"I'll show you what I can do," I said to myself, every time some moron made fun of me. Yet, feeling awkward about my physical appearance didn't mean guys didn't try to touch me in inappropriate places. They thought they could toy with the outcast, from a dare or mere curiosity; to practice their groping skills behind closed doors. I hated them all so much. But never said anything. Fighting back didn't help when no one cared about my feelings.

Kara didn't know about that part of my life. The emotional abuse I was subject to every single day was a secret I worked hard to keep hidden from her. When we were together, we only surfed and ate In-N-Out burgers, and laughed about stupid girl stuff.

First time I laid eyes on Dan, my heart took a giant leap. And every time he walked down the hallway, I almost had a heart attack. Hormones controlled all my reactions.

Out of all girls, I shouldn't have fallen in love with him. Yet there he was, proud as a peacock. I shut down my feelings the best I could, obviously.

Once Dan asked me to do his homework for him, I became his go-to girl. Must have thought I was pretty smart to trust me like that. Yeah. Gosh, how did I manage to fall so low? I still tried to shush the blooming infatuation. Try stopping a Boeing 747 from taking off with your bare hands. Exactly. Unless you're David Copperfield, I wish you luck.

So there I was, heading full speed towards a collapse of atomic proportion, Dan being the key to my release. And I couldn't, I just couldn't, get him out of my thoughts. He invaded my dreams. He became my main reason to wake up in the morning. I even worked on improving my nerdy looks by iron-curling my short hair and wearing tighter clothes—although I felt extremely uncomfortable in them. I wanted to please him, and bent over backwards to show him how attractive I could be.

But nothing I did really mattered, because he never loved me back.

6

I sighed. Susan was staring at me.

"What? I'm good," I said, looking away.

Miko covered my flank.

"You're remembering," Susan replied.

I snorted. "Yeah, right, all the uncomfortable high school teenage crap. Delightful. And you were part of it, by the way."

"Oh yeah?"

"Yeah, giving me warnings about Dan."

She smiled. "But you didn't listen, otherwise you wouldn't be here."

I scowled. Susan led the way. We exited the football field and entered the locker rooms, which looked just as bad as the inside of the main school building.

"Why was Kara acting so weird?" I asked.

Susan sat on the edge of a bench. "She's angry, man."

Miko nodded. "Very angry."

I took a deep breath.

"I don't understand. She was my best friend."

Miko busied herself checking the room, opening every locker, even browsing the inside of the showers. I sat next to Susan and buried my head in my hands.

"Clear," Miko said, before leaning against one of the walls and crossing her arms.

"The darkness is powerful," Susan said.

"I don't know anymore. I feel awful," I mumbled.

"Kara comes and goes. You're the reason she exists in this evil form, after all."

"When will I remember?"

Miko smiled at me, and Susan patted my back.

"It all has to do with how ready you are, girl. These things take time," she said.

I didn't know what to think about that, so I changed the subject.

"So the eye-glowing thing, what is it exactly?" I asked.

Susan laughed. "Oh, it's quite simple. The eyes allow us to cast light, and read what's inside your mind."

"Aren't you inside my mind already?"

She chuckled. "Yeah, we are. But you still control the game. We're mere players, trying to show you the way to go. You make all the final decisions."

"Does that mean I can get rid of Kara anytime I want?"

She shook her head. "You can't get rid of her just because you want to get rid of her. She's your memory. But you can certainly change the way you feel about her, and the way her memory affects you."

I sighed. "So I'm stuck here until life gets better, huh?"

"Remember, you gotta fight the darkness," she said.

I nodded. "Evan used his eyes on me."

"Did it work?"

"Yeah. The cough and headache went away. I found it a bit freaky though."

"That's normal. But you shouldn't worry about it. You can make your eyes glow too, you know?"

I raised my eyebrows. "How?"

"Well... You're not able to do it yet. Once you're more relaxed and see things for what they are, you'll be more in control. Your anger is still very strong. It powers the darkness inside this world, and makes memories like Kara very feisty. You got upset earlier, and Kara took the opportunity to show up. As you discover what happened to her, you'll grow more upset and she's going to be very vengeful. And she will come back, probably not alone."

"Who-Who's with her?"

"The other folks you hurt," Susan said. "Dan, and his friend Michael."

"I-I can't remember." I broke down in tears again.

"It's okay. You will."

"I'm in so much trouble."

"It's all part of growing up, girlfriend. You do stupid stuff and you learn from it. When the balance of light and darkness is compromised, a solution must be found. Your cry for help was heard, even though you thought you could run away forever and sweep all the stupid stuff you did under the rug. Punching Melissa in the face was the last straw. That's why The Mighty Listener brought you here." She smiled.

"But where does that Mighty Listener come from?" I asked.

Susan pointed her index finger upward. "She's a spiritual helper. She comes from another dimension. Her job is to save people from ruining their lives. Call her a guardian angel if you want. I don't really have a definition for her."

"She drugged me."

"You took something that would trigger the recovery process."

"Where am I now? Am I under? Am I in a coma in some hospital?"

Susan shook her head. "Girl, where you are doesn't matter."

I stared at her in disbelief. "What?"

"You are here," she said.

I started pacing the room. "I'm stuck in my own crazy mind! But where is my body?"

She shook her head. "Sorry. I don't have an answer to this question."

"Shizzle," I said under my breath.

"You're at a point in your life where you can think, go back, face the things you did, and decide to make a drastic change."

"Like what, make amends?" I asked. "Meanwhile my body is rotting in some dark alleyway, behind a one-dollar store?"

"Learn to forgive. Move on. Become a better person."

Miko nodded and the weight inside my chest crushed my lungs.

"Hey guys." Evan's voice pulled me out of my state of panic.

Susan hugged him. "Man! What happened to Kara?"

He laughed. "She's gone for now."

I was relieved to see him alive. Although that thought was a bit ridiculous, given I'd only known him for the past hour or so.

"What happened to you?" he asked me.

"Oh, I just got scared," I replied. "Seeing Kara all mean. You know, not easy stuff to witness. Plus the whole stuck in my own mind business without knowing where I really am."

"Right," he said.

Susan and Miko were staring at me.

I chuckled. "It's okay, guys. I'm fine. Not like I'm going nuts or something."

Evan gave me a hug I happily welcomed.

"Trust me, no one likes to face the ugly truth. But this is your wake-up call."

He broke the embrace but held onto my hand. Feeling his touch made me all mushy inside. I liked the warmth of his skin against mine.

"I think we did well for a first dip in murky waters. I hadn't expected Kara to show up so soon, but this is a good sign. Things should improve quickly. Let's go back underground," he said to me. "I'm sure you're tired."

I nodded.

"You can talk more with the others, too, at dinner," Susan added.

I smiled. "Okay."

We all exited the locker rooms.

Back outside, I glanced back at the football field. The goal posts now stood upright, as if some magic hand had lifted them back into their original position.

"What happened here?" I asked.

"This is a sign your mind is trying to replace the bad with good," Susan piped up.

"Does that mean Oceanside will look perfect again once I'm done here?"

Evan nodded. "That's the whole point. But one step at a time. These posts might lie back on the ground next time we come here. Don't be fooled by these temporary changes. The darkness won't be defeated easily."

My eyes met his glowing pupils.

"Okay. Baby steps," I said.

My parents and I moved out of Oceanside right after my fifteenth birthday. Dad had landed this hot executive job at one of the movie studios, following years of struggling to break into the Hollywood world. Before that, we never starved but never splurged either. After scoring a deal for a movie that became a blockbuster, over the span of a few months Dad swapped his small fish suit for a big shark tuxedo, and our life dramatically changed. Dad was thrilled to earn loads of cash and make a name in Hollywood. Mom supported Dad's decision. My parents sold our condo, right by the water and, despite Mom working to convince me there were beautiful beaches all around Los Angeles, I couldn't keep up with the revolution that was hitting us all in various ways.

At first, I didn't agree with the move. I refused to leave my best friend Kara behind. I put up a valiant fight, but Mom just rolled her eyes and placidly told me to check whether my room was packed.

When we left, something had broken in my heart, and I didn't care about Kara or Oceanside anymore. I actually welcomed the change of pace and the new scenery. I could become someone else. Land in a town where no one knew me, and build a whole new identity.

Eager to forget my past, I decided my life would start all over again. Julie Jones would look, think, and act differently.

Shortly thereafter, mood swings began controlling my actions. Happy one day, and depressed the next, I thought I was just going through the normal, rebellious phase every teenager experiences. But the anger grew. It was a feeling I held onto like a treasure. I started arguments. Physically attacked people.

The last time I got into serious trouble, the school principal awarded me with a one-month suspension. My self-defense argument had fallen on deaf ears. I argued the kid tried to grope my butt and deserved his just punishment, and I didn't care if he weighed two hundred and fifty pounds and was a senior. Nobody touched me without my consent. A hefty and aggravating civil lawsuit was avoided after Dad agreed to cast the kid's older sister in a horror chick flick that scored a few hundred million at the box office. She played a tiny role that landed her in the bathtub with her throat slit from ear to ear. Yeah, that movie sucked.

My life went on as if nothing had happened.

And the anger remained.

If Oceanside held the answer to why my anger blew out of proportion, I wanted to know. I didn't feel good about what I did to Melissa. Or this kid who touched me. Did he even touch me? Maybe he brushed my arm, and I took it personally too quickly.

I wasn't sure anymore.

But I knew I didn't want to be a criminal for the rest of my life.

"Are you alright?" Evan was watching me while I was lost in my thoughts.

I nodded. "Yeah. Tired. That's all."

"We have rooms where you can rest. I'll show you."

We walked through the Dome and entered one of the tunnels I had noticed earlier. His green glow illuminated the way before us. I really liked the idea of having magic pupils that could work as flashlights.

He stopped by a tiny opening in the wall.

"I'm sorry it's so dark in here, but we're working on it. Actually I should say, you're working on it." He smiled.

The dimple in his left cheek showed and I was sure I blushed. Thanks to the overbearing darkness, he wouldn't see it.

"Susan told me about my glowing power," I said.

"Ha, yeah, you'll get it too. In due time. For now, you'll have to rely on mine."

"I'm okay with that," I replied.

"Good. There's a bed in the corner. You can take a nap. I'll come get you when food is ready."

"Okay."

I lay on the twin bed, rudimentarily put together with planks of plywood and a foam mattress that had seen too many guests to still feel cozy. I was soon too exhausted to think much about my comfort and, as my eyes closed, my mind drifted once more.

7

I was sitting in the passenger seat of Mom's car. As we cruised on the freeway, I found myself playing a mindless video game, a tile-matching puzzle, on my cell phone. I had always been good at it—practice, practice, practice—but never managed to beat the last level—the pieces flew way too fast for me to catch and position them in time. Five seconds later, I restarted the level for the one-millionth time.

I cast a quick glance at my mother as the game loaded up.

"Who's the guy?" I ventured, fully expecting Mom to give me the same cold treatment as Dad had earlier today, when I ran into him in the kitchen.

"Richard Gold. He was top of his class at UCLA Law, received lots of awards and published a few articles in the press. The best of the best," she answered, and smiled at me.

The bad cop/good cop strategy being exercised full turbo ahead by my parents didn't ease my distrust of them.

"And? How did you find him?" I surely hoped he'd be the best of the best with a name like that. Did he hand free candy bars to all his clients too, just to make them happier with his "golden" services?

"Your father got a referral. We believe he will help you with your issues. You can't sacrifice your future because of this incident," she said, and I sensed a touch of condescension in her forced, friendly tone.

I scowled. "It was self-defense. There's no denying it."

"I know, but one small mistake can't prevent you from succeeding."

"Small mistake?" I repeated with derision. "There was no mistake."

"Oh, honey, don't be so hard on yourself."

She cast me a glance that made it seem like she actually cared about me. For one second! Was I indeed more important than her Cartier watch or her latest Lexus sedan? Only time would tell. Right then, I remained very skeptical.

Would this tough crap lawyer really change anything? I guess for appearance's sake in court I was better off with smarty-pants Richie by my side, or I'd say something stupid that'd send me down to the pit of hell in the blink of an eye.

"Right," I said, unconvinced. "Are you coming with me for the interview?"

"Yes, honey. I'll be there."

She didn't smile—and the same gut feeling kept nagging me that I couldn't trust either of my parents. Mom only called me "honey" when she wanted to prevent me from getting mad at her. Like it really worked.

We pulled into the garage located beneath a giant glass tower in the center of the financial district in downtown Los Angeles. Of course the law firm would be there, in a building that probably cost more to build than most cities. Referral or not, I didn't want to meet with an attorney.

After a small elevator ride from the garage, we entered the lobby of the building. Everything was disproportionately immense and looked very modern—i.e., cold and robotic, almost too futuristic, with a remote, sci-fi vibe. I didn't like this place. This suit Mom had made me wear stuck to my skin, and all I wanted was to toss it off and put on a pair of jeans and sneakers. Criminals weren't supposed to look better or nicer because they wore a suit. Stereotypical pre-conceptions that made me mad beyond belief!

I huffed and puffed as my eyes idly browsed the entire lobby. Two rows of escalators, illuminated by blue LED lights on each side of the steps, led to a higher level, equipped with more elevator banks. A large, abstract sculpture occupied most of the space by the main entrance area. The glossy metal projected the reds and oranges of the afternoon light into an improvised kaleidoscope on the floor. Made of stainless steel, the wide and ominous reception desk proudly bore "Gold and Associates, P.C." in gold letters across the front.

Fear struck me hard in the stomach as we walked towards the guy in a black suit, standing behind the reception desk. I could tell he wouldn't like being messed with. Just like a bouncer outside a nightclub, although I always managed to bribe those guys with a smile and a wink. Not sure whether that strategy would work here.

"May I help you?" he asked both my mother and me, without the hint of a smile.

"We have an appointment with Mr. Richard Gold," Mom replied in the same flat tone. Well, at least those two would understand each other. Me, on the other hand...

"IDs please," the guy in the suit continued, and extended his hand in an automated motion, ready to receive our driver's licenses like a ticket for a roller-coaster ride.

I ruffled through the contents of my purse and, after a few tries, found the wallet that had disappeared into the deepest and farthest corner of the bag—naturally. Why had I even bothered bringing my purse? I wasn't going out. I was going to see an attorney. And that bag weighed a ton.

We gave our IDs to the guy who took them without a thank you. Automated machines at an amusement park were more polite than that.

While the reception dude played with his computer and searched our names, a small group of men in business suits went up the bluish main escalator. Lawyers. They all looked too slick and boring. I huffed. My experience with members of the legal profession was very limited—mostly based on movies. With my luck, my lawyer would be the least slick guy in the entire office. I hated this place. Make it quick, make it quick. The movie studios where my father worked were way more entertaining than this joke of an office. People walked around in costumes and funny makeup. Not black or navy pin-stripe suits. The color palette around here would bore me to death.

"Main reception is located on the thirty-fifth floor." The guy handed back our driver's licenses, along with two visitor's passes.

"Thanks," I mumbled, and stared at the pass in my hand. The guy had snapped a picture while I wasn't looking straight at the camera. That profile of me was quite scary. I didn't like my face. Could we snap another?

"Have a nice day," the reception guy spat out and looked at us with a blank stare. I guess the alien face on the pass had to do. I said nothing in reply. If I had to be nice, it would be with the attorney I was about to meet. And I wasn't convinced I'd be nice to him either. As I said, I didn't like attorneys.

We ascended to the second elevator bank. Mom checked her cell phone every two seconds.

We didn't chat for the whole ride up to the next reception desk, where the same exchange and lack of eye contact played out. Were these people subjected to a lobotomy after being hired?

Once our identity and appointment were confirmed, we sat on a comfortable couch facing a panoramic view of downtown Los Angeles. Mom remained glued to her cell phone's screen. I didn't bother to pull mine. I had grown tired of playing video games and losing all the time.

From boredom, I moved away from the couch and paced around the floor. This office also served as a museum. Interesting. These attorneys had some feelings after all.

Expensive artwork was displayed on the walls. I killed time while waiting for Gold. I was more and more convinced we were meeting with the firm owner. Who else were Gold and Associates, if he wasn't the main guy?

As I idly gazed at the surrealist interpretation of a still-life of a cup of fruit on a wooden table, the man who appeared before me and proceeded to shake my hand, while giving me a commercial-like toothpaste smile, couldn't be more than thirty years old.

"Miss Jones? Hi, I'm Richard Gold. How are you doing today?" He asked this with such a confident tone, I lost my train of thought. Gold stood roughly six feet tall, built, with short dark hair, bright blue eyes, a tan complexion, and a cute dimple in his chin. Darn, he was cute.

I pinched myself.

"Nice..." I swallowed my words, "to meet you."

"Likewise. You found the firm alright?"

He seamlessly led us from the reception area before stopping by the elevator bank again.

"Um, yeah," I replied with an awkward smile. Even if we thought we had entered the wrong building, the huge name on the reception desk was a dead give-away. *It's a building you can't really miss.* But I'd save the smartass comments for later.

He laughed softly, and I instantly melted, like a scoop of butter on warm toast. How the heck did this guy manage to get his name on the firm? Strong connections? An iron fist? Extraordinary intelligence...?

"So who's Gold and Associates?" I fired.

The elevator doors opened and an automated voice welcomed us inside. "Thirty-fifth floor."

Gold smiled. "He was my great-grandfather. That firm was founded in 1906." He pushed the button to close the doors.

So Gold was a dynasty type of thing. Now I got it.

"Wait! This thing has no buttons." I looked at him, and he gently put his hand on my shoulder. Woah! The melting process quickened. Oh boy, had I suddenly ascended to heaven? Get a grip girl. This guy was your lawyer, not your date. Hormones, hormones...

"I selected the floor on the touchpad outside the elevators while we waited," Gold replied.

"Oh." And in addition to blushing up to my forehead, I felt completely stupid.

Looking at Mom, who acted like it was the most ordinary thing in the world, I sighed. Gold laughed again and forced a smile out of me. Yep, the ascension to heaven was under way. And I didn't hate this place so much anymore.

I couldn't think of anything else to say. Gold seemed to accept my silence as he removed his hand from my shoulder and shifted his gaze to the small TV located within the elevator. His touch still lingered through the thick fabric of my blazer. I was thankful he was completely absorbed by the Wall Street business mumbo jumbo playing on the screen, because I couldn't help but stare at him from the corner of my eye. Heat invaded my core as I studied his navy, pinstripe suit, perfectly tailored to fit his broad shoulders. I suddenly wondered what sport he had played in high school and college. Maybe football? He could easily have been the quarterback.

"Are you okay?" Gold asked. Darn, he was looking at me now. Could he tell I was feeling butterflies in my stomach? Locking eyes with his, I mostly read a hint of concern in his stare.

"Yeah." Brushing a strand of hair from my face, I forced a smile.

Gold awarded me with another slight pat on the shoulder, and the elevator doors opened.

"Twenty-fourth floor," the automated voice announced.

"Everything will be okay," he said. "As long as you have me around, you'll be fine."

His perfect smile made me believe every word that came out of his—beautiful—mouth. I was sure he had charmed many clients before me, so I realized I was not that special, but that did little to calm the flutters in my stomach. He looked too handsome to be real. I pinched myself again.

We proceeded down a narrow corridor, and passed a series of offices. I peeked inside each of them, and saw family pictures on the walls, expensive furniture, and tons of papers and brown folders scattered around the desks and floors. I studied the rooms until the final turn took us to Gold's solitary aerie, located in the farthest corner of the floor. I thought corner offices were for important people. So Gold, despite his youth, was a well-connected prodigy. Send me to Girl Scout camp! If this guy couldn't save my sorry butt, I didn't know who could!

"Are you thirsty?" Gold asked, as we sat down in the visitors' chairs. "I can offer you tea, coffee, hot chocolate or water."

His radiant smile made me feel so mellow.

"Water is fine. Thanks," I replied.

"Same for me." Mother finally opened her mouth, while not losing track of the latest alerts on her phone, which were obviously more interesting than her own daughter.

"Great, I'll be right back." Gold stepped into the hallway.

Since Mom wasn't keen on paying attention to me, I browsed Gold's office. It was very neat and organized. I stared at the degrees and certifications proudly displayed on the wall. Some were in English and others in Latin. He definitely held impressive academic credentials, as Mom had said. I could see no family pictures or girlfriend photo-booth snapshots discarded under a pile of legal documents. Oooooh. Stop it.

Besides the two guest chairs, the furniture consisted of a corner desk facing an immense window with a view of downtown Los Angeles, and a big, black, leather chair that seemed too comfortable for someone to stay awake in. I ran my fingers along the dark wood of the desk and pictured myself working there ten to twelve hours a day, answering phone calls and typing confidential letters at my computer, addressed to an important client—who could easily be my father.

I sighed.

"I didn't expect to come back and see a more somber face," Gold said, handing my mother and me each a plastic cup with ice and water. "Are you still worried about what might happen to you after what you did to this guy?" He closed the door behind him.

I shook my head. "It was self-defense. I said it a million times already."

Gold patted my shoulder again before sitting behind his desk.

"Well, let's relieve some of your concerns."

Pulling out a pad, he shuffled through several pages covered in notes until he found a blank spot. I drank silently, chewing small cubes of ice. The cold melted in contact with my tongue and gave me brain freeze. Ah, I didn't feel so hot for him right now. But Gold was too busy preparing his notes to watch me play like a child with my water. Gold finally lifted his head, glanced at my mother, and then focused on me.

"Alright, since you're still a minor, and it's your first criminal offense, we can get you off with probation and community service, and then expunge your record. This is the worst-case scenario. We'll also deal with the civil suit the plaintiff has started against you, asking for damages. You're sixteen years old. You come from a good environment and you're ready to make amends, yes?" Gold asked.

He now spoke like the guys on a TV show.

At the word "amends", I stared at him in bewilderment. "How am I going to make amends to someone who tried to assault me sexually?"

"Is that what you're going to claim in court?" he asked. "We could avoid a trial and work on some arrangement with the state and a settlement with the plaintiff, ultimately pushing him to withdraw his claim—"

"Wait, he attacked me. I defended myself," I interrupted.

He shook his head and frowned. He still looked too darn cute, even with a frown.

"Okay... He claims you punched him in the face without his initiating any physical contact."

He paused and doodled something on his notepad. "The judge will weigh the evidence from both sides and, right now, although it's his word against yours, the claim is backed up by photographs of his face, showing severe bruising and a cut on his lip."

I rolled my eyes and he put down his pen.

"Listen, your dad hired us because a criminal sentence on your records would seriously hinder your chances of going to a good college. So here's the deal." He started playing with his pen between his fingers. My level of uneasiness increased by the second. "You will apologize for what you did and cooperate with the state. We work on reducing the charges against you, and ultimately we want the civil claim to go away too."

I scoffed. "Dad should be able to work out a deal. I don't see why I have to apologize to a pervert who groped me because he can't get any otherwise. Why am I even here?"

"Julie, I understand you're frustrated, but I know you're a smart girl and realize the consequences these lawsuits against you will have on everyone—not only you—but your family too."

"So it's about Dad! His job! Great!" I threw my hands in the air. Mom stayed silent. Let her phone commit a crime and we'd see her reaction then!

"Talk with my father. I've got nothing to do, especially not to make amends to someone who hurt me."

"So we're going down the self-defense route?"

I groaned. "Yes. We are. I don't see why this seems so complicated. And Dad will work his magic and everything will be fine."

Gold's eyes narrowed.

"Fine," he said. "I'll speak with your father."

"Good," I replied, looking away.

8

I woke up drenched in sweat.

That lawsuit was nothing but a bad dream. The kid backed down because of money, and the judge assigned on the case believed my lame apologies and got rid of the entire thing to give me a second chance. Because I did apologize in the end. Gold worked hard to convince me it was the right way to go, and I followed his advice.

Maybe Melissa would do the same. My chances of getting another judge nice enough to let me walk with just a slap on the wrist were slim, though. And if my father refused to help me out again, where would I find the cash to make her shut up about what happened in school? I broke her nose before an entire audience of other kids, who I was sure were dying to bury me six feet under with exaggerated allegations.

My anger wasn't that bad. I couldn't help it if I had a short fuse!

I scratched my head and ran my tongue around the walls of my mouth. My throat was completely dry. I needed water. My stomach started making gurgling sounds too.

I slid off the bed. Since the room was pitch-black, I used my hands to find my way out.

"You're up!" A voice I didn't recognize startled me.

A light bluish glow illuminated the room, and I realized I had walked to the wrong wall.

I turned around.

"Hey," I said.

"Jeremy Sloan." He extended his hand.

His ashen hair was disheveled, like he had just woken up. He wore an XXL t-shirt that fit loosely on his slender body, and long baggy shorts, with gray-washed Vans sneakers.

"Hey, Jeremy," I replied, reciprocating the handshake.

"Call me Sloan. Jeremy is for morons."

I smiled. "Okay, Sloan."

"Dinner's ready. Are you hungry?"

My stomach made gurgling sounds again. "Starving," I said.

"Good, then let's go."

I followed his glow until we reached the center of the Dome.

A table had been set up, and Evan, Susan, Miko and another kid I hadn't been introduced to yet, who was Sloan's mirror image except for the apron, busied themselves with platters.

"Is that your twin brother?" I asked as we approached the table.

Sloan nodded. "Yep. His name's Sky. He's the cook here. His feelings get hurt easily, so don't tell him his cooking sucks or else..."

"I got it."

He smiled and led me to a seat next to Susan.

"How was your nap?" she asked, as I sat down.

"I had a dream," I said.

"What kind of dream?" She handed me a platter of watermelon.

Seeing food made me salivate like crazy. I pushed a bunch of watermelon cubes onto my plate and started eating.

"I dreamt of my attorney," I replied with a mouth full.

The watermelon melted on my tongue and the sweet flavor immediately made me feel better.

"And..." Susan prompted.

"The first time I met with him, after I punched this kid in school. He got me out of a lawsuit. Well, Dad and he did."

I kept on chewing. Sloan sat between Miko and his twin across from Susan and me, while Evan occupied a seat at the end of the table, separating Miko and Susan.

Another platter came my way, this time covered with weird looking critters.

"What are those?" I asked.

"Rats," Susan replied. "Here have one." She stabbed one of the creatures in the abdomen and put it on my plate.

I grimaced at the sight of the tiny legs and shrunken body.

"I... I don't know if I should." I gulped down more watermelon.

"Try it. It's delicious, I swear," Susan said. "Sky's extra touch makes them taste like chicken."

She ripped one leg off the rat she had on her plate and gnawed on the thing.

Cautiously, I cut a tiny piece of the animal with my knife and bit into it.

"Wow," I said. "This really tastes like chicken."

Susan laughed. "Yes."

"Why rats?" I asked.

"We gotta eat what we find."

"You could eat fish."

She scoffed. "Right. You haven't seen the state of the ocean lately."

I remembered the beach in Oceanside. Kara and I used to sit and watch the sunset. The sky always turned bright pink and purple before the sun disappeared below the horizon, and stars lit up like diamonds. We took our boards and surfed at night. The water spread like crude oil as the moon played hide-and-seek behind a thick cloak of clouds. Darkness stretched for miles around, and I listened to the ocean. Waves whipped the shore in an even rhythm, bringing my heartbeat to a perfect pitch. The moonlight kissed the surface in irregular patches, as I slowly paddled against the current. I felt no fear, just anticipation of the first outline of water I'd get to tame before the clock struck midnight. The countdown started in my head. Five... Four... Three... Two... I caught a wave and a thrill ran through my body like a jolt of electricity. I was one with the board, one with Mother Nature.

"So tell me about this attorney of yours." Susan brought me back to the harsh reality of the Underworld.

I shook my head. "The judge on the case liked me, so I walked free. As for the kid's family, my father worked his money magic and agreed to cast his sister in one of the movies he was working on. I didn't go to jail or anything. Like nothing happened."

I ate a bit more of the rat, but my stomach tensed up.

"Do you have water I could drink?"

"And then you go on with your life, and punch Melissa in the nose, huh?" she asked.

I nodded. "I've never had to pay for what I did."

"I don't know, this lawsuit sounds like a big deal to me. We don't have clean water for you, yet. If things improve around here, we'll get you some."

The knot in my stomach tightened, and I discarded the half-eaten critter on my plate.

"Great. I guess the watermelon will do, then. Where did you find it, anyway?"

"We have a greenhouse," Sloan replied.

"And it was left untouched by the explosions and the rain of ash?"

"Yep. For now the greenhouse still stands."

"This is weird, that memories have to eat," I remarked.

Susan chuckled. "Ha, yes, well, we are alive here. And it's a myth that superheroes don't need food to survive." She winked.

"Because of your powers?" I gulped another cube of watermelon. "So how did you guys develop the glowing eyes? Are the rats and fruit radioactive or something?"

She laughed, and Evan took over the explanation. "Not quite. See, the Underworld is a special place. Many mythologies use the term Underworld when they want to refer to death and the afterlife. In Greek mythology, for instance, the Underworld is the place where the dead travel, their soul becoming a full person—looking exactly like they used to in the world of the living. Here, the Underworld is a place where lost souls like yours go to find forgiveness and redemption. And the eyes are the mirror of your soul, the light that never stops burning, even buried under layers of thick black dust."

"I never killed you in real life, did I?" The knot inside my stomach was making me nauseous now.

He smiled. "You don't need to kill us in real life for death to feel real."

"You said this Underworld was a place for the dead," I pursued. "Last time I checked, I wasn't dead."

"The Underworld shows you all the secrets your mind holds. Buried treasures, memories you've repressed, thoughts, fears, fantasies..." Susan continued. "The question is not about being physically but emotionally dead. Once you decided to forget about your past, and ignore certain events that made you who you are today, you denied yourself the right to be whole. You killed a part of yourself when you left Oceanside, and you killed us in the process too, because we're memories. The Mighty Listener decided it was time for you to take a trip here, and learn why you needed to accept what happened to you. Before you lost yourself completely."

"You mean, before I went completely nuts?" The need to throw up was unbearable.

"You don't like the word crazy. This word makes you angry," Sloan observed.

"Yes, it does, but..."

Susan grabbed my hand and placed it between hers.

"You need to take a step back and observe. The Underworld is showing you the way to the truth. The dream you had about your attorney is a good sign you're questioning your past deeds. Do you regret punching Melissa in the face? Or being involved with this kid who you claimed assaulted you?"

I stared at her while my insides turned as hard as a rock, until it became difficult to breathe.

"Yes."

"Julie, are you alright?"

I shook my head.

"I'm not feeling great. All the things you're telling me..."

I retched.

She grabbed me by the waist and pulled me off my seat. "You need to rest."

"What's wrong?" Evan left his seat.

"Maybe it's the food," I replied.

Sky threw his hands in the air. "Oh no, don't blame me!"

"Told you not to criticize my brother's cooking," Sloan added.

"That's alright," Susan said. "We're not going to leave the headquarters until you feel okay to move forward. Come with me."

"I'll tag along," Evan piped up.

"Okay." Susan walked me out of the Dome into a tunnel, and he followed.

We returned to the car, and I didn't say a word. The meeting with Gold had left me drained and tired. Now all I wanted was to go home and sleep. A little bird told me, however, that Mom would surely take advantage of the ride to bombard me with questions, until she knew exactly what was going on in my head; and also maybe play nice again and try to bribe me with a motherly treat.

"Well, that was an interesting meeting," she said, before pushing the start button of her brand new hybrid sedan. Even if people felt the urge to be environmentally friendly in California, Mom's farts would surely never smell like roses.

I nodded. Sitting next to her made me sick to my stomach. I didn't want to talk to her. Too many thoughts cluttered my mind.

"You hungry?" she asked.

My eyes ventured along the dashboard, then moved to the cream leather seats. My father had bought her the latest luxury car as an early birthday present—most likely a make-up gift for whatever mistake had caused her to lose her temper—my family was so magazine centerfold perfect. A real dream come true. Maybe Mom had convinced herself her farts smelled like fresh roses. It was easier to lose oneself in superficiality than deal with the hefty mess her daughter had left in her trail. Granted, though, she was making an effort by being friendly, even if she didn't say much during our meeting with Gold.

And yeah, actually, I was hungry.

"In-N-Out?" I buckled my seatbelt.

Why did I think of the burger joint Kara and I always loved? Kara did love In-N-Out burgers. She used to say there was something so gratifying about the feeling of your arteries clogging after a long day surfing. We would laugh before biting into our calorie-filled burgers like ravenous beasts.

This had certainly been a long morning, and an artery-clogging In-N-Out burger sounded like the perfect remedy. Something made them taste just right. Plus, I hadn't been to an In-N-Out in ages.

"Deal," my mother replied, like she had suddenly morphed into my best friend.

I disliked her tactics, trying to wrap me around her finger. Whatever kind of bribe she used to bait me, my mouth would stay shut.

"Are you alright?" I realized my mother was staring at me. We hadn't left the garage yet.

Barely pulled out of my funk, I nodded like a bobblehead.

"Yep, all good. Just... starving." My smile would do the trick and stop all lines of questioning, right?

"You know, I'd like to help you. You can talk to me," she said, while casting me this loving, motherly look I didn't know she was capable of displaying.

Not now. I didn't need the mother-daughter talk. Witnessing her trying to act like my friend was already too much for me to handle.

"Yep," I repeated, building fake confidence into my tone. "I'm good. He's a great lawyer. He'll do his job and then, yep... I'll be fine. Just... fine."

I sounded like a broken record, and stood no chance of convincing Mom to keep off. On the contrary, with an attitude like this, I was inviting her in and she'd never leave me alone.

"I'm sorry I reacted like that," I continued, "but why should I try to bend the truth and say it wasn't self-defense? And he told me everything would run smoothly. Dad will make everything better anyway. That's always how things work in this family."

My mother's eyes grew wider by the second. "Why are you so angry with Dad?" she asked.

I jeered. "Dad loves his job more than he loves me."

My tone was on the verge of becoming a little too high-pitched. I was freaking out inside, my heart pulsing erratically, like a clock about to break down; but on the surface I pretended to be as cool as a cucumber. My sweaty palms stayed glued to my legs.

Mom remained silent, as if drawn into a deep mental struggle, trying to find the right words with which to shatter my shell, with one single, powerful blow.

"I don't know where you get these ideas!" she finally spat out.

"You didn't really show much interest either, Mom. Stop pretending you care. Your phone is more important than me."

I turned my head in her direction, and locked eyes with her.

Now, drive and feed me instead of asking more questions. I hoped she'd read my message.

Not a muscle in her face flickered for several seconds. I didn't look away, although I badly wanted to. Holding my breath, I thought I'd turn blue before she reacted.

"We're worried about you. But you shut us down. You don't talk to us. You don't tell us what's going on. I try, Julie, I really try. But it takes two to tango. You can lead a horse to water, but you can't make it drink. I-I really would like for you to finally open up," she said.

I shrugged and chuckled. "Well... I went to see Gold today, didn't I?"

She moved a strand of hair from my face and gently tucked it behind my ear. A caring touch I hadn't felt in a very long time, and my speeding heart slowed down a little.

"Yes. I'm proud of you," she added.

I looked away and frowned.

"This is my life, Mom. I deal with morons in my own way."

"Do you want to go to college?"

I huffed. "Why, every time I do something wrong, does the college talk have to come up, as an incentive to make me stop? You really think I care about getting a degree? You really think my life is gonna get better? There are too many guys in college anyway. So many more morons I'm going to punch in the face because they want to get inside my pants. That's all men want, isn't it? My personality, no one cares. But my bootie, yeah, let's all go for it. Free for the taking! Don't even need to ask permission."

Her face adopted that sad expression, like she understood what I was going through, but I knew she didn't.

"What happened to you, honey?" she asked, in a mellow tone that drove me completely insane.

I looked at her, on the verge of tears.

"I'm hungry. Let's just go, okay?"

She stared at me a while longer, before finally shifting the car into reverse.

"Okay. Ready for a delicious burger?" she asked, as the car moved backwards.

I nodded. "Absolutely."

"Then let's go."

9

"Why are we back here?" I asked, as we set foot on the street.

Susan smiled at me. "Fresh air will help you feel better."

I grunted and looked at Evan. "Fresh air? You call this murk fresh air? And I thought I was going to rest."

Smoke cluttered the atmosphere and a thick rain of ash poured down on us. Not what I'd define as a healthy breathing environment.

"Do you feel a slight difference in your anger already?" Evan asked in return.

"I don't see a huge difference in Oceanside, if that's what you imply."

"The town is changing though." Susan smiled. "And a walk can do wonders."

"Yeah, so can a nap." My gaze shifted to Evan. "You warned me about these temporary changes, so I'm not paying attention to them. How will I know when a change is permanent?"

"Be mindful that these temporary changes can become permanent, unless you decide to revert back to your original angry state."

"Buildings still look ready to collapse at the first sneeze! Sure, there's less debris on the pavement. How can I be sure the state of decay isn't increasing, though? I can't remember every single piece of trash covering this city."

"Patience. Everything will make sense soon. Don't focus too hard on the appearance of this town, okay? We have more urgent tasks to deal with."

I huffed. "Okay, I'll ignore the smoke, and the dust, and these horrible explosions. So why are we back here? And don't tell me again it's for the fresh air."

"We're taking a stroll to the school library," Susan answered.

"What will we find in the library?"

"Memories," Evan piped up.

An explosion popped in the distance and I jumped.

"I don't take that sound as evidence of improvement."

Susan and Evan seemed unaffected by my distress.

"How about ignoring the explosions," Susan suggested.

"Right, easier said than done." I took a deep breath. "Aren't we supposed to get there fast so Kara doesn't catch up to us, since she's so evil and all?"

"Kara won't show up if you don't provoke her with your anger," Evan replied.

"Oh, right. Like I have control over my anger."

"Well, do you feel angry right now?"

I shook my head. "No, just unsettled by this mess I caused."

"Oceanside will look better, I promise."

"No, I was talking about Melissa, and the other stuff..."

"Ah, yes, the thoughts that bothered you during dinner," Susan interjected.

I nodded. The rain of ash kept falling upon us in flurries. "So, tell me, who are Sky and Sloan?"

She laughed. "They attended the same school you did."

"Yes, I figured, but I can't remember them either. I actually can't remember any of you."

She shrugged. "You experienced a pretty traumatic incident, so when you decided to wipe off the past, you weren't really paying attention to whom or what you removed. You put us all in the same basket."

"I remember Kara, though."

"Of course you do. She was your best friend. You loved her like a sister."

"But Dan... I loved him too."

"Yes, you sure did."

"Why, then?" I persisted.

"Why what?"

"Why didn't I love any of you?"

We slowed our stride, and Evan put his hand on my shoulder.

"Because you were lost in your own little world, where none of us belonged. I like to think you antagonized us because we were different, and you wanted to fit in so badly. Kara was the perfect example of the girl you would die to be. She was popular and pretty, attractive to most men at least."

"Why do you say that? Didn't you find her pretty?"

He shook his head. "Oh gosh, no. I've never been attracted to girls."

I stared at him. "What, you're gay?"

He laughed. "Yes, darling."

My heart skipped a beat. "Wow."

Susan and he laughed.

"Oh come on, don't tell me it's the first time you encountered a gay kid," he said.

"No, no." I felt heat rush to my face. "I just didn't think..."

"That's okay. Just because I'm nice doesn't mean I want to get inside your pants."

I didn't respond. I felt very stupid. Hormones had made me believe he was interested in me. He was just a memory... But I liked him. Crap.

As soon as I moved to Los Angeles and started my transformation, guys liked to be around me. For the first time in my life I didn't feel used, but wanted. And I loved it. I enjoyed having the upper hand. If a guy didn't want to be with me, I made it a challenge to conquer his feelings, before crushing them. It had become a game I enjoyed playing. Until I met Mark. And he was the one who broke my little heart.

I clenched my teeth.

"You shouldn't get upset," Evan said.

"I'm not upset."

"I can read your thoughts."

"I-I... I am not upset!"

I pushed him away from me, and crossed my arms over my chest.

"I'd like for us to reach the library before Kara makes an impromptu appearance," Susan urged.

"Okay, let's go then." I resumed my walk.

Something didn't sit right with me. I wanted these feelings to go away, but they kept harassing me.

"I'm going to tell you a story, okay?" Evan said.

I shrugged. "Okay."

We turned a corner and continued down the two-way street leading to the school. The area still looked desolate, but as I stared at the ground I noticed tiny blades of grass growing in the cracks of the sidewalk. Temporary changes...

"I was thirteen years old," Evan began. "My family was the typical church-every-Sunday type of deal. I went to Catholic school and learned everything there was to know about good and evil. Very early on, I knew that a boy who liked other boys was a big no-no, so I fought my feelings as hard as I could. I played with girls, and even made my parents think I had a girlfriend. Here I was, trying to fit in. I decided I could be like every straight person out there, and my feelings wouldn't get the better of me. Until I met George, the choirboy."

I laughed. "You fell in love with a choirboy?"

"Hey, don't laugh. He was just perfect. Not only was he cute, but also smart and kind. I couldn't resist being near him, although I don't believe he was gay. But, like me, he was afraid of what his family might do to him if he turned out like me. After months of being very close friends, I spent the night at his house. We were in his room, talking, laughing, and sharing stories. Everything felt so natural. He lay on the bed, and I sat next to him.

When he wasn't looking, I brushed his hand with my fingers. He didn't protest. So I went further. I lay next to him, our shoulders touching. Next thing I knew, we kissed. And my heart exploded inside my chest. This felt right. This felt normal. And I wanted to feel this way forever. I fell asleep holding his hand."

"Don't tell me this story ends well," I said.

He shook his head. "The next morning, his father kicked me out of the house, beating me with a broom. He yelled that I was the reason for all evil on earth. But I wouldn't corrupt his son. George was pure, innocent, and I was the serpent luring him. I couldn't sleep well after that. My parents heard what happened and sent me to boarding school. They thought distance and isolation would help them cope with the fact I was homosexual. I was with boys twenty-four seven!"

He chuckled. "I returned to Oceanside when I was sixteen and decided to go to public school. After one year, I couldn't take the boarding school environment anymore. But there was one truth I knew: I was gay. I'd always be gay. And being homosexual didn't mean I had to live in denial. So I embraced my true nature. I came out to my parents, and told them I would always be their son. They could hate me if they wanted, but I would always love them in return. It wasn't their fault I was born this way. If God truly wanted me to be happy, then he had chosen this path for me. My dad didn't talk to me, but he didn't kick me out of the house either. I ran into George shortly thereafter. He ignored me. I could have been resentful. Instead, I let him be. He couldn't change who I was. And he belonged to the past. I had all life to look forward to. I didn't close the door on anything that had happened to me. I accepted the past and moved on.

"See, you will remember what happened to you, and you will get angry. Very angry. Kara, Dan and Mike will show up. But you will decide what happens to you. These people, no matter how badly you treated them, or how badly you think they treated you, don't deserve your hatred. They deserve forgiveness and love. The stronger you are, the weaker they become. You will accept your true nature. And by accepting your true nature, this world will be kind to you in return."

He smiled.

"How can you be so brave?" I asked.

He put his hand on my shoulder. "Because I've accepted. I didn't try to forget."

I lowered my head. "I don't know if I'll be able to accept anything."

"Chin up," he said. "We've arrived."

The library profiled itself in the distance.

"What am I going to find there?" I asked, and a lump formed in my throat.

"Answers," Susan said.

Another day in the school week. Crossing the gates gave me anxiety. I felt self-conscious. The short hair made me look like a boyish version of myself, and there was nothing sexy about my oversized jeans and my plaid shirt. Plain and simple: I didn't belong there.

Taking detours through classrooms I wasn't even supposed to enter, I hid in the bathroom for a while, crying in silence in a stall. No one I knew would see me today. I'd work hard to avoid any talk, any glance, anything at all that would spark a conversation.

I was late for class. Math, with Mr. White.

As I returned to the hallway, my plan for not interacting with anyone fell into disarray when I bumped into the hallway monitor.

"Shouldn't you be in class by now? Where's your pass?"

Barry, five feet tall and at least five feet wide, could have been the perfect poster child for the negative effects of eating junk food as your daily diet. He stared at me from behind his huge glasses, his eyes magnified like in a fishbowl. He thought his glare would make me run away with my tail neatly tucked between my legs. But his strong lisp made me want to burst into laughter.

Trying to maintain my composure, I displayed an apologetic smile.

"Um, this will sound completely crazy, but I forgot where the classroom was."

Barry remained completely unmoved by my lie. There was a long pause. I wondered if some slow, thinking reaction was taking place inside his brain.

I waited patiently.

I could almost hear the sound of crickets in the background.

"Right. And I'm the Queen of England," he finally said. So, that's what took so long. He was trying to be funny.

"Well, under certain circumstances, you might well run for office. I mean, who wouldn't respect your authoritare?" I fired back.

The Eric Cartman line may have been a little too much.

"Go back to class before I send you to the principal's office," he ordered, with his finger pointing along the empty hallway.

"Yes, Sir," I blurted, before taking off.

Now, facing the barrier to math class, I knocked on the door and entered.

All eyes were on me.

"Ms. Jones, glad to have you with us. Please take a seat."

Mr. White looked like his last name. Blending with the walls, he was the most vanilla human being I had ever met in my life.

Kara didn't share my passion for math. But Dan did. Of course, since I authored all his homework.

Refusing to look at him, I picked a seat at the back of the classroom and pulled my notepad. Oddly, I sensed eyes boring holes in me.

Dan sat two rows ahead of me, staring at me.

Glorious.

"Okay, everyone, we're ready for our thirty-minute quiz. All materials away besides your pencil," Mr. White announced.

I sighed. Dan smiled and focused on his desk. Did he bring his cheat-sheet with him so he'd get an A on this one?

I hated surprise quizzes, but being forced to look at a piece of paper for thirty minutes was actually a great way to ignore Dan's ominous presence.

After the test, though, I had to find a different way to distract myself. So I focused on what Mr. White was scribbling on the blackboard.

Make Dan go away, please.

Oh, and there he was, staring again. Did I have a funny Sharpie design drawn on my forehead?

I had never felt happier to hear the bell signal recess.

As I packed my bag and the crowd of students left the classroom, I didn't look once in Dan's direction. I wanted to ignore him. Once all my stuff was in, and I was prepared to leave, I finally dared look... To realize he was gone.

I felt a hint of disappointment, because I still secretly wanted him to talk to me. This crazy infatuation would lead me into more trouble than I needed. Why couldn't I get rid of these feelings for him? Loving him wasn't a good idea.

As I strolled down the hallway I passed the water fountain, and then the vending machine. No one was paying attention to me. I ignored everyone like they had the plague. Bodies stood and chatted. I was so pre-occupied with my train of thought that I bumped into Susan.

"Is everything alright?" she asked.

I refused to look at her. All I wanted was to vanish from the surface of this planet.

"Yeah, yeah..." I mumbled and kept on walking.

Perhaps I was ashamed of my looks, but hers were off the charts. I couldn't be friends with a bunch of Goth freaks. Or a single freak, because she seemed like a loner.

Next class was Spanish. Not something I excelled at. Funny how my French-born mother never taught me a single word of her mother tongue either. She always told me I was better off speaking English, and with an American accent to top it off. I didn't mind fitting the stereotype, that Americans were awful linguists. But sometimes I thought it might be nice to be able to speak a different language.

I picked a seat at the back of the classroom again and waited for everyone to sit. My dear, vixen, red-haired Goth friend had chosen a chair right at the front. In addition to being a devil worshipper, she was also the teacher's pet.

I pretended to pay attention in class, but lost myself in my thoughts again. I felt too smart for my own good. I hated myself for loving Dan. Because I did love him. That love ate me whole, creating a hole in my heart like a dough-nut, and I didn't know what to do with myself anymore.

Before I realized, it was lunchtime.

Grabbing a ham and cheese sandwich at the cafeteria, I headed outside and walked until I recognized the bleachers bordering the football field. Not sure why I wanted to watch Dan practice, my feet walked me there more than my head. Or maybe it was my doughnut heart leading the dance.

As I heard the familiar sounds of players shouting obscure instructions to each other before each play, my chest tightened a little.

I loved football. Every lunch period I made it my goal to sit on the far top of the bleachers, away from the crowd, to munch on my bread and listen to solid masses of muscles tackle each other. Most girls liked football because of the players. I loved football because of the game. And Dan. Yeah, I couldn't fool myself. I had learned every play. Knew the strategy. Kara didn't really care about that stuff.

My eyes scanned the field. Dan was running through obstacles, agile as a cat. As his hand released the ball, the arm expertly aimed at a running back positioned a few feet ahead, I held my breath. A chunk of bread stuck to my tongue. I didn't swallow my food until the passing play was successful. Right into the end zone! The whole action lasted less than ten seconds.

Even if he wasn't a bookworm, Dan deserved that scholarship. He was a real football star. All eyes were on him, mine included. I honestly found it hard not to stand and cheer from the bleachers, like a perfect football groupie.

The team practiced some more and my eyes never left him. I burned to be close to him, to smell the sweat on his jersey—even if it was utterly the last thing I'd dream of doing. But with him, I'd do anything. He could ask me to follow him to Mars to do his home-work and I would. I wasn't yet fifteen, for crying out loud! Three years older than me, he'd be off to college next year. My love for him was hopeless and desperate.

Crushing the wrapping paper of my sandwich into a tight ball, I swallowed my frustration with a gulp of soda and moved down the bleachers to be closer to the field.

The team was done playing.

When I reached the edge of the grass, I made sure to pretend I just got there. I didn't want him to know I had been looking at him the whole time.

I pretended to pay attention to another player. Too bad I didn't wear sunglasses—it would have been easier to hide who I was looking at.

"Okay guys, good game!" the coach shouted from the sideline. "See you tomorrow."

As the players scattered, my eyes followed Dan. He grabbed a Gatorade from the cooler and chatted to the water guy and the other players standing nearby.

I couldn't stop watching, feeling like a spy. Drink half full in hand, Dan waved at me. The black streaks under his eyes had smudged onto his cheeks because of the sweat. Boy, he looked so handsome. I suppressed a jolt of pure excitement as he walked in my direction.

"What's up with you, nerd?" he said with a raspy voice I found super-duper sexy. Kill me now!

"Nuthin'," I replied with a shrug. "Nothing exciting, at least."

His face welcomed my comment with raised eyebrows. "Oh really, so..." And he proceeded to brush the side of my arm with his fingers. I couldn't contain myself, and an army of butterflies was unleashed inside my stomach.

"You really like football, don't ya?" he said, giving me a dreamy smile.

I nodded. "Yeah, football's awesome."

What was with the sudden conversation? I only did his homework. We never chatted about football!

"I heard you're leaving soon."

Ah, so that was it.

"Yeah. Newsflash, huh?"

"Yeah, news gets around pretty quickly."

I looked away. "Good. I mean, okay."

He laughed. "Mike's planning a big party for his birthday at the end of the month. You wanna join?"

Hold on to your horses.

I shrugged to pretend I didn't care much. Just because... I didn't. I really didn't.

"Ah, yes." I cleared my throat. "I have much packing to do. No clue if I'll attend. Plus, I'm not a drinker. So..."

He brushed my arm again. Lordie have mercy, did he know the effect he had on me?

"But... it'd be a way to celebrate your departure, and your upcoming birthday too, am I right?"

He grinned, and I was dying to land a kiss on his beautiful mouth. I really didn't know how to kiss a boy properly, but with him, I'd surely learn real fast.

"You should come."

My turn to raise eyebrows. "Really?"

He nodded. "Really."

He took a sip of the Gatorade. Whatever he did looked so darn killer. I was on the verge of dissolving into a puddle of pure lust.

Stupid hormones.

"Well, I'll see. I..." my voice trailed off.

As he leaned toward me, I recoiled. But he kept going, to give me a slight kiss on the cheek.

Now my heart was dancing the salsa inside my chest.

And the puddle of lust? Yes, it was coming too.

Boy. Oh boy. I was in trouble.

"You've been kind enough to do my homework. You know, it's only my way of saying thank you."

He winked.

The heart attack would happen in one, two...

I brushed the air with my hand. "Sure, of course. No problem."

"So I'll see you there?" he asked.

"Right, yeah, I'll do my best to come." As I answered, my voice climbed two octaves in the span of two seconds.

He smiled again. "Great. I'm gonna jump in the shower. I'll catch you later. Probably in the library, huh, nerd?"

I chuckled. "Right. My favorite spot on earth."

As he stared at me, my legs turned to jello.

"Gotta go. See ya, nerd."

He ran back to the locker room. I was mesmerized by his stride. His back, his legs, his butt... How would I justify going to this party to Mom? Nonsense. I'd find a way.

The joy I felt inside made me want to fly.

10

my fingers gripped the back of a chair.

"Are you alright?" Evan's glowing green eyes locked onto mine.

I took a deep breath.

We stood inside the library, behind shelves still carrying books. The destruction I witnessed outside hadn't permeated here. There were study tables along the wall. I sat down and put my head between my hands.

"This place still looks the same," I said.

"It was always your safe harbor, wasn't it?" Susan replied, taking a seat across from me.

I nodded. "I remember you. And Dan invited me to a party. I-I'm not sure why he did it, but he invited me. Out of all things..."

"This is a major breakthrough!" Evan exclaimed.

"I don't understand why being in the library made me think of him." I sighed. "I feel so stupid."

"Because this place used to be your sanctuary. The place where you hid from the world, where you had no secrets," Susan said.

"I can't take this!"

Tears rolled down my face and I buried my head in my jacket sleeves.

"This building holds answers to your questions. We came here for a reason," Evan added.

"Come on, Julie, let's go," Susan suggested.

"Are you sure this is a good idea?" I sniffled.

Susan grabbed my hand and I stood.

Following them, I sniffled my sorrow away. We passed a series of shelves and, when we stopped, I read "Sciences of the Occult and the Unknown" on a label stuck to the wood.

"What is this?" I asked.

"You'll see. Where is..."

Evan browsed the content of the shelf, his finger running along the spines of books. Then a grin spread across his face.

"Aha!" he exclaimed and pulled out a notebook.

He handed it to me.

I stared at the cover and read: "Julie Jones's Journal—Keep Out."

"Why is my journal here?"

"Well, it's a good spot if you don't want people to snoop. Come on, let's have a peek! Aren't you curious to see what's inside?"

I frowned and looked at Susan. "I'm not sure this is necessary."

She smiled, and Evan made a funny face while pointing at the journal.

"Okay, yeah, sure. I need to learn more about my convoluted past." I opened the journal at a random page. "Here goes nothing."

I started reading out loud.

I had this dream last night. Dan called and offered to pick me up. I didn't know what to wear. To ease my nervousness, I decided to have dinner at Kara's. After eating, I was stuffed. Holding my stomach with my hands, I let out a big yawn while still at the table. My yawn wasn't unnoticed by Kara's mom.

I frowned. "My writing style needs some serious improvement."

Evan tapped me on the arm. "Go on."

I sighed, and continued reading.

"Ready for bed?" she asked with a giggle.

Actually, no. I had a party to attend.

"Um, I heard there was a party going on at Mike's tonight, and I was thinking of going," I said, while playing with my fork.

"Oh, very well," her mom said.

Would I even have the strength to go to this party? My eyelids were dropping shut.

Kara watched me, a weird look in her eyes.

"Do you even have anything to wear?" she asked.

Her question caught me off-guard.

I shook my head. "Not really. It was a last minute decision."

She smiled. "I have something perfect for you. Come."

I pushed my chair away from the table and left my plate and utensils in the sink.

"Good night, Mrs. Burke. Thanks so much for the delicious dinner."

I stood in front of the fridge, looking at a picture of Kara and me. We both wore our surfing gear, holding our boards upright next to us, with the backdrop of the ocean stretching behind us. The bluest, cloudless sky added the last touch to the perfect pose and smile, flawless testament to our unbreakable friendship.

"I love this photo," Mrs. Burke said.

"Yeah, it's a really great shot."

"So proud and strong, don't you agree?"

I nodded.

She smiled. "Well, ladies, have fun. And be careful." She proceeded to wash the dishes.

"Thanks, Mom," Kara said.

"Thanks again," I added.

Kara and I entered Kara's bedroom. I sat on the edge of the bed, while she shuffled through her closet before pulling out a dress and showing it to me.

When I put the dress on, my initial reaction was not what she expected.

"Are you alright?" she asked.

"Yeah..." I replied. "Yes, I'm good. Stuffed from all the food. And tired too. I won't stay up late tonight."

She laughed. "You say that now. What do you think of the dress I picked for you?"

The dress in question was short, very short, and red, very red, with a bustier that cupped up my small breasts into an outrageous display of obnoxious right-in-your-face-take-advantage-of-me-now boobage.

I frowned. If Mom saw me like that, she'd send me to Catholic boarding school on the spot, although we didn't believe in Jesus Christ.

"Are you sure?" I uttered, staring at my reflection in her full-length mirror.

She cooed with excitement.

"Yes, I'm sure. It looks so perfect on you. Everyone's jaw will drop."

Did it mean Dan would finally see me for more than the nerd he said I was? A girl with a real girl body, no longer hidden under layers of hideous clothes?

"Seriously?" I asked, still uncertain whether the makeover was absolutely necessary.

"Yes! I'll do your hair and makeup! Come on! Let's make you duper pretty!"

After straightening and styling my short hair, piling tons of foundation on my face and black, glittery eye shadow on my eyelids, and painting my lips in dark burgundy, I stared at my reflection again. The girl in the mirror looked nothing like the Julie I was used to. This new Julie actually looked fierce. Growl! Without the glasses, obviously. But I could navigate without my binoculars as long as no one asked me to read anything.

"Do you like it?" Kara asked.

"Yeah!" I said, unable to look away from the mirror.

Those red lips especially were killer.

"You're going to make heads turn tonight," she whispered, and my ego took a boost I had never experienced before.

I closed the journal.

"This is nuts," I said.

"Well, does it help you understand what happened?" Evan asked.

I scowled. "It was a dream."

"You were thinking about that party," Susan continued. "You remembered Dan asking you to go. You wrote about it. This party is the key. Do you realize that?"

Their sudden excitement made me more confused. I didn't remember attending a party. Anything I wrote in my journal was only meant to be read by me. And most of the stuff I wrote was a product of my own making. That note was a dream. Nothing else.

"I don't know. I can't remember any of it. I am so... tired."

My hand fell to my side, and the journal slipped through my fingers.

Evan picked it up.

"Okay, then let's go to something else you wrote. Not a dream. A memory."

He opened the journal again.

"Uh hum, your attention please," he said, and started reading.

"Gimme one valid reason why I should agree with you," I said, attempting to skid a small rock over the ocean surface. Despite a promising throw, the pebble landed in the water with a faint plop and sank to the bottom.

Kara sat behind me with her knees to her chin and her arms wrapped around her legs. Still in her bathing suit, her skin looked very dark in the failing light. Our surfboards lay side by side on the sand, our wetsuits thrown in a pile on top of them. Staring at the pink and purple sky, a pinch pricked me in the chest.

Turning away from the beautiful vista, I crawled over and grabbed one strand of Kara's long, blonde hair. Long, blonde, sea-salt-improvised dreadlocks, I should say.

I chuckled, "Kingdom for a shower, girlfriend!"

"No need to get so upset. I just want your opinion." Ignoring my comment, she sheltered her eyes from the setting sun with her hand.

"Okay." I silently watched the sun crashing into the horizon and waited for her to continue.

"You know..." she said, "I really like him."

I suppressed an angry snort. "So you said. To which I said, I can't protect you if something ugly happens." Despite my best intentions, or maybe because of them, my bitterness came through loud and clear.

"Really, the world will come to an end if I date him? Out of all guys?" She stared at me, and I read the disappointment in her eyes. She wanted me to support her in her decision to ask Dan out. "Out of all guys..."

Dan looked much hotter than every guy out there. Here was the list of his physical attributes: six foot three, two hundred pounds of solid muscle, young-Brad-Pitt-in-Thelma-and-Louise-blonde hair, and hazel-green eyes that would make you cut off your own arm just to stand in his vicinity. That was, of course, if you didn't die of excitement first. Or blood loss. Or a combination of both. And besides looking good, Dan played quarterback for the school's football team. Hanging out with him was like finding the Holy Grail.

This guy could date anyone he wanted.

Except me.

I stayed awfully quiet while she bored holes in the side of my head with her eyes.

"Soooo... Tell me," she whined.

Exhaling, I picked my words carefully.

"I'm scared."

"What are you so scared about?"

Drop the attitude, would you? As if it wasn't hard enough to be "honest." I swallowed hard. "Dan is a player. You're going to fall in love with him. And he's going to break your heart."

"You're lying."

Love was blind, so blind.

I shook my head.

"But he is so perfect..." Her voice trailed off. "Why did you never warn me? You interact with him more often than I do, given you do his homework."

Great way to remind me of my weakness.

"I don't know. I probably mentioned it. Before." I so hated repeating myself. Though, admittedly, it might not have been in so many words. "It doesn't matter now. I just... Whatever. Be careful."

White and yellow trails crisscrossed the darkening sky, as waves threw themselves against the shore in a fruitless display of aggression. As fruitless as this conversation.

"I'm crazy about him," she said.

Yeah, me too! Oh Lordie! The key was to stay diplomatic. "Listen, I don't want you to get hurt, that's all."

I should have listened to my own advice.

"People say he's a player because they're jealous. And you know what I think about rumors."

"Dan went out with Lilly, and she said he had been horrible," I added.

I made that one up. The only person who had warned me about him was Susan.

She scoffed. "So you base your opinion of him on what one girl said?"

And here we went. Distractedly playing with sand, I let it clump between my fingers.

"You're right," I replied. "What do I know? Nothing."

She smiled at me. I didn't smile back. The sky was now completely dark; time to head home.

"Thanks for being such a good friend." Her comment sealed the lid on the coffin. I shivered. "Let's get dinner. My house?"

I could always do dinner at her house. In fact, I had dinner at Kara's almost every evening, because my own mother mostly liked microwavable stuff, which tasted like plane food. Kara's mom was very sweet and always asked me what I liked. Often threw together my favorites, too: creamy spinach and baked potatoes, or corn on the cob and roasted chicken breast...

We walked until the beach became the street and Kara's house, the third on the left, winked at us with its dim streetlight.

Evan shut the journal. "I don't know why you think your writing sucks," he said.

Listening to him, I had wanted to grab the journal and burn it.

"So, Kara was in love with him too. And I apparently got invited to a party. What does it have to do with anything?"

"What this journal tells you is that your feelings for Dan were exacerbated. Knowing your best friend loved him too and had an actual shot at dating him made it so much worse. Were you afraid of losing her?" Susan asked.

I sighed. "I don't know what to think. She's roaming this world now as a bad memory. This whole hunt is becoming exhausting."

I stepped away from the occult section and walked back to the entrance of the library.

"Kara became a bad memory because her feelings were hurt," Evan said.

I turned around. "Yes, I know that. So were mine."

"Using your pain to justify hurting other people isn't right, Julie. If you focus all the attention on yourself and play victim, you'll never move on," he replied.

I threw my hands in the air. "I'm not playing victim, okay? I was hurt, and sad, and heartbroken. There. Happy?"

"You're getting angry again."

I huffed. "No shizzlenit, Sherlock."

I reached the front desk and stared outside. The rain of ash was still pouring down, blackening the ground.

"This is the world I chose to forget because thinking about it doesn't make me happy. I'm not strong like you are. I don't know how to accept things. So why bother?" I fired.

"Oh, because you consider yourself happy now?" Susan asked.

"No, I'm not. Dan did his thing, Kara abandoned me, and crap hit the fan faster than a fart in a hurricane. Why should I look back and feel all this pain again? Don't I have enough pain to deal with already?"

A loud explosion popped outside, and I ducked for shelter under the front desk.

"This is too much for me to take!" I grunted, struggling to keep my heartbeat steady, and my undies unsoiled. I needed a shower!

"Well, well, well, if that isn't simply touching," Kara said.

II

I groaned. "What does she want?"

Evan and Susan crouched next to me.

"She comes when you lose your temper," he whispered. "I already told you that."

"Oh yeah? She thinks she scares me? I'm going to tell her once and for all what I think of her!"

"No, Julie, that's not a good idea!" Susan said.

Of course, I didn't listen and stood to stare straight into Kara's soulless, purple eyeballs.

"What do you want?"

"Oh, friend, I do remember you being mean to me," Kara snarled. "Why, I thought we could talk—"

"Oh yeah, you want to talk? Funny, I'd like to talk too. But I'll let you speak your mind as long as you don't attack me like last time. I accept a civilized conversation, not a scratching fest."

She leapt and landed with a whoosh on top of the desk. Evan emerged from his hiding spot and positioned himself between her and me.

"Back off," he said.

She laughed.

"Oh come on, she wants to talk. So... let's talk."

"You don't want to talk," he replied, looking at her, and then at me.

"How do you know what I want?" she asked.

"Because I can read your mind."

She smiled. "And what am I thinking about now, tough boy?"

He clenched his teeth. Susan got up, put her hand on his arm and stepped between him and Kara.

"You should go before anyone gets hurt," Susan said.

Kara laughed. "Is that so?"

"No way can she hurt me," I mumbled under my breath. "I have too much hatred against her. If she wants to fight, I'll join the dance."

"Trust me, fighting her won't solve anything. Quite the contrary," Susan insisted.

Kara pointed her finger directly at my face.

"You destroyed my life!" she shouted. "And you think you're not scared. But you are going to piss yourself again, little girl! You know why? Because Julie Jones is a coward! She hides behind all that anger but, deep inside, she's frightened. Look at her. She can't even live with herself!"

She stomped her feet on the desk, grunting and grimacing and, without further ado, my bladder released its load into my pants.

Donkey crap on a banana peel. Did I need anything else embarrassing to happen to me right now?

"You don't know what you're doing here," she continued, "but you're certainly not in control anymore. I'm the one telling you what to do!"

I was angry, really angry, but frozen in place. Despite my best efforts to demonstrate strength, I couldn't hold back tears.

"I'm sorry, I'm so sorry," I said in a shaky voice.

She laughed louder. "You are so pathetic!"

"Stop this!" Evan shouted, moving me out of the way and igniting his green beams. Susan followed his lead.

"Oh no. Not this time, big boy. She still has a lot to learn about herself. I won't spoil the fun. We'll see each other again very soon." Kara propelled herself into the air. Floating against the ceiling of the library, she spread her arms wide and stared down at us like a vulture ready to fall on its prey.

Evan and Susan were ready to fire at her, but they waited. I had no idea what the signal was for them to beat her sorry butt, given I was swimming in shame.

"I have been waiting for this moment for so long," Kara continued. "And you taught me patience, Julie. When you're ready, you'll come to me begging for forgiveness."

"W-What what the heck is she talking about?" I asked.

"Oh, you love me. You love me so much deep, deep inside. But your heart is filled with so much hatred! How do you think you'll ever be forgiven for what you did? You'll drive yourself insane first!"

Her eyes glowed brighter as she kept talking.

"You will beg me to spare you, while you never offered me that choice, did you? F.Y.I., I really want you to feel the way I felt on that fateful night, and every night since. But," she paused, "your time will come."

My body shook like a blade of grass beaten by a storm. As her deafening laughter filled the space, she vanished from sight.

I looked at Evan, in shock.

"W-What the heck w-was sh-she t-talking about?" I stuttered. "W-What f-fateful night?"

Evan grabbed me by the waist and pulled me toward him. "She's gone. We should return to the Dome. Speak with the others."

"Tell me what she meant!" I shouted.

He brushed my hair with his fingers, while I released a torrent of tears onto his shoulder.

"Not now. I promise we'll answer all your questions, but not now and not here. Please come," he said, dragging me outside.

"The truth will be revealed soon," Susan added.

"Do I get to at least shower? I feel disgusting."

Evan nodded. "Yes."

Looking forward to eating my double-double and sipping a vanilla and strawberry milkshake, I picked a spot in a corner by the windows, while Mom bought the food. Placing a pile of condiments at the center of the table, I played with mayo and ketchup packets, forming words and funny faces to kill the wait. The place was crowded.

"Alright, ready for this? I haven't eaten junk food in years," Mom said, as she put the tray in front of me.

I quickly moved the ketchup and mayo packets away, deleting the name that started with a K in the process.

"This ain't junk food, it's pure heaven!" I replied, grabbing and unwrapping my sandwich. The smell of meat, cheese and bread hit my nose and made me salivate like crazy. Mom, despite her best intentions to have a mother-daughter moment, didn't look as keen to take a bite. She seemed really jaded about a lot of things lately.

"Well, that's what the makers of this would say so you'd eat it. But"—she pointed at my fries and shake—"you know it isn't technically healthy for you."

I sighed. Would my mother really ruin this meal with her dull remarks? Chewing a bite as big as one quarter of my burger, I could only manage to blurt out, "Okay."

I ate quickly. My belly felt full before I could finish all the food on the table. Mom took her time, and at that rate would probably be done in an hour. Her demeanor completely defeated the purpose of eating at a fast-food restaurant.

Leaning against the hard bench to give me more room to breathe—I hadn't eaten that much in months—I peeked at the ocean outside the window. It was a perfect day for surfing. The cloudless sky looked so inviting. I could already picture myself running bare foot on the hot sand, with my wetsuit on, ready to tackle a few waves. Something I hadn't done since moving to Los Angeles.

"So, tell me." My mother interrupted my train of thought—a specialty of hers. "What happened to you?"

Her questioning made me uncomfortable again. Just when I had started to relax a little, with happy thoughts.

"The guy cornered me," I answered, while eyeing a group of surfers riding the waves. "I had no escape route."

"The police found you wandering outside school after you attacked him. You seemed disoriented," she continued.

"Mom, lots of stuff happened."

Those surfers were having so much fun. Two in particular. I couldn't see their faces from there. Could we cut the interrogation short so I could mingle and enjoy myself?

"Honey, do you do drugs?" Mom asked out of the blue.

I choked on my own saliva and proceeded to take a sip of my milkshake to let the air flow down my pipes again. Oh crapola. Here we go. The drug talk. I was pretty sure my face expressed exactly how I felt about that question. What was I supposed to answer?

"What?" My body jolted backwards, as I threw her a glare filled with as much outrage as possible.

"It's okay if you do. Just tell me the truth," she continued, speaking with the same impassible tone of voice. Like she wouldn't freak out if I broke the news I shot heroin and smoked crack on a daily basis. Which I certainly didn't. I was only a recreational drug user, not an addict, and she didn't need to know about that, even if she said it was okay.

Since when had she become so willing to learn more about my personal life?

"Mom, I'm serious. This is not something I do." I locked eyes with her to make sure she didn't continue along that tangent.

"I'm worried about you!" She put the rest of her half-eaten burger down and pushed the tray aside. Grabbing my hands in hers, she begged me with her eyes to spill the beans.

"I am fine, Mom," I repeated.

"Okay." She let go of my hands. But her exaggerated sigh demonstrated that she wasn't convinced. "Then what happened to you? What happened to my little girl?"

I shrugged and looked outside at the two surfers again. "I told you," I said, a little annoyed now.

"The person who punched this guy isn't you. So if you don't do drugs, why did you do such a horrible thing?" she fired again.

Seriously, what did she want me to tell her?

"Did Dad ask you to have the talk with me?"

She sighed again. "Your dad works hard for this family. He's worried about you too."

"Right."

My focus was dead on what was happening on the beach. The surfers were still there, having their fun, while I was being grilled like a hot dog on Memorial Day weekend. My mother had certainly chosen the perfect opportunity too, after eating, when all the blood was concentrated in my stomach rather than my brain. Devious, devious strategy.

"Mom, what do you want me to tell you?" I sensed she wasn't ready to give up so easily with her annoying and obsessive questioning.

She gave me a really stern stare.

"I want you to look me in the eye and swear to me this is the last time such a thing will happen; and that you will finally act like a responsible young adult. We can't live with the fear we'll find you passed out in an empty alley, drugged up, hurt, in jail or even dead. We just can't," she said.

Her voice wasn't calm anymore. She was actually angry with me? Okay, I understood. She wanted me to grow up. And that was a legitimate concern, given all the crap I had put her through. But I didn't need her scolding. I couldn't change overnight! Despite my best intentions, my farts would never smell like roses.

I just wanted to go to sleep. I never wished to be an angry monster. All I prayed for was to find my purpose on this earth. And be left alone by perverts. So my mother, with all her questions about my drug use, was far from hitting a homerun on this one. And actually, this conversation tired me, rather than being in any way, shape or form constructive or remotely helpful.

Yet, if I didn't promise her I'd work on my issues, she'd stalk and harass me night and day until she was convinced I'd make an effort at being more open with her. So, make Mother Dearest happy, and then go back to business as usual. Pretending to be a good daughter wasn't that hard. After all, Dad pretended to be a good husband all the time! A little white lie here and there wouldn't hurt.

"I swear," I said, "to be good." My tone and glance seemed convincing enough, because she exhaled loudly and leaned back against the seat of the booth.

"Alright."

My turn to sigh deeply with relief. Knowing her relentless nature, I had honestly expected a little more questioning from her, but she held off for the moment. She took one last, slow bite at her burger. She was too upset to be hungry. I could have said other things to reassure her, but what for?

Right then, I needed to focus on my own problems. And gosh knew there were more than could be solved in a fifteen-minute-long conversation at a burger joint.

12

Everyone was waiting for us at the Dome.

"So, how did it go?" Sloan asked.

"Steady progress," Susan replied.

"Hungry yet?" Sky walked up to me, and I forced a smile.

"Sorry, buddy, don't take it personally, but I'm not really in the mood for a snack."

He shrugged. "Oh, no worries."

Miko gave me a hug.

"Feel better soon, promise."

"Thanks, Miko."

I turned to Susan and Evan. "I feel really gross."

Susan smiled. "Of course. Evan will take you. We'll be here."

"Ready champion?" Evan asked.

I nodded.

He guided me through the darkness towards a room I hadn't visited yet, and my heart took a leap.

"Oh gosh, I can't wait to wash off this dirt!" I said.

He laughed. "Yes, but don't get too excited; it isn't a five-star hotel."

"At this point, I don't care."

"Good."

Rudimentary was the first word that popped into my mind when we stepped inside. A shower head was suspended by a pipe from the ceiling. At the center of the room, several hoses were attached to a kitchen faucet. These led to the ceiling, where gutters had been installed. Water trickled into the gutters and down through the shower head.

Simple but effective.

"So, where does the water come from?"

"The sewer."

I shrieked. "What?"

"Don't worry, it's not super dirty. No one lives in this town anymore."

"Yeah, and what about all that crap I've seen above ground?"

"The ceiling acts as a filter. Here, try it. If you don't trust it, you can sit in your pee-scented pants for the rest of the journey." He smirked. "No one is forcing you to wash yourself."

"Fine," I huffed. "Not like I have a choice anyway. Like you said, it's not a five-star hotel."

"Okay, then take off your clothes."

"Hold on, you're going to stay here while I shower?"

He laughed.

"Well, you better turn around, mister, because I'm no exhibitionist!"

"Not like I haven't seen it all before."

I placed my hands on my hips and stared at him.

"Fine, fine, as your majesty commands."

He turned around, and I took off my jacket and my top. My pants, socks and shoes followed.

"You got soap by any chance?" Still wearing my bra and my pee soaked underwear, I positioned myself under the shower head.

"Um, no. Sorry," he replied.

I sighed. "Yeah, even a one-star hotel has soap. Whatever. Will the water be hot or cold when it comes out?"

Evan glanced at me.

"Hey, what did I say about not looking?" I shouted.

He raised one hand in the air. "Calm down. The water will warm up if I use my beams. So if you want a decent, hot shower, you're going to have to let me aim at the head, which is right above you."

I huffed. "Oh crap. Whatever. I feel gross. Fire away, Captain."

"Okay. Then turn on the faucet."

I complied, and a gurgling sound came from the gutters as he ignited his magic eyeballs.

When the water hit the top of my head, I screamed with joy.

"Holy banana split, this is the best thing ever!"

I closed my eyes and stood under the hot stream for a while, rubbing my skin and the fabric of my underwear vigorously to remove the dirt and pee smell. It seemed like eons since my last shower. Just as I began truly relaxing, the water flow stopped.

"Alright, this is good enough for now." Evan had sneaked up behind me and switched off the faucet.

"What the heck? But it felt so good!" I whined.

"The shower lasted long enough. Don't complain."

"Right, it lasted one minute."

"No. Longer than that."

I scoffed. "One minute and fifteen seconds."

I stared at the pile of clothes on the floor. "Do I get a change of outfit, at least?"

"Yeah, Susan might have some stuff to lend you."

I frowned. "Susan is three times my size."

"Oh, Miko then?"

"Extreme, much? I'm not extra small."

"Then you keep what you have."

I grunted. "This is ridiculous."

"Well, your mind didn't provide extra underwear," he replied.

"And this glitch should be fixed pronto," I mumbled. "How about I wash what I have and you zap them dry with your magic beams?"

He raised an eyebrow. "Without soap?"

I sighed. "Yeah."

"Okay."

I placed my clothes under the shower stream and rubbed the fabric as hard as I could. Evan's beams acted as an improvised dryer.

Grabbing my pants and top, I dressed.

I squeezed the dampness from my long hair, then put on my socks and shoes and, finally, my jacket. I didn't feel exactly like new, but at least a bit better.

"Alright," I said.

Evan smiled. "Great. Let's go see the others now."

Back at the Dome, everyone looked at me as if I was being prosecuted for assassinating the President. Gathered around the table, the memories didn't pip a word until I sat down next to Evan. Did I still smell like pee? That must have been it.

"Kara pushed you too far." Susan broke the uncomfortable silence. "She is uncontrollable."

"You need to remember," Sloan said, staring at me.

Miko nodded.

"Think hard about what you did," Sky added.

"How can we help her remember if she doesn't want to?" Sloan asked his brother.

"She will remember," Susan replied. "Julie, we need you to be strong, okay?"

I had no idea how strong she wanted me to be exactly. The smell of pee was certainly still strong.

"Well, does anyone have a change of clothing I could borrow?" I asked Susan, who looked away.

"No, we don't have anything," she replied eventually.

I sighed. "Worst feeling ever."

Our eyes met.

"You need to remember on your own," she said. "We can't force things upon you."

I huffed. "Great."

"We could tell you everything right now, and get it over with, but..." she continued.

"So tell me!"

Evan's hand rested on my arm.

"Your job," he said.

Shaking off his hand, I grunted and stood.

"My mind is rambling."

"You need to find peace in your heart," Susan said.

"ENOUGH!" I pounded my fist on the table. "I will not change. My mind is screwed up! And all of you died for a reason. So, my friends, today I decide to stop playing this game. Now send me back to the real world so I can rot in jail, but at least get a fresh set of clothes!"

"You don't know what you're saying." Susan answered in a calm tone of voice that angered me more.

"Don't! Just don't try to make me believe any of this is good for me. I want to be alone. Leave me alone. ALL OF YOU!"

"Kara will show up if you don't stop this—" Evan began.

"Shut up! Shut the fly up. Kara isn't my friend anymore. She's gone. I walled her in and she won't get out. So, I'm going to go to sleep, and when I wake up, I want to be back in Los Angeles, understood? And... I won't smell like pee anymore."

"This isn't something we can decide, you hold the key—" Sloan said.

"*You* hold the key. You made me come here!" I fired. "Kara can burn in hell for all I care!"

I stormed out of the Dome and into the tunnel I believed would lead me to the room where I had slept earlier. I needed some time off.

"Wait!" Evan shouted. "This is not—"

"Just let her go," Susan said. "Let her find it all out by herself."

Anger coursed through my body. Heat invaded my core. Blood pounded inside my head. My breath quickened. I wanted to scream until I had no voice left.

Did I really want to go back to Los Angeles?

Of course not.

I balled my fists and punched the air. Since the tunnel was so dark, I couldn't see anything in front of me. My fist hit the wall, sending spikes of pain through my arm. But I didn't back down. Physical pain was better than the emotional turmoil I was experiencing, asking questions I knew didn't have answers.

Inside the tunnel, I felt sheltered from my own fears. No one could tell me what to do or think here. I was on my own. And alone I would remain.

Anger breathed through me like the devil. I was in control. I had always been in control.

I punched and punched, my fists becoming numb, the skin on my knuckles probably cracked and bleeding.

It felt good to release all the tension bottled up inside.

A purple glow broke the darkness.

"And here you are," Kara said.

"I'm not afraid of you." I clenched my teeth. "Why don't you finally tell me what I did to you, huh?"

Her shrill laughter echoed around me.

"Do you think you can handle the truth?" she asked. Her face appeared inches from mine.

I stared into her purple eyeballs.

"Try me," I replied.

She laughed again. "Fine. But I don't think you'll like it."

"I don't care what you think!" I shouted back. "Stop playing with me!"

"But playing with you is so much fun!"

I sneered. "Because my anger keeps you alive?"

"Because..." She pressed her index finger onto my forehead. "You don't know how to deal with life without it."

She pushed me backwards and I fell to the ground.

She proceeded to twirl in place.

"Let me show you something."

When she stopped twirling and looked at me, my eyelids fluttered, then closed completely.

I lay in bed, my bed, in my room in Los Angeles. The house was dreadfully silent. Where were Mom and Dad? I needed my cell phone.

Rolling out of bed, I shuffled through my bag and looked under the mattress, the pillow, inside the laundry basket, even in the bathroom, but my phone was nowhere to be found.

Why didn't I have a cell phone? Didn't I need one?

"Why?" I asked out loud.

That question remained unanswered. I stepped outside. No people on the street. No cars driving by. Only deserted houses in a neighborhood empty of life, and me wandering among them like a ghost.

And, in the distance, downtown Los Angeles and the tower where my attorney, Richard Gold, worked.

The building was a tall tube of glass, lost among other tall tubes of glass, like a tree lost in the middle of the forest. I thought the building was miles away but, after a few steps, my feet took me inside the giant lobby, where no one welcomed me behind the ominous reception desk. The double row of escalators remained perfectly still, having become plain stairs I would have to climb to reach the elevator bank.

Once there, I stared at the calling panel, not sure what to do next.

"What the heck?" I mumbled. "Not going to take the stairs."

My finger pressed the up button and the light came on.

"Okay, so there's electricity in this gosh forsaken place."

I entered the elevator, and the doors closed on me. The ride ended shortly thereafter.

"Thirty-fifth floor." The automated voice welcomed me into an unoccupied space. What used to be the reception area was now an empty floor, stripped of all paintings, couches, chairs and conference rooms. All that remained was a bunch of construction tools on a tarp. A window-washing cart hung outside, also empty. Wandering along the windows, I noticed a light blinking faintly in one corner of the floor. A thick, red candle, like the ones I saw in church, was burning next to a small bouquet of dying white roses.

A small note accompanied the flowers.

I picked it up and read it out loud.

Forget me not,
Wherever you go,

> *Memories are like daggers,*
> *And your heart holds the truth within.*

No signature at the bottom, but I recognized the handwriting.

It was mine.

My fingertips ran over the surface of the card, retracing each word.

The flame of the candle vacillated slightly from left to right, as if a draft of air had passed over it, although no window was open. I picked up the flowers and brought them to my nose. Closing my eyes, I remembered that smell. Kara's fragrance. I threw the flowers on the floor and stomped all over them. When I had exhausted my anger, the candlelight died with one swift wisp, as if someone had extinguished it with a single breath.

Looking at the horizon from behind the windowpanes, I watched the cloudy sky quickly turn black. Darkness was near, ready to take over and bury me under its heavy cloak. My relentless anger wouldn't shatter it. My defiance wouldn't defeat it.

Staring at the crushed petals smearing the floor at my feet, I balled my fists and dug my fingernails into my palms.

The pain, even slight, felt real. I knew how to hold onto that feeling. And that ache throbbing inside my heart was my ally. My faithful companion.

How could I let go and not feel the dread anymore? How could I stand alone against the world and fight all the memories that drove me completely insane? Tears didn't relieve me of my burden. My shoulders couldn't carry all the weight I had imposed upon myself for all these years.

I had stopped growing since leaving Oceanside.

The realization of that truth was heartbreaking. Sickening.

Nausea gripped my stomach as I stepped away from the window. Pressing my hands against my abdomen, I took a series of deep breaths. But the nausea grew more intense and I threw up on the tarp.

Once I regained control of my bodily functions, I grabbed a power drill and weighed it. That thing was heavy.

I returned to the window where I had found the candle and the flowers, and threw the tool at it.

The glass cracked.

I grabbed the drill again and threw it harder.

The window shattered, and shards as small as flakes fell like snow on the floor. A strong, cold gust of air stormed in and forced me to the ground.

Crawling on all fours to the edge, I closed my eyes, and cold, humid air whipped my face. I pictured the beach with its hot sand under my feet, the sunlight shining bright in the bluest sky, and the salty air teasing my nostrils and entangling my hair. Kids jumped into the waves and laughed, the thrill in their voices making me smile. A young guy wearing a Lakers cap walked his white labrador and played fetch. I longed to join in and share the happiness.

I reopened my eyes and looked down.

Melissa could sue me all she wanted for breaking her perfect nose. If I was dead, she couldn't bother me anymore.

I wouldn't have to deal with Mark and the breakup.

Or my parents and their rules.

School.

All my problems could be solved right now.

With one jump.

It would feel nice, for once, not to worry anymore.

My heart held the truth within.

And my truth was anger.

One jump, and my life would be changed forever, either in the abyss, or up in the sky, amongst the clouds...

Who was I kidding? I didn't belong in heaven.

13

"**S**top what you're doing right now!" Evan's voice pulled me out of my funk.

Kara was gone. He stared at me with his green, glowing eyeballs.

"What do you think you're doing?"

"I-I saw her. She showed me—"

"Kara didn't show you anything! Don't you get it?" He lifted me off the ground like a wet rag. "You let her do these things to you because you refuse to accept what happened. But you know the truth. You know it!"

He shook me and I didn't fight back. Instead, I only started crying. Again.

"This anger of yours is a cop-out. Well, I'm tired of you trying to ruin your life. So I'm gonna take you somewhere, and you will remember! This pity party is over, you hear me?"

"I'm sorry," I said. "I didn't want to upset you."

"Your apologies are unnecessary. You think taking one step forward and then two steps back will help?

You're worth so much more, Julie. There's goodness in your heart. Now stop!"

I sniffled. "Okay. Okay."

"W-What are we doing here?" I asked with a shaky voice.

"Just wait," Evan ordered.

Oceanside's cemetery. That kingdom harbored tombstones from the eighteen and nineteen hundreds, from when the town was officially created. It belonged to the old Mission San Luis Rey de Francia, and was the oldest cemetery in the north county of San Diego still in operation.

I used to go there just because it looked so beautiful and intimate, with its trees and gardens, a real haven for the dead; and for me too, when I sought isolation from the world.

"This is the reason Kara's mad at you," he said, pointing at a tombstone.

I read the inscription.

"Kara Elizabeth Burke, beloved daughter and friend. An angel has passed. RIP."

My breath caught in my throat.

"Do you want more?"

I didn't know if I was ready to see anything more disturbing than this.

"Come on," he added.

I walked a few feet down the same row of stones, and read: "Susan Mary Welldorne."

She died the same day as Kara.

"Let me show you all of them," Evan insisted, and soon I was paying my last respects to a bunch of my high school classmates.

The lump that formed in my throat grew to the size of an apricot when I read: "Daniel Ray Goldberg."

Also dead on the same friggin' day.

Collapsing to my knees, I sobbed harder.

"What happened to them all?"

"I've got the best one for you."

"Evan Michael Fallone," I read out loud.

He nodded. "That's right. You killed us all. You buried us all here the day your life in Oceanside ended. And for what? What did you accomplish by erasing us completely?"

I didn't know what to say.

"You died too. Your tombstone is right here, right next to mine."

He pointed his finger at my name.

"Julie Erica Jones."

More tears flowed.

"But what for, Julie? This anger that you love more than you love yourself? This cemetery is now your home. You decided you were better off dead than alive. Why, Julie, why?"

"I DON'T KNOW!"

"Yes you do. What happened on that day? Tell me what happened!"

I buried my face in my hands. "I can't!"

"Yes you can! Yes you can!"

He pulled my head around and forced me to stare at the tombstone that bore my name.

"That day, I went to the party..." I blurted.

"And what happened there?"

"I... I saw... I saw..."

☾

Dan's car. He had picked us up, Kara and me, and was driving us to Mike's party.

Sitting on the backseat, I tried to avoid his repeated glances in the rearview mirror.

"I see you made a special effort to look nice tonight, nerd," he said.

Kara giggled.

"Yeah," I answered, not sure if he was making fun of me or giving me a compliment. Maybe a bit of both. Still, his smirky eyes bothered me. Could he look at the road instead of me, please?

"I helped her with her outfit," Kara added.

"You did a great job," he replied, casting another glance in the rearview mirror.

I looked away. I felt shy, uncomfortable, and more eager to go pack boxes than attend a stupid party with stupid people I didn't even talk to because they all hated my guts.

I knew trusting my feelings would be a bad idea. Strike that. I knew trusting my hormones would be a bad idea.

And, of course, the uneasiness grew as I followed Kara and Dan inside Mike's house.

The music blasted in every room. People had gathered like livestock in a slaughterhouse. How many were there, anyway? Hundreds? I recognized some faces, but I had no clue who most attendees were, and didn't care to get acquainted.

Of course, there was alcohol involved. Tons of alcohol. Marijuana too. And probably other drugs I wasn't privy to at the time. Fifteen-year-old Julie Jones wasn't much of a party girl.

I couldn't see well without my glasses—and if I put them on, I'd destroy the sexiness of the whole attire Kara had spent so much time squeezing me into, like a tight little sausage—so I walked around the house in an artistic blur, trying to find a spot where I could sit down and just kill time.

Because Kara had made it very clear she'd hang out with Dan, and I'd be the third wheel. Oh, and hang out she did. Right after we passed the threshold, she vanished from sight, hand in hand with the love of my life.

Witnessing that awful reality hurt more than any slap in the face.

I cringed in silence, holding back my tears, since no one cared about my feelings.

My only goal was to find a spot in a dark corner and be left alone.

"Hey," I heard. Mike stood right before me, two full, red, plastic cups in hand.

Dan's best friend and football teammate. With his strong jaw, fierce blue eyes, jet-black hair, and muscles to make any girl squirm, he definitely belonged to the prom king realm.

But I wasn't interested in him.

"Hey," I answered.

"You thirsty?"

I had drunk beer before, but never in the context of a binging night. A sip here and there out of Dad's bottle was all I knew about drinking. Was I remotely interested in getting hammered?

"Come on, have some." Mike waved the cup and I grabbed it.

I guess one gulp wouldn't hurt.

"Attagirl. What are we celebrating? Oh yeah. Now I remember. Your awesomeness."

I scowled.

"Oh, sad face!" he said, and scooted next to me on the empty couch I had decided to occupy for the rest of the night. "Come on, let's cheer."

I stared into his glassy eyes and fought the urge to run away.

"Cheer to what?" I asked.

He grinned. "Let's cheer to freedom. And fun. Lots of fun."

He had spiked his hair into a Mohawk, and was wearing a black t-shirt that read: "Lethal Hazard".

"What's that about?" I pointed at his chest.

He laughed. "It's the name of my band. You like it?"

As I looked at him, a spark lit up inside, giving me the confidence to spew my next line.

"Yeah. It's hot you're in a band." I leaned forward and brushed the skin of his arm. "What do you think of my outfit? You like?"

He grinned, and then scooted closer until our hands touched.

"Yeah," he slurred.

"How much?"

"Woah! A lot!"

"Then kiss me," I ordered.

His lips lingered a few inches from my mouth, and I smelled his alcoholic breath. "We should go upstairs," he mumbled.

There was no hesitation in my heart, and I gulped the rest of my drink.

When we entered the bedroom, he gave me a shot glass. I wasn't sure what the pink liquid inside was, but I didn't care to ask. As soon as the alcohol warmed my throat I begged for more, because it tasted just like sweet watermelon.

The more I drank, the faster the world spun. My inhibitions melted away. I longed for Michael's touch, and he kissed me, oh he kissed me a lot, but I wanted more. Always more. Kisses couldn't quench my thirst for attention.

I lost all sense of space and time.

Finally, Julie had found a way to let loose and enjoy herself.

Until a hand grabbed my arm and twisted the skin.

I cringed.

Tried to pull back.

The grip became tighter, and hurt me so much I screamed.

"Don't make it difficult, nerd."

Mike was holding me from behind by the wrists, pushing me onto the bed.

"What are you doing?"

He wrapped his arms around me and forced my hands behind my back, hurting me in the process. I could feel his hot breath on the skin of my neck. My brain couldn't register the events quickly enough. The alcohol was messing with my thoughts.

"You're so ripe, my friend," he said.

He pulled tighter on my hands while I kicked and twisted sideways to free myself. The drunken slo-mo didn't help my cause.

Soon enough, he lay on top of me, his weight crushing my hips.

"Let me go!" I begged, tears spilling onto the side of my face.

He laughed.

No one cared about me. I had become a piece of meat these animals could pound until they were too tired to play, and I'd be tossed to the curb like a used Kleenex.

I shut my eyes, praying to forget everything that was happening to me.

I still heard fabric rip. Smelled beer. Beads of sweat trickled on my skin. I bit my lip, and blood coated my tongue.

And then someone laughed. A girl.

"I can't!" I threw my arms around the tombstone, pounding the cold surface with my fist.

"Finish it!" Evan ordered. "Remember!"

The heavy blur of my fateful interlude with Michael popped right back, reminding me how drunk I was. But for some crazy reason, I passed out only at the end. Aware of my surroundings, I had been tied to the bed, prisoner in that bedroom that wasn't mine. Michael and Dan were looking at me like I was a prize. A disgusting prize in a cheap costume, I'd say.

I hated every second of that torture—the gloomy reminiscence of a life I had long forgotten. Each memory crawled back to the surface like an insect buried within a body. Their legs tickled inside, impatient to burrow an exit and be set free. I understood now why I had blocked everything out.

Everyone in that house wanted to hurt me. Kara wasn't there to help me out of this mess. She had abandoned me.

When I heard her laughter, my sanity was consumed and my anger unleashed.

I remembered her sitting on the back seat of Dan's car.

I remembered swerving and losing control.

I lost my breath. Caught it again.

The vehicle flipped and landed on its roof.

I managed to get out. Dizzy and disoriented, I realized Kara was still stuck in the car, hanging upside down. When I pulled her out, she didn't move.

Her face was smeared with blood, tears and makeup.

"What did you say?" I crouched on the ground and leaned closer to her mouth. "Did you say, 'I'm sorry, Julie?' I might have heard wrong. How can you be sorry now, huh?" I looked at her and couldn't help laughing. "Not so pretty anymore!"

I punched her in the stomach. My violence was of no use because she didn't react.

She was gone. So far gone.

And so was I.

14

Deep sorrow washed over me like waves on the shore, hitting me harder with every breath I took, burying me until I felt completely submerged.

As the rain of ash fell upon Evan and me, I held onto my tombstone like a plush pillow, and there wasn't a thought in my mind that didn't make me want to cry harder.

I was overwhelmed with disgust. I couldn't live with myself. Yet, the truth couldn't be ignored.

What Mike and Dan did to me was unforgivable. Worse, Kara's failure to protect me was a nasty stab in the back.

But I wasn't sure what her involvement actually implied. Did she watch the whole thing? Did she know about Dan and Mike's evil intentions?

How could she betray me like this?

Her best friend?

Kara.

Kara.

Kara.

KARA!

Sadness consumed me until I felt nothing but absolute darkness.

"So..." Evan eventually spoke up. "You will have to learn how to transform your anger into something more constructive."

"How?"

He smiled. "Don't you dream of having these magic, glowing eyes?"

"I don't understand. You want me to use anger to light up my eyeballs? I thought my anger attracted Kara."

"Well, your anger certainly fuels the darkness of this world, because it produces nothing but negative energy. But if you turn that same energy around, you can accomplish great things. Here's the catch. The more you fight the darkness, the more the darkness will retaliate, and play tricks against you to make you weak and vulnerable. You must not give in to it. You must stay strong no matter what. And Kara will certainly try to break you down. So be extremely mindful."

I stood. "Can she kill me?"

He looked down.

"She doesn't have to do anything to make you feel as though you want to die, Julie. You are your own worst enemy."

"But you know how I feel right now," I said.

He nodded. "Yes. That's why I'm going to stay with you at all times and help you jump over this hurdle." He raised his eyes. "Homework's not done yet. We should return to the Dome."

☾

Sitting at the banquet table, I stared at the critter lying before me with utter revulsion. Who had the brilliant idea to serve me dinner after I was forced to live through the horrid memory of my own rape?

I grabbed the fried rat with two fingers and tossed it on the floor.

"Hey what do you think you're doing?" Sky stared at me like I had just thrown the recycling into the main garbage disposal.

"I'm sorry."

He pointed at my empty plate. "You want another one?"

"I'm not hungry."

"Okay. Well, I'm supposed to give you food."

I raised an eyebrow. "And who made that decision?"

"I did." Sloan approached the table, and pulled up a chair.

"Right," I replied. "Well I don't want to eat."

He smiled. "Trust me, you're famished."

I laughed. "Haven't you heard the latest? I just remembered the most traumatic memory."

"Oh, I know," Sloan said. "But trust me, you're hungry." He looked at Sky. "Give her another one."

A fried critter landed on my plate and I grimaced again.

"Come on, take a bite," Sloan ordered.

I suppressed a gag and brought the rat to my mouth.

"Attagirl," he said.

To my shock, I couldn't stop chewing, and devoured the critter in a few seconds.

"Nicely done," Sloan commented. "Would you like another one?"

I nodded. Sky put another rat on my plate and I proceeded to eat this one at the speed of light.

"I'm sure Evan told you about the glowing eyes?" Sloan asked. His palms face down on the table, he looked very serious.

"Yep," I said in between bites. "Although I'm not sure how it's supposed to help me."

"Aren't you curious to hear about the whole process?" he inquired.

"What process?" I asked with a full mouth.

"The recovery process," he answered, his eyes glowing their familiar bright shade of blue.

I felt tired again. Crying all the time and eating this meat made me want to take a nap.

"You seem distracted," he continued. "Is what I'm saying boring you?"

With droopy eyes, I gnawed on the last bit of my rat leg.

"I'm waiting to hear what you have to say," I replied.

He scoffed. "I don't think you've been listening to a word I said."

I shook my head. "Absolutely I have!"

"This is a crucial moment in your recovery."

My eyes widened. "What?"

Sloan leaned closer. "What are you going to do about the anger?" he asked.

I shook my head again. "I don't know! Evan asked me the same thing."

"You're a ticking time bomb."

I wasn't sure where he was going with that statement.

"That's enough," Evan interrupted. "She deserves to be here. With us." He picked a seat next to me and patted my back.

"And I think she should be kept away until we're sure her anger is under control!" Sloan replied.

"Why should I be kept away?" I asked. "I'm not psycho."

Evan looked at me. "We thought we should temporarily isolate you."

"What?" I snapped. "But you didn't tell me this!"

My eyes locked with Sloan's. "And why do I need glowing eyeballs?"

"This is a matter of life and death. I don't see why there has to be a discussion. We all agreed to this. That was the point of the whole exercise!" Sloan pounded his fist on the table and the vibrations shook my plate.

"Alright, let's all calm down," Susan intervened, choosing a chair next to Sloan.

"What the heck is going on here?" My body tensed up and my pulse quickened.

"It's okay, Julie. We are trying to help," Susan said.

"Help? How can keeping me in the dark be helpful?" I was boiling inside.

"Evan, why do you think Julie's better off with us here?" She ignored my question and focused on Evan.

I fumed under my breath. From the corner of my eye I spotted Sky. With a quick head movement, I indicated I wanted another fried critter. Since no one cared to hear what I had to say, I'd dedicate my full attention to a dead rat. Better than make Kara appear again.

"I know what she's been through," Evan replied.

Sky dropped a rat on my plate and I ate it like I hadn't touched food in days.

"I understand her state of mind," Evan continued. "Complete isolation is dangerous. She needs someone by her side to guide her through the process. I know we've discussed this. I don't think this is a good idea."

As I chewed, a chunk of rat meat firmly lodged itself inside my throat.

"How can you be so blind to the reality of her condition?" Sloan fired.

What? That I was choking on rat meat? Oh boy. And this one piece felt especially big. Anyone know how to work the Heimlich maneuver around here?

"I can tell she's still in denial!" Sloan persisted, unmoved by my imminent choking.

Eyes tearing up, air was missing down my pipes. Grabbing onto the table, I tried to spit out the lethal chunk but none of my self-help techniques did the trick. Glancing around in a panic, I searched for Evan's eyes. But he wasn't looking at me.

"Julie Jones, so eager to show the world she can be better. I only see darkness in her soul," Sloan added.

My fingers clawed at the wood as my chest tightened with every missing breath. Seriously, darkness or not, I'd be dead in two seconds if no one came to my rescue pronto!

"It doesn't matter what I say to you, you are too stubborn to listen! Way too stubborn," Evan replied.

I slammed my hand against the table as one last cry for help.

"If she slips, we all die," Sloan said.

Was I turning blue already?

"I agree with Sloan, Evan," Susan added.

"I demand to cast a vote," Evan said. "And if you all decide she should stay away from us, I still ask to remain by her side," Evan said.

"You could be killed. And you're one of the toughest members in this group. Are you sure this is a good idea?" Susan asked.

Evan nodded. "Positive. Please."

A grunt erupted from my mouth, and my face hit the table.

I was suddenly grabbed from behind and lifted off the flat, uncomfortable surface and, after a violent slap on the back, I spat out the chunk of meat, which landed with a mushy plop on the table. A side-glance indicated my savior was Miko. At least she didn't arrive when it was too late, like the cavalry.

As I recovered my spirits and my precious breath, the other memories stared at me in disbelief.

"Are you alright?" Susan asked. Oh, now she was paying attention to me?

"I choked," I replied, still fighting to regain full control of my respiratory functions. "While you were talking about me like I wasn't in the room. No one told me I had to be isolated. Where are you going to send me?" I asked bitterly. "And what the heck am I supposed to do with glowing eyes?"

Sloan's eyes narrowed.

"Are you willing to overcome your anger?" he asked, with equal bitterness.

I groaned. "I don't necessarily like to feel this way, if that's what you want to hear. But tell me how you would feel the day you learn you were raped by the boy you love and his best friend, and then stabbed in the back by your best friend. Then we can talk about my darkness all you want."

He didn't reply. Thought so, smart butt.

Evan turned to me. "This is not something I wanted."

"You still kept me in the dark, and I don't appreciate that. I thought we were tight," I said.

He frowned. "I'm sorry, Julie. Your perception is still flawed. But I'll help with that."

I scoffed. "Yeah, right."

"Alright, despite what was originally intended, we will vote," Susan interrupted. "And our decision will be final. All in favor of Julie being isolated until she over-comes her anger, raise your hand."

Arms rose like spikes, ready to impale me through the heart. Except Evan and Miko.

"Alright," Susan said. "Julie, Evan will stay with you until he decides you can come back."

Evan grabbed my hand and pulled me away from the table.

"What is going to happen to me?" I asked, as we exited the Dome and walked toward one of the adjacent tunnels.

"Nothing will happen to you. You're going to let go of all this awful energy festering inside, and you'll return as a brand new person in no time," he replied, without looking at me.

15

"Why am I being cast away?" I asked. "It's not like my anger is new to anyone."

Evan's green glow illuminated the tunnel, and I absorbed his light, wishing time would stop right there, right then.

"They're afraid you're going to give in to your darkness. And if you do their survival is compromised."

"And what am I going to do then?" I asked.

He glanced back and winked at me.

"It's okay, Julie. It's understandable you're scared, but I'll be with you, okay?"

We entered another chamber and I noticed a dark mass moving by my feet.

"What is this place? Another shower room?"

"I call it the Cave. Well, it's not really a cave. Just the sewer." He laughed.

"Good Lord, what's up with you and the sewer?"

An acrid stench was concentrated in this small space. Not a fragrance I'd use every day. I started retching.

"Sorry, I forgot to do something," Evan said. He grabbed my face between his hands and stared at me. A few seconds later, the horrible stench was gone.

"Do you feel any better?" he asked.

"Yeah, yeah. Relatively speaking, of course. Thanks."

I sure liked his glowing eyeballs. The sewer on the other hand...

"What was the point of me taking a shower in sewer water if you had already decided to bring me here?"

"Filtered sewer water. The Cave is a nice place to reflect on yourself," he answered.

"Oh, because I haven't reflected enough?"

He laughed. "It's going to be fun. Trust me."

I shook my head. "Yeah, I don't know about that..."

"Here's the deal," he continued. "I'd like you to let go of your negative energy by fighting."

I choked. "Fighting? Isn't it something I've been doing all along? And how? Who?"

He laughed. "Oh this little beast won't be defeated easily, but you can't get hurt. Consider it a simulation."

"W-What beast?"

He pressed his fingers against my lips and I responded with raised eyebrows. "Listen." Squeezing my hand tightly, he whispered very softly in my ear. "Don't fret, but I have to turn off the light for a minute."

"Ooookay," I mouthed back.

The comforting green glow vanished almost immediately, leaving pitch-black in its wake. Evan touching my arm didn't stop me from freaking out. Breathing as quietly as possible, I waited for something terrible to happen. What should I be listening for?

Then I heard it. Through the constant dripping and flowing of water, a very low murmur pierced the murk. It sounded like a cat in heat, meowing to find a mate far, far away. Okay...

"You hear it now?"

I nodded, but then realized he couldn't see me.

"Yes," I said.

"Relax." He paused. "I'm going to get its attention while you run at it. Then it's all you."

"A-Are you going to stick around and help me?" I asked.

"Yes. I'm sure the others aren't keen on letting me be with you," he said, "but they know it's the best way to restore you to sanity."

I cringed. The nervous knot in my stomach gave me cramps.

"Are you feeling okay?" he asked.

"I-I could use some of your powers to relax me a little, I admit."

"Okay, why don't I give you this instead?"

Evan's hand suddenly abandoned mine, and complete agitation exploded in the pit of my stomach.

"Evan?" I needed him.

When his hand brushed mine, I jumped. "Are you crazy? You almost gave me a heart attack!"

He placed something in my palm. "You should eat this."

"What is it?" I felt the edges of a small, round shape as smooth as a pebble.

"Eat."

"I don't understand."

"Just do it. Come on." As soon as I felt the pebble on my tongue, I swallowed it.

"Did you eat it?" he asked.

"Yes."

"I didn't hear you chew."

"Uh, well, I gulped it."

He laughed. "Okay."

I couldn't tell whether he was making fun of me.

"Are you ready to have crazy powers?" he asked.

"What?"

And then, my chance to say anything else poofed out like a curl of smoke from Bilbo's pipe.

A rapid surge of adrenaline blasted through my entire body, as if I was about to slide down a roller coaster very, very quickly, my heart thumping hard and nearly bursting from my chest. The scenery around me changed. The Cave lit up with a purplish hue so captivating I almost stepped into the sewer water, suddenly turned plasma. Flashy oranges, yellows, and reds undulated uncomfortably near my feet; and ahead, a bluish mass of goo bubbled in the distance.

The beast looked five times my size. I had to calm down and focus.

"Evan!" Cold sweat trickled down my back.

"What is it?" His touch put me a bit more at ease. Taking a slow breath, I searched for his eyes. Through my new psychedelic vision, he looked like an Andy Warhol portrait.

"W-What did you give me? And what am I supposed to do now?"

"Don't panic. The stuff you took won't last very long, but it will help with your energy levels. I'm going to use my beams. The beast is going to move toward us. You jump at it, and let out all the anger. Whatever you feel, let it out. It doesn't matter what you think of, use these thoughts to fight it," he said.

I shivered from head to toe. A little bird told me jumping at this unidentified mass of goo wouldn't end well.

"Are you ready?" he asked.

No, but I wasn't left with much choice at that point.

"I'm firing in three, two..."

His eyes lit up and the green laser pierced through the purple murk, directly at the mass of goo. I heard a loud growl.

"Go!" Evan ordered, pushing me forward.

Energy spiraled through me like electricity.

Well, here goes nothing! I figured a giant superhero leap would easily cover the distance between me and the mass of goo. Securing my balance, I jumped like I was about to break a record at the Olympic Games.

Holy banana!

I extended my arms forward to prepare for a perfect landing, while the creature, now quickly rising, was ready to swallow me in one gulp.

I avoided the giant, gaping mouth and landed on my target's back. Without thinking twice—which perhaps I should have done—I crawled toward the top of the pile of goo.

Every superhero flick teaches us to aim for the eyes whenever the goal is to disorient a stronger enemy. In my superhero playbook, however, I usually went for the groin. Worked every time! What was I doing now? Was I even reaching for the head? Was this the front end? Who knew how that beast was configured? I had to expect anything. No user manual was provided when Evan ordered me to defeat the thing. Did a mountain of slime even have a face or a groin?

My fingers probed the goo and, naturally, the monster growled and snarled, trying to shake me off. I doggedly held on. Grabbing the ears—I had convinced myself they were ears—I twisted them against the increasingly violent shaking. The giant shrieked. Oooh! Achilles' heel! Unfortunately, whatever kind of heel it was, it didn't solve my problem. I was drowning in goo. A fleeting thought passed through my mind, of Freddie Kruger and his claws severing heads with a single blow.

A tingling sensation flared to life in my fingertips, and the more I scratched at the beast, the more my nails seemed to grow into blades. Whoot! Reborn as a blood-thirsty serial killer, I let 'er rip, until I had shredded the creature's insides. A primal rage dominated me as the beast yelped and cried, and its bluish hue bled into a darker, unhealthier color.

"Keep going," Evan's voice popped in the distance.

My wrath increased. My arms and hands became as strong and sharp as swords and continued destroying until there was nothing left to destroy. Once the beast's slimy substance leaked into the plasma river, I stood on solid ground, catching my breath.

"Use your anger," Evan said. "Use it to fight."

"Why? I just killed this thing..." my voice trailed off.

The slimy substance reappeared surface side, slithering to the edge of the pool and reassembling the monster all over again. Over the span of a few seconds, the beast looked as big and as terrifying as before. It growled and opened its mouth, ready to bite my head off.

"Use your anger now, Julie!" Evan shouted.

Right. Great advice. But I wasn't fully prepared to fight this thing for one more round. The effects of whatever Evan gave me earlier were starting to wear off. If only I could unleash fire from my eyes...

As this thought crossed my mind, two very powerful orange beams poured out of me, straight at the beast's body. The light pierced the goo, melting it like wax.

I kept burning until the beast vanished completely.

Once all goo was gone, for good this time, I collapsed on the ground, and the orange light was extinguished.

"Here, here, look at you!" Evan said, pulling me upward.

Yeah, right. I felt exhausted.

"What the heck did you give me?" I asked, as the plasma water reverted to its original state, and the Cave was immersed in darkness. Evan laughed and lit up his green glow.

"Oh, a piece of chocolate," he replied.

"W-What? Like what the old lady gave me?"

"Something similar, yes."

"My vision changed, my hands, my body. I felt so strong, so invincible," I said. "Do the others know you're giving me magic pills?"

"It doesn't matter what they know. The beast distracted you. You put all the focus on the goo instead of yourself, and you defeated it. Job well done!"

"But the others, what are they going to say?"

He brushed this away with his hand. "Worry about you. You can spend days mourning and lamenting, asking yourself what you did wrong. But the journey is meant to teach you how to use bad memories and grow from them."

I nodded. "Yeah, I get that. But the goo monster isn't Kara. I don't know what I'm going to do once I see her again."

He patted my back. "Don't project. Stay in the here and now. Practice."

"Whatever you say, I guess."

"Come on, there's more work to do," he said.

The chocolate left me hungry for real food. I wasn't talking fried critters—no matter how good a cook Sky was—but a juicy, delicious burger in my friggin' mouth. Salivating just at the idea, I reminisced about In-N-Out's double-doubles.

It was one heck of a hot day in September. Kara and I had been surfing all afternoon, and we decided to take a break before sunset.

"Dinner at my house?" Kara took off her wetsuit and packed it neatly in her oversized beach bag. After slipping into a pair of shorts and a t-shirt, she pulled her tousled hair into a ponytail.

"Nah. I shook my head. "I'm in for some deliciousness at the burger joint. You game?"

I removed my wetsuit and put on loose sweat pants and a tank top. Stepping on the hem of the legs, I rolled them up to mid-calf.

"What about our surfboards?" she asked.

"I'll go get the food while you wait outside. We can munch on the beach."

I ran my fingers through my short hair to spike it, and looked for my glasses in my pants pocket. I didn't wear contacts when we surfed.

Binoculars in place, I enjoyed my 20/20 vision again.

"Alright," she said.

In-N-Out was located a couple of miles north from where we were. We carried our surfing gear while strolling on the beach, taking our time.

While we walked, my eyes caught sight of two boys skating on the pavement. Their boards made an awful lot of noise as they used the sidewalk to slide and do acrobatic tricks.

"Bunch of showoffs," I mumbled when we passed them.

"What?" Kara asked.

"Nothing." I looked ahead at the burger joint, drawing closer. "Darn, I can't wait to feast!"

Kara stayed outside and watched our surfing gear while I entered In-N-Out. The place was packed, and the wait time longer than usual. When I finally made it out with the food, Kara was talking to the two skater kids.

Moving toward them, I huffed. Who did these guys think they were? I had expected to enjoy my meal in peace with my best friend.

Kara saw me and waved.

"Hey! We got company!" She smiled like it was the best day of her life.

I put on a fake happy face and handed her a burger.

"Yeah, we do."

The two kids looked exactly alike—twins—with disheveled blonde hair, bright blue eyes and freckles all over their faces.

One of them extended his hand for me to shake.

"Hey, I'm Sloan," he said.

Based on his boyish appearance, I didn't expect his voice to sound so deep.

"Julie," I replied and grabbed his hand.

The handshake was firm, a sign the kid felt confident and sure about himself.

"This is my brother, Sky." Sloan introduced me and I shook his brother's hand.

"Nice to meet you," I said.

"Yeah, pleasure," Sky replied. His handshake felt more like a dead fish.

Kara cooed. "Did you know Sloan and Sky just moved here from LA? And they're attending our high school."

I snorted. "No, I didn't know. Thanks for the newsflash."

I looked at Sloan. "Why come to Oceanside? Was LA not good enough?"

Sloan laughed. "LA was fine."

"So why move?"

"Parents got divorced," Sky answered.

"Oh," I said. "That sucks."

Sloan shrugged. "Once you know they're happier apart than together, you learn to make peace with that new reality. Nothing's really changed for us. We still get to skate and have fun."

Sky stayed silent, which made me wonder whether he felt the same way. His handshake definitely told otherwise.

"Well, you wanna join us?" Kara piped up. "Burgers and fries, and milkshakes? Huh?"

Sloan laughed again. "Yeah, sure, that sounds like a plan."

Sky nodded. "I'm hungry."

Kara clapped her hands. "Yay! It's a date!"

Not that I didn't empathize with the whole divorce ordeal, but In-N-Out was Kara and my thing. We never invited other people to join the fun. What the heck was happening?

My stomach growled.

"Wanna wait for us while we order?" Sloan asked.

"Yeah, take your time!" Kara replied.

I clenched my teeth, trying not to say something rude, although I was dying to tell these kids that no, I couldn't wait.

"Yeah, yeah, hopefully the line won't be too long," I mumbled.

Sloan patted me on the shoulder.

"Neat. We'll be right back."

He and his brother entered the burger joint and I stared at Kara.

"What?" she asked.

"Nothing. I'm tired and hungry. I think I'm gonna head home after we eat," I said.

"Oh, okay. Well, maybe the boys can walk us back and help us carry the boards?"

I took a deep breath.

"Right, yeah, whatever works."

She smiled. "Great."

I forced a smile in return, and looked at the ocean.

16

"**D**arn," I said.

Evan glanced at me. "Oh, your thoughts are wandering again?"

I brushed the air with my hand. "Yep."

"Did you like igniting your eyeballs?"

I nodded. "I admit, this was fun!"

"Okay, then you're gonna jump in," he replied.

"Where? In the sewer water?"

"Right."

I clapped my hands. "Sweet! What am I gonna fight this time?"

He laughed. "Oh you'll see. I don't like to ruin surprises. And I'm going to dive in with you."

He stepped closer to the water.

"Are you going to give me a magic chocolate again?" I asked.

"You liked what it did to you, huh?"

I shrugged. "Duh."

"Tell you what, how about we try to fight without any magic trick this time? You know how you felt, right?"

I nodded.

"So use those feelings. Believe in yourself," he said. "Ready?"

"I guess. Although a kick wouldn't hurt..."

"Give me a convincing answer, girl."

"Well..." I sighed. "Yes."

"Good, then let's go!"

He dove and I followed.

My primal reaction was to keep my mouth closed so as not to swallow any liquid and drown. While using my arms and legs to push me forward, the pressure inside my lungs kept increasing, indicating there wasn't much O_2 left. Evan's green glow served as my guide through the dark water, which I realized was also really icy. The pressure inside my chest squeezed my lungs like wet sponges. To spare a few seconds of precious air, I stopped my swim, but the cold of the water was too overpowering.

"Where are we going?" I asked Evan in my thoughts, since he could read them. "I need some air."

"Have you tried to... breathe?" he inquired.

"Underwater? You want me to drown even faster?"

"Believe in yourself," he said again.

Shizzzzle nizzle.

The pressure inside my lungs forced me to release all the CO_2.

This was really no joke, to be playing little mermaid. Little Antarctic mermaid, I should add.

I closed my eyes and mumbled a few comforting words.

"I am okay. I will not drown."

I reopened my eyes and, as the pressure inside my lungs became unbearable, let my mouth gape open to let water enter my airways. The sensation of having liquid instead of air inside my pipes was very unsettling—and my entire body twitched and convulsed as more liquid entered my throat. Fog filled my head but, as I drifted into the darkness of my own passing, the pressure quickly lifted off my chest.

"See, not that bad, huh?" Evan asked, interrupting my mermaid morphing process.

"What?"

He laughed. "Are you breathing again?"

I ran a test, inhaling and exhaling very carefully at first. Then, as I grew more comfortable with the idea that it was totally possible to breathe underwater in this world, the inhaling and exhaling process became more natural.

Darn, this actually felt amazing.

"Told ya," Evan said.

Out of pure thrill, I tumbled into an upside down flip. The sensation of freedom was unbelievable. As oxygen reached my muscles, I stretched my limbs into the shape of a star.

"How are ya feeling?" Evan asked.

"This is the most balls to the wall thing I've ever experienced!"

"Glad to hear!" he answered.

I tumbled some more. I couldn't stop doing this—it was too much fun!

"Uh hum," Evan piped up, as my pirouette exhibition continued.

"Oh, nice, now you're gonna kill my buzz," I replied.

"Well, you weren't sent here just to toy around."

I huffed. "I know, I know."

I did a flip once more just for the sake of it. "So, where to next?"

"We're going to swim to the bottom and look for the big fish," he replied.

"Big fish? Like sharks?"

Pushing my weight downwards, I continued my descent to the unknown, following Evan's green light.

"Time to enjoy yourself," he said. "Not with sharks. Just a big fish."

"Are we doing a simulation again? Why do I have to fight a big fish? Kara's not a fish!"

He laughed. "Kara's not a fish, and we're not here to fight Kara but help you channel this anger of yours. Think of everything you can do once you can control it. First and foremost, we need to rebuild your self-confidence. Once you believe in yourself again, you'll find it easier and easier not to use anger as a response to every challenge you're confronted with. And since you always loved to go surfing and swimming, doing things underwater seemed like a great way to help you release some tension and be content with yourself. You shouldn't focus on Kara right now. Trust me, she will come later."

"I don't know if I can stop thinking about Kara. I'm really mad at her," I said.

"Yes, she's part of the process. I'm not asking you to forget about her, simply to put your focus on something other than her right now."

"Alright, alright, I get it. So where's the big fish?"

"We're getting closer."

"Can I turn on my beams?" I asked.

"Can you turn them on without burning everything in your way?"

"What do you mean?"

"Learning how to control your anger also means learning how to control your energy levels. If your focus is on destroying, the light pouring out of you will not just be for esthetic purposes."

"How do I learn to just turn on the light without burning everything?" I asked.

"Self-control. Balance your emotions. One step at a time, okay?" he replied.

"But I love to do things fast!" I protested.

"Oh I know. That's why the big fish is going to teach you patience." He paused. "There, do you see it?"

I squinted, but without any additional light source it was difficult to see anything.

"Nope," I replied.

"Okay, wait until we get real close. And beware, the big fish is blind. The only way it can sense you is if you touch it."

"What? Like I'm here to play with this thing?"

"Yep," he added. "Learn to tame your emotions by learning the fish's weak spots. Trust me, this animal may be blind, but it's not stupid."

Oh crapola. The fish wasn't the only blind one in this game.

"Okay. And then what? Do I kill it?"

"No, Julie. Is destroying the only thing you can do?"

"Eh, I don't know. I'm used to it by now, you know."

"Right, well break the bad habits and get to work."

"If I could see anything!"

I slowed down my strokes.

"What about the psychedelic vision? Can I do that again?"

"Not without the help of a chocolate," Evan replied.

"Crap. So give me one more!"

I felt like a child who had to learn everything from square one.

"No. Use my glow as guide," Evan replied. "Without any substance altering your mood and sensations. This is a simple exercise, don't overcomplicate it."

I sighed. "Okay, okay."

I secretly wished I were high so I could change the colors of my surrounding environment or, better, ignite my eyeballs.

Evan's glow finally gave me a glimpse of my target.

"Do you see it now?" he asked.

"Yeah."

Time to assess the size of this blind fish.

It measured at least ten to fifteen feet long, and was covered in a thick carapace, like a turtle. The face had a narrow beak, with a second mouth hanging from the neck—or whatever I should call that part of the body—with a deformed, oblong skull that expanded way past the torso. That thing looked nothing like a fish! The six legs were equipped with long, sharp claws. And last but not least, the back ended with a tail—a lizard type tail that flicked from left to right as the creature cruised through water like a crocodile.

Shizzlenit.

I had to touch this thing?

Deep breath. From my swimming and surfing days, I remembered following schools of fish while underwater, and watching them swarm around me like I was bait. All I had to do was pretend I was a fish myself by mimicking the movements of the animal. I would remain unnoticed and could move real close.

I started my journey toward the creature, undulating my body like a dolphin and making sure to keep my legs together so the thing would believe I had a tail too. Although maybe all those efforts would prove fruitless since that fish was blind. But sharks didn't have great vision either. They sensed movement. They tasted blood in the water.

"Evan, am I going completely crazy here?"

"Keep swimming," he replied simply, in answer to my internal *National Geographic* monologue.

"Fine," I grunted.

Reducing my breathing to a bare minimum, I kept undulating my body, using only my arms to paddle me forward.

Dude, that thing was ugly.

The carapace looked like it had been made from hot, dripping wax, with ridges and uneven bumps all over. There seemed to be no logical pattern to its appearance and shape. In the mouth I noticed rows of razor-sharp, toothpick teeth. The two eyes on top of the head were as small as needle heads.

Who the heck was in charge of creating monsters in this world? I sure never imagined a goo monster or this fish reptilian thing.

I kept my swimming smooth and slow. The creature moved in wide circular motions and didn't seem bothered by my presence. My nerves were shot. Could that beast sense fear?

Drawing slow breaths, I reached the top of the animal. I extended my fingers and grabbed the edge of the scales. A sharp pain immediately burrowed through my skin.

Crap.

"What the heck was that?"

"Small defense mechanism. Keep going," Evan said.

Okay. That flesh wound would do. No need to ask whether I'd die from such a wound. After all, I was immersed in sewer water. That concern had to be suppressed for now.

I focused on the creature and went for the scales again.

Try grabbing onto a thin, razor sharp ledge, while hanging one hundred feet above ground. Despite being underwater, I had to use all my strength to hold on. Gosh, Evan, what did you make me do?

"Wouldn't it have been easier to feed me a magic chocolate?" I asked.

"No," he replied. "You need to try doing things without an artificial kick."

"What if I like that kick?"

"The fish won't care either way. Now, stop debating and get ready."

"Ready? What for?"

As the beast pulled me along, a strong electrical current ran through my hands and arms, the pain shooting straight through my spine and sending a surge directly into my brain. My jaw locked as I cringed, until my teeth almost shattered into little bone crumbles. For a few seconds I lost all sense of space. My vision blurred and I saw stars.

I released my grip. My breathing quickly returned to normal. The pain was definitely acute but didn't last longer than a few seconds. Note to self: the shock was a surprise but in no way lethal. Good to know. Still, I'd not like to repeat that exercise. What would happen if I kept being shocked over and over again?

"The multiplication of such electrical neural activity in your brain will just cause more pain," Evan said.

"Well, you could have warned me. Ouch, that friggin' hurt!"

"Yeah, better avoid that next time, shall we?" he added, in a derisive tone. "Are you going to be able to keep on touching it?" he inquired.

"Besides cutting me too, which was another defense mechanism you could have warned me about," I groaned.

"Listen, do you get a user manual on how to live life? No, you improvise and adapt."

"Seriously, what's all the fuss about? This fish is so ugly."

"Don't be deceived by appearances."

"I'm not willing to get hurt again," I whined.

"Julie, if you want to make progress, you'll have to make sacrifices. Now get back to your homework," he ordered.

"Fine, fine, I'll try one more time."

"Go on."

I swam and grabbed onto the scales, now securing my body to the animal. I could tell it didn't like me touching it, as it swam faster and rolled over to shake me off.

I felt the electrical current course through my body again, but held on.

"Okay, now what?" I asked, preparing myself to unleash my beams, just in case.

"No destroying, Julie! I know what you're up to!"

"But this thing wants to hurt me," I replied.

"Do you believe this fish has anything against you and wants to get you?"

"Yeah, it hurt me already."

"Gosh almighty, listen to yourself. It hasn't attacked you. You made the first move and the creature simply reacted to your hostile touch." He sounded annoyed.

"You told me to touch it!" I protested.

"Listen, just proceed with the exercise. Feel love instead of fear. Tame instead of destroy," Evan replied. "Why don't you try to make this baby your friend?"

My friend? Like my pet?

"Dude, this is getting weirder by the minute."

"The purpose of this exercise is to explore other options. Use your emotions to understand yourself. How far are you willing to go? How much time are you willing to invest? You don't have to take the high road every time a challenge comes your way. Love and patience, Julie."

I huffed. "How exactly am I going to overcome my anger by taming this thing?"

"Ask yourself how you can change your perception of certain events, instead of judging a book by its cover and throwing in the towel right away."

I took a deep breath.

"The fish doesn't mean anything to me," I replied.

"Just because it's unfamiliar and doesn't look pretty enough according to your beauty standards? Do you realize how twisted your thinking is?"

"My thinking is perfectly fine. I'm entitled to think this creature is fugly, and I don't want to touch it or tame it, or make it my personal assistant, okay?"

"You're not entitled to anything in this world. And this fish, as ugly as you think it is, is still a living thing. Please, accept that simple fact."

I shook my head. "This is bullcrap. I don't care about this friggin' fish for crying out loud!"

"Then you don't care about getting better, and you'll stay stuck here forever," Evan answered in a flat tone.

"I'm gonna stay stuck in this sewer forever? This is bigger bullcrap!" I said.

"Nothing comes easy, girlfriend. But if you're willing to improve, you'll have to work hard on yourself. Trust me, the end result always pays off."

"I don't know." I sighed. "Gosh, what did I get myself into?"

"You have no choice. Meanwhile, all this time you spent arguing, you still held onto the fish despite the electrical current coursing through your body and causing you discomfort, which shows me you want to change."

My heart sank. If only I hadn't punched Melissa in the face I wouldn't be in this stupid situation today. Imprisoned in my own mind, with memories as my only companions. Memories that gave me orders, too. And gosh knew how much I hated receiving orders.

"You're right, although I don't want to admit it," I said.

"Baby steps, Julie," Evan answered.

I still let go of the fish after it rolled over a million times to dislodge me from its carapace. This thing was giving me a headache, on top of the increasing pain in my muscles. And the taming appeared to be a complete failure.

I wanted to go home.

But I couldn't. I grunted. "So what's the plan exactly?"

"Learn to be patient," Evan said. "You can't win every time."

Watching the fish swim below me, I focused on the tail, flicking from left to right, as if nothing had ever bothered to touch the creature in the first place.

"Okay," I replied, defeated.

Yet, a part of me wanted to win that battle. I couldn't stay stuck there forever. That creature just didn't like me, probably because it felt threatened by me. If I used gentler moves, I could show I had no intentions of hurting that thing.

So I swam toward the fish again and extended my arms without touching it. As I let my fingers hang a few inches away from the carapace, I mimicked the animal's movements, like they were my own, in an improvised dance under Evan's soft green glow.

17

After class was over I sprinted to the library, almost leaving a trail of fire and smoke behind me.

Ignoring text messages from Kara, I walked past the computer lab and into the shelving area, finally feeling at home.

The library, despite its small size, held an impressive number of volumes. My favorite spot was the occult section. I browsed the contents of the shelves. *Science of the Dark Side*, *Witches' Hunt*, and *Old Tales of Black Magic* caught my eye. Books I'd never read, but their titles made me laugh.

I pulled one volume from the shelf.

"Interested in black magic?" I jumped as Susan walked up behind me, and the volume I was holding fell with a light thump onto the carpeted floor.

"Um, no not really. I was just... checking things out," I said.

She smiled. "Hmmm mmmm. I see."

She picked up the book and examined the cover.

"Yeah, this one isn't that great. A lot of it is pure speculation. If you really want to learn more about that stuff, you should read this one." She went to the bottom of the shelf, pulled out another thick volume and handed it to me.

I read the title out loud.

"*Secrets Behind the Doors of Your Soul: What you already know and what's left to discover.*" I took a deep breath and looked at her. "How do you know what book to pick?"

She chuckled. "I'm proud to admit I've read them all. Lots of them are repetitive. So you can forget about those." She pointed at the top shelf.

I nodded. "Right."

She smiled. "Come on." She put the book back into place. "Aren't you curious to talk to me about Dan? Has he asked you to do his homework yet?"

I scowled. "No, and it doesn't mean I'm going to comply when he does."

She laughed. "Seriously? Think you can fool me?"

"Right, how do you know he's gonna ask me to do his homework anyway?"

"Let's have a little chat."

She winked as we headed to a spot in the back, where there were tables and chairs.

"Since when do you follow rules, Julie Jones?" she asked and sat down.

I raised an eyebrow. "What do you mean?"

She chuckled. "You're not much of a follower in any sense of the word, even if you teamed up with Barbie Doll over there. That, I must admit, puzzles me. But I'm sure you got a good explanation for this, right?"

My turn to sit.

"I've known Kara for a long time," I said. "She's my best friend."

"I figured. Still, people change you know."

I inhaled deeply. "Yeah they do. Why are you so interested in my life?"

She smiled.

"Oh, don't play dumb with me. You know exactly why. We aren't like everyone else, you and I. Even if you try your hardest to fit in, you won't. And people will use you, and you will please them because you think doing what they ask you to do will make them like you more. But the truth of the matter is, they won't." She shook her head. "You have a gift. You're smart and good looking, despite what you think."

I swallowed slowly, the lump in my throat growing in sync with my quickening heartbeat.

"So what did you want to tell me?" I asked.

"How about you ask me questions and I provide you with answers?" she asked back.

I looked away, unsure what to ask first.

"Are you a lesbian?"

She rolled her eyes. "No."

"Are you a stalker?"

"Heck no."

"Were you Dan's girlfriend at any point in time?"

"I wish, yeah!" She sighed. "But no, he never went out with me. In my dreams he did."

"Okay." I paused. "Then why did you warn me about him?"

"Because he had the same effect on me. He was charming and nice, and one day he asked me for a small favor. I thought doing his homework would make him like me. But he used me. And crushed my heart in the process. That's okay though. I learned my lesson."

"Even if I do his homework, it won't last forever," I said.

"Nah, of course not. He's going to graduate at some point. Thanks to our combined efforts."

I sighed. "What makes you think I have feelings for him?"

She scoffed. "Girlfriend, the world isn't blind."

"I don't like him like that. I don't even know him."

"Oh yeah, then how do you like him?"

I took a deep breath. "Why are you being friendly with me?"

"Do you think I have an agenda?" she asked, smiling.

"I don't know what to think."

She shook her head. "Oh Julie, your guard is up in all the wrong spots."

"I'm fine," I replied with clenched teeth.

She grabbed my hand.

"No, you're not. But who am I to tell you that, huh? Nobody."

I pulled my hand away.

"Exactly."

She laughed. "Gosh, we're not so different, you and I. If only you could open your eyes and see the world for what it is."

"My eyes are open."

"Then why do you come to the occult section?"

"Because no one else does."

"I do."

I exhaled loudly. "Susan, I'd like some time alone. Would you mind?"

She nodded. "Okay." She stood. "Just know that I don't have bad intentions. Have a good day."

"Okay," I replied, looking at the ground.

She stepped away.

Once I made sure she was gone, I unzipped my backpack and pulled my journal. Opening it at a new blank page, I started writing.

There was too much bitterness in my heart.

Susan sensed my ill-being right away, and I ignored her warnings. Falling for Dan was only the tip of the iceberg. As I went through puberty, and my anger grew with me, I didn't take the time to pause and deal with myself. I lashed out at everyone around me: my parents, teachers, schoolmates, and Kara.

I remembered this one incident. Kara stopped by the house as I was packing some boxes in my room.

She entered my bedroom and radiated happiness, like those angels painted on big murals by Michelangelo.

"OMG, you'll never believe who just asked me out!" she said.

I looked at her, not sure what she was talking about.

"Dan!" She burst into laughter and gave me a hug I didn't reciprocate.

"He asked you out?" I asked, trying to stay calm. "For real? Not just in your imagination?"

"Yes! He asked me to be his date at Mike's party!"

I felt frozen in place. "Wow, congrats, I guess," I said in a flat tone. "Yeah, you've been infatuated with him for some time, so yeah, that's, uh, wonderful news."

She punched me in the arm when I scowled. "Gosh, you had the same reaction at the beach. Can't you be happy for me? Friends are supposed to be happy for each other!"

"I can't," I replied. "I just can't."

"Is it because you're afraid he might break my heart?"

I sighed loudly. "I, uh, don't know. I'm busy here. Can we talk about this at a better time?"

"You're really something else."

"What do you want me to tell you, huh? The world won't stop revolving around its axis to watch you two lovebirds exchange your first kiss. You're going out with him, that's great. See, I'm happy for you."

"No, you're visibly upset."

I laughed. "No, I'm not. You on the contrary..."

Her face had flushed fifty shades of red. "Really, Julie?"

I knew my next words would hurt her, but didn't care at that point. I just refused to see Dan with another girl, my best girlfriend at that. The move to Los Angeles was inevitable. It had been inevitable for the past three months. And during those three months, life had changed at the speed of light. Long distance friendships didn't last. Out of sight, out of mind, right? Too irritated to think clearly, I wanted her to leave me alone.

But I also wanted to make her cry. Hurt her like I was hurt. He could have given me a chance. The nerd who did all his homework in secret for him. A slight chance was all I asked for.

"Whatever! If you want this guy for a boyfriend, you might as well stop being my friend," I said.

She shrieked. "Are you asking me to choose between you and him?"

I couldn't look at her. "That's not what I meant." I stared at the ground.

"Your words tell otherwise. I can't believe this!"

She paced back and forth across the room. I didn't move.

"This is insane! You're a miserable, selfish human being. All you care about is you! And don't act like you care about this friendship too, because you clearly don't. So if you're really asking me to choose, say it now!"

She stared at me, her eyes begging me to say what she wanted to hear.

"Fine," I said. "Yes, I'm asking you to choose."

Her eyes teared up as she clenched her jaw and balled her fists. "Why, Julie, why?"

I shook my head. "You wouldn't get it. It's fine. I'm leaving town soon anyway. Good riddance, right?"

She began crying and I didn't console her. I just watched her like I would a movie. And all I felt inside was anger.

When I couldn't watch her sob any longer, I turned my back and continued packing.

"You're pathetic!" she shouted. "And you'll never love anyone more than your stupid anger."

I stopped midway. Then, slowly shifting around, I delivered the final blow.

"I'm not the one wailing like a brat. It doesn't matter whom or what I love. You, on the contrary, seemed to have moved on quite nicely, despite me still being here. Maybe you are the insensitive, selfish bitch, and you're showing your true colors now."

She fumed for a few seconds, her skin blazing like an overcooked lobster, then raised her hands in surrender.

"Fine. Be that way. Deny, deny, deny! I'm done with you. I've put up with this attitude for way too long. So, Julie, have a nice life!"

I said nothing in return, and just stared at her. When she left the room, I tore boxes apart and punched the walls until I felt less hotheaded.

The problem was, I didn't like fighting with her. I tried to make amends, but every time I ran into her at school, this nagging feeling of failure kept tugging at my heart. Our friendship couldn't die in this awful manner.

What did I do to make things better, though?

We patched things up a week before the party. I even had dinner at her house prior to going. She took me to her room afterwards, said everything between us was okay. We hugged, and she gave me that dress—an awful tight black dress, not red like I had written in my journal—with ruffles at the top and bottom. When I glanced in the mirror, I didn't feel in my comfort zone. But she did or said nothing to imply we might be on bad terms. She acted like her usual self, and even complimented me.

Why didn't she protect me from Dan and his best friend? Why did she let them take advantage of me?

As mad as I was, I would never have done that to her.

I needed closure. Would she give me an explanation next time I ran into her?

Or would she attack me because I drove us off the road?

I should have backed down.

I was hurt. Terribly hurt.

Dan and Mike had violated me, but she had ripped my soul apart.

And the only response I knew was anger.

I wasn't the type to stop fighting. I needed the last word. I needed to make an impression.

For what outcome?

All I caused was pain. Pain around me. Pain inside me.

And forgetting the past never really helped me. The wound festered until I became one with my suffering.

Julie Jones had forgotten how to be happy. She had forgotten how to enjoy life. All she did was fight the ghosts of her past. And today, those same ghosts were fighting her.

Love for a boy had distracted me from the important things. The stuff that mattered so much to me became trivial when in Dan's presence. I would have died to be accepted by him, and rejection hurt me more than I thought it would.

He used me. He made me feel like I was invisible.

And I let him do those horrible things to me because I loved him.

I couldn't force anyone to love me. All I could do was be myself. And all I knew was how to be angry with myself.

Fast-forward. The breakup with Mark proved once more I couldn't tolerate rejection. He told me so many times I was too mad at the world. I didn't listen. I thought he was the one who did everything wrong. And maybe he did. But maybe he didn't. I considered him the enemy, and convinced myself it was right to be angry all the time.

And now look where I had landed. In a sewer pool with an ugly fish that didn't love me, just as no human being I had ever met loved me. The creature sensed I wasn't there to make friends, so it wouldn't be friends with me. Plain and simple. If I wanted to tame the beast, I had to tame myself first.

My fingers brushed the carapace slightly and I felt the electrical current course through my hand again.

The swimming lasted forever. I lost track of time. When my body began to fatigue, I slowed my strokes and watched the fish continue its relentless journey, until it vanished from sight, undisturbed by my emotional uproar.

"We can take a break if you want," Evan said.

I had never met someone so patient and willing to wait for me to learn.

"I can keep going," I replied, although my muscles were starting to cramp up.

"I can tell you've been working hard, but remember, nothing comes easy. We should go back above ground, get some rest. You'll come back down here later," he said.

"Okay."

We found shelter in a corner of the Cave. Evan lit a fire with his magic eyes, and we roasted a few rats that we proceeded to eat while our clothes dried.

Living in this world almost seemed normal to me now. Despite the destruction, the ash and the dirt, and the scarce food, I felt alive for the first time in a long time.

"So where did you find the magic chocolates?" I asked, while eating.

"The Mighty Listener gave to each of us one piece of candy. Depending on how things go here, you have the choice to ingest them or not," he explained.

"Does that mean Kara has one too?"

He nodded. "I would assume The Mighty Listener doesn't discriminate."

"Who is this person? Susan was vague when I asked about her. What does she do exactly?"

He cleared his throat. "Her birth could be described as the most extraordinary event, yet the most clichéd story ever told since the dawn of men. Many tales mention supernatural creatures, granted with eternal life, some good, some bad. You know, vampires, werewolves, fairies, goblins, wizards, shape shifters, witches... The list is long. Demons even. And angels. Humans have used all these names to describe beings beyond this world, who possess supernatural abilities, and can travel through dimensions in the blink of an eye. The Mighty Listener is the spawn of many generations of supernatural beings, who have fought each other since the dawn of time. Good and evil, darkness and light, the yin and yang of everything in the universe. Two polar opposites never supposed to stick together. Yet they did, because love and harmony were stronger than hatred and chaos. Their interlude should never have given birth to her, since it was genetically impossible. But the Creator of all living things had a brighter purpose in mind, I suppose. Because the war between the polar opposites didn't stop, He ordained her to bring balance back into this world, and every world beyond. That's why she was born. That's why her powers are so great. She chooses who needs to be straightened out." He laughed. "In this case, she sent you to the Underworld to seek and understand the truth about your nature."

"You mean my mental obsession?"

"That and other things about you. The Underworld is a place where your mind is exposed for what it truly is, a maze of memories and feelings, thoughts and dreams. I am only a guide meant to help you find answers to your questions."

"So you're like the voice of my subconscious," I suggested.

He nodded. "Yes, I am a part of your psyche."

"And the others? Sloan was so mean to me today. Not the way I remember him."

"He represents the scolding and untrusting part of your psyche. Susan is a mediator. Miko, a silent helper. Sky likes to tease and be playful. He's your sense of humor. Kara, Dan and Mike, well... They're the self-loathing and unforgiving part. We are all pieces of the puzzle that is you."

"But I don't remember ever hearing your story. What you told me about being gay, and how your family treated you."

"You heard it somewhere. You didn't make this one up," he said, and smiled.

"Does it mean it's your story though? Or is it someone else's, and I'm applying it to you?"

"Well, I'm evolving along with your emotional development throughout this journey."

I took a deep breath and rubbed my palms against my legs.

"Yeah, I think I'm going crazy."

He laughed. "You won't lose your mind here, if that's what you imply. It's a bit overwhelming, but you'll adjust."

"These magic chocolates, what do they do to me?"

"They alter your mood. But they don't heal your pain," he explained.

"The one I took felt good." I sighed. "Is that why it was so hard to tame the ugly fish?"

He nodded. "Yeah, you had to use your unaltered emotions to deal with this particular challenge."

I pouted. "I like those chocolates."

"Julie, I'm only here to give you suggestions. You'll decide next time a chocolate is offered to you whether to take it or not."

"So once I'm ready, I'll exit this world and return to Los Angeles? And face jail?"

"The Mighty Listener won't help you clear your criminal record," he said. "I can't give you more details about what awaits you in the real world."

"Right. Surprise!"

He stared at me. "You'll be fine, Julie. Just have faith. I listened to your train of thought and found hope in your heart. You would like to understand everything right away, but life is complex." He smiled. "You were born to do amazing things. Deciding that your life ends because you made mistakes isn't the way to go. Failure isn't an option in your book; but failure is necessary for learning and growth. Once you accept failure, you will accept forgiveness."

I stared at the dancing flames in the fire and pictured myself as one of them. Bright, bold, and powerful.

"I would like to feel free. And happy," I said.

"Well, your anger extends to everyone around you: your family, your friends, yourself, and also God, if you believe in Him. The truth of the matter is that your anger hides fear. Fear of the unknown, change, secrets about yourself you have refused to deal with for years. You may believe anger is strength and can be an anchor, giving temporary structure to the nothingness you think your life is made of. It feels like being lost at sea: no connection to anything. Then you get angry with someone, and suddenly you have this structure, your anger toward them. The anger becomes a bridge over the open sea, a connection from you to them. It is something to hold onto, and a connection made from the strength of anger feels better than nothing. Yet, anger is like a curtain of smoke. Once it dissipates, you're left with yourself."

Tears welled in my eyes.

"I don't want to feel this way anymore," I said. "But I don't know how to stop that pain from growing stronger every day."

"I know. Turn that pain into love. Your mental obsession is blocking you from that love you want to feel."

"My darkness..." I sobbed.

"The overbearing cloud of fear looming over your head."

"So I need to learn how to handle fear," I sobbed. "Without chocolates."

"That's right." He wrapped me in his arms.

"What part of my psyche are you?" I asked, when we broke the embrace.

He smiled. "Acceptance."

18

The sky darkened as the storm approached. Newscasts had been blasting us with severe weather updates all day. The alerts on my phone didn't stop, and they annoyed the heck out of me. I had been hiding in the library, studying a little, but writing in my journal for the most part.

When I left the building, rain had started falling, and the wind blew too strongly for me to use my umbrella. I sprinted through rain drops, trying to beat the odds of coming home drenched.

My phone rang and I ignored it.

"Another stupid alert," I mumbled.

The rain intensified, and I quickened my pace. Visibility decreased, and a car almost ran me over as I crossed the street.

My phone rang again.

"Oh for crying out loud!" I grunted, and fumbled through my pants pocket to find the device.

Running and looking at a cell phone is never a good idea. I wiped rain drops off the screen. I had two missed calls from Mom. Great. She must be wondering where I was. Slowing my stride, I unlocked the phone. I accessed the menu panel, opened a new text message, and started typing.

"On... my... way..."

Now send.

"Hey, watch it!" I heard from behind me.

"What?"

I turned around and saw a boy.

Then, I stepped in a puddle.

The water soaked my sneakers right away. Crap.

"Oh, that's really my luck!" I exclaimed.

The boy walked in my direction. He was wearing a black poncho that covered most of his face and upper body. His green eyes stood out when he spoke to me.

"You okay?" he asked.

The rain was hitting hard. I had no time for a conversation.

"Yeah, yeah. I gotta go. My mom is waiting for me."

"Hey, I got an extra poncho if you want one," he said.

"Oh wow, you're a free poncho distributor?"

He laughed. "Yeah, that stuff takes no room in a bag. I got a bunch at the one-dollar store. You never know who might need one. Here."

He unzipped his messenger bag.

"Thanks," I said, tearing the plastic wrap.

Pulling the poncho out, I scowled.

"Dude, bright orange?"

He laughed again. "Yeah, the rain isn't color racist. Plus, now cars won't run you over when you cross the street."

He helped me with my heavy back pack while I suited on.

"Better, right?" he asked.

I nodded. "Yeah, now I feel like a Halloween pumpkin. My feet are soaked though."

"Sorry, rubber boots take too much space."

My turn to laugh. "I am a doofus. I should have left school earlier."

"Admit it, this storm came as a surprise. Not like we were warned or anything today."

"Right, I'm amazed my phone hasn't exploded yet from all the weather alerts I received. Well, I feel much better. Still going to try to make it home quickly. Thanks for this."

He patted my arm. "Anytime. You attend Oceanside High?"

"Yep."

"Me too. I'm a junior."

"Oh, freshman."

"What's your name? I'm Evan."

I shook his hand. "Julie."

"Nice to meet you."

"Same."

He smiled. "Well, I won't hold you back. Get home safe."

"Thanks. I'll give the poncho back when the weather clears."

"Nah, keep it. You never know when you might need it. I'll see you around in school anyway, if I need a favor." He winked.

I chuckled. "Nice. I thought good Samaritans existed only in fairy tales."

He laughed. "You're funny. Alright, girlfriend, get going before your mom scolds you."

"The scolding will happen anyway."

"I hear you. My parents gave up scolding me."

"How did you manage this miracle?"

"Long story. The short version is that I'm gay."

"Oh."

"Ah, no worries. Life. I'll see you around. Be safe."

"Okay, thanks again."

"Anytime."

Evan and I parted ways, and I resumed my fast walking.

When I finally made it home, Mom was waiting for me in the kitchen.

"What did I tell you a million times? Pick up your phone when I call you. I was worried sick with this weather." She sounded pissed.

"I sent you a text I was on my way," I replied.

She waved her phone at me. "I got nothing."

I pulled my phone. "I sent you a text. I even stepped in a puddle while doing it."

Accessing the text message panel, I showed her my screen.

"See!"

She shook her head. "You didn't press send."

I looked at the phone.

"Right. Well this guy distracted me by giving me a free poncho, and my shoes are ruined..."

She raised her palm to my face. "Just dry yourself up, and pick up the phone when I call."

I huffed. "Fine. But this guy—"

"This guy was kind enough to give you something you needed, so don't use him as an excuse. And no, I won't buy you a new pair of sneakers."

I looked down. "Right."

Going to my room, I thought how nice it would be not to be scolded anymore. Evan had it easier, but I couldn't turn gay to avoid it. My life sucked.

The fire had died when I woke on the floor of the Cave. I felt as though I had slept three days straight.

Stuck in the darkness, I shivered from the cold. The humidity in the air didn't help.

"Evan?" I called his name but received no response. "Evan, where are you?"

Maybe he had gone to another part of the Cave while I was asleep. Without him by my side, I felt abandoned. Fear settled in the pit of my stomach, and questions unraveled inside my head. What if he had left me for good? What if I never made it out and was stuck here forever?

"No, he must be somewhere," I mumbled to myself. "He promised he'd never leave your side."

Unable to see anything in front of me, I ran my hands along the walls. Listening to the soft murmur of the water flowing nearby, I fought the feeling of dread that roamed inside my abdomen, causing my stomach to cramp up. I took a series of deep breaths to relieve the pressure, and my drifting thoughts brought me back to the downtown Los Angeles office of my attorney, Richard Gold.

He didn't look at me when he put away his notepad. He didn't even seem annoyed by my decision to plead self-defense. Gold was a professional, probably used to much worse. I played in the amateur league, although I didn't consider myself an amateur.

"Okay," Gold said to close the meeting. "I'll stay in touch then."

Glancing at Mom, who was glued to her cell phone, I sighed. My sweaty palms stuck to the fabric of my pants. Instead of leaving my chair, I moved to the edge of my seat.

"Can I...? Can I ask you a question?"

Gold exhaled loudly. His hesitation, coupled with my nervousness, cast a weird vibe within the room that even my mother was not insensitive to. She lifted her head and looked at both of us.

"What can I do for you?" Gold bore a comforting smile.

I looked at the ground. Ignoring my mother's interrogating stare, I carefully picked my words. "What if we don't settle, and I have to do time for what I did?"

"Well... Even in the worst case scenario, I don't think you'd do time. You're not a murderer, Julie," Gold said. "But it seemed from what we discussed you were opposed to the idea. Why are you thinking about it now?"

"Who wouldn't? My father could refuse to bail me out of this mess." I choked, working my hardest not to cry.

My mother had to go. She prevented me from speaking honestly. Glancing at Gold, then at my mother, I didn't pip a word and grabbed a pencil instead. Playing with it helped me focus on what to tell my attorney once Mom left the office. Would he get the hint that I wanted her out?

"Mrs. Jones, would you mind leaving us alone for a minute?" Gold asked.

Smart kid.

"Is that necessary?" she snapped, still staring at me. I avoided locking eyes with her and kept playing with the pencil.

"Mrs. Jones, I sincerely believe it would be better if you waited outside. Please?" Gold insisted.

"Alright." Despite her obvious reluctance, she pushed her chair back, and Gold escorted her to the door.

Once Gold and I were alone, he sat in the guest chair Mom had occupied.

"So what's on your mind?" Gold asked.

"I'm just scared..." I replied with a broken voice.

"Is there something else you want to tell me about?"

Tears rolled down my face and a torrent of sadness was unleashed. Meanwhile, Gold didn't talk. He kept looking at me, his blue eyes expressing nothing but understanding, and handed me a tissue. I cried relentlessly. Not the pretty crying either. We're talking full-on snot dripping from my nose. My breathing sounded more like gulps of air, with odd hiccup noises thrown in. Who was this little girl, weeping in her lawyer's office? Didn't she know showing emotions wouldn't play any role in court? Minutes passed, until I felt strong enough to speak again.

"I'm so scared."

"Could you please tell me what's wrong?" Gold begged.

"I just don't know what to do anymore." I sniffled and blew my nose. "I want to make things better but I can't."

"Why?"

Looking into his eyes, I imagined the color of the sky just before a big storm. Would those eyes ever show anger and pain, like the turmoil of emotions that ran havoc inside my heart right then? Would Gold ever reveal the true face that hid behind the mask of the attorney, who claimed he'd be able to help me, but in all honesty was just doing his job and couldn't produce miracles? My expectations were always disproportionate to the actual outcome, which explained why I was always so disappointed and jaded.

"I really want to trust you," I said.

"You can trust me, Julie. Nothing you confess to me will be repeated. I'm held by secrecy when it comes to communications with my clients." He shook his head. "But I can't help if you won't talk to me. So why do you think you can't make things better?"

"Because..." Sensing the cavalry of tears pushing again to break the dam, I took a deep breath. "Because I'm not a good person," I replied.

Gold's facial expression didn't change.

"It's true. I'm not a good person. I know it sounds crazy, but whatever I do, I screw everything up."

"Please stop," he cut me off.

My eyes widened and my lower lip dropped until I had achieved the perfect puppy look. Gold awarded me with a heavy sigh.

"Well your fear is understandable. If I was in your situation, I'd be afraid too. Listen, sometimes people make impulsive decisions that result in horrible consequences. This is not the case for you. You have a chance to make things right. So, you have a choice. If you plead self-defense, you face the judge, and whatever sentence he thinks is appropriate he'll give you. If you apologize and plead guilty, you can get off with very little. It's that simple."

"I-I... I punched him, but he touched me," I said.

Gold sighed again.

"Do you understand what I'm going through?"

"Yes, yes I do. And it breaks my heart to see you like this. I will do everything in my power to help you," he replied.

Our eyes locked, and at that exact moment I knew he couldn't help me, because he wasn't God. He couldn't bend the legal system sideways for my benefit. No one could. I was screwed. I crossed my arms over my chest. "I just don't want to go to jail. So we'll stick to the plan. And if anything changes, you'll let me know."

He nodded. "Of course."

I pushed away my chair, and he walked me to the door.

"We will do what's best for you," he said.

"And I'll be fine. Just fine."

He handed me his business card. "In the meantime, and please don't take this as disrespect, but you might want to talk to someone more qualified if you feel you have a heavier burden to lift off your chest. Friendly advice of course. I wouldn't dare pass judgments."

"My father already made an appointment," I replied, wiping snot from my nose.

He nodded again. "Okay. Was there anything else you wanted to tell me?"

I shook my head.

"Okay, then." He opened the door before shaking my hand and smiling. "Well, Miss Jones, I'll see you again. In the meantime, take care of yourself, okay?"

My turn to smile. "I always take care of myself."

"Good." He opened the door wider, and my mother made her lovely appearance.

"What happened?" she asked Gold. I could hear her made up concern, as if I may have sustained some horrific trauma during her absence, and desperately needed her comforting presence.

"Oh, your daughter wanted to confide a few more details about the course of events. But everything's in order now. We discussed the basics of the case today, so why don't we see each other in a few weeks, when things move on? You have my card?"

Mom nodded.

"Excellent. I'll walk you to the elevator lobby."

"Oh, it's not necessary. We can find the way back," she said.

Yes, she wanted to pry and know what the talk with Gold was really about. Good luck with that.

He gave me a last pat on the shoulder. "Miss Jones, it was a pleasure to meet you. Feel better, alright?" He smiled.

"Thanks."

As we walked away from Gold's office, my mother's stare drilled holes in the back of my head.

My little meltdown wouldn't be repeated again. I didn't like to open up like that. Made me feel all fuzzy inside, and I hated being all fuzzy, like a stuffed teddy bear. Fuzziness was weakness.

So I brushed everything off and entered the elevator as if nothing had ever happened.

Still stuck in the dark, my thoughts wandered further.

Even faced with serious consequences, I didn't want to acknowledge I had a problem. I thought I could work out all my issues on my own.

I remembered the day Dad picked me up from the principal's office, after being told I had beaten this kid unconscious.

"When are you going to grow up?" Dad fired, as soon as I sat in the passenger seat of his latest obnoxious Mercedes toy. I barely had time to buckle my seatbelt before he dashed out of the school parking lot.

I couldn't talk to him. He couldn't talk to me either, apparently, because all he did was stare at the road like an enraged bull ready to lunge upon his target, the unsuspecting matador. He didn't glance at me. And if not riveted to the asphalt, his eyes stared at his smart phone every time we stopped at a red light.

Despite my best intentions, I couldn't find the strength to explain myself. I didn't even attempt one of my lame apologies. I didn't cry or beg, or basically do anything. I just let Dad fume as I watched the side of the road, lost in my thoughts. Being a passenger gave me the opportunity to observe the outside world without leaving the wind- and rain-resistant interior of the Mercedes.

I should have stuck to simpler things, like piano and dance lessons, instead of fending for myself and beating up everyone else around me. Sometimes I lost track of time, woke up with a hangover sensation, not really aware of what I had done. The beating felt like a dream. A great uppercut right into the bridge of the kid's nose.

When I sat in the uncomfortable, fake leather chair in the principal's office, with Dad next to me, glaring at me like I was a psycho-killer, I only thought the kid deserved his just punishment.

"You're meeting with the lawyer tomorrow," Dad said, pressing his foot harder on the gas pedal as traffic cleared.

The outside world blurred more and I frowned at the idea. Lawyers were just a bunch of stuck-up obnoxious know-it-alls who ran after only one thing: money. Dad surely had enough money to hire some well-known big shot in the courtroom.

I sighed.

"You've got to learn your lesson once and for all, young lady." He dangerously swerved into the left lane of the ramp to enter the freeway. "What you did is unacceptable. I hope you get a grip. Because if you don't..."

I stopped listening. On most occasions, I was little more than a mouth to feed in his eyes. The few times he decided to treat me as his daughter were never to congratulate me, or tell me he was proud. Instead, they were reserved for scolding me, or correcting whatever wrong he felt I had committed.

Father of the year award, right? What a hypocrite. He made me sick to my stomach. He didn't care much about what I did. His career at the movie studios mattered more. His beloved daughter wouldn't ruin his empire. So fine, I'd better myself to make him look good at his next executive producer meeting.

"Oh, and one more thing. I booked an appointment with Dr. Ronstein. Your first session is on Wednesday."

I clenched my jaw and took a deep breath to calm myself. "Dr. Ronstein?"

"Your shrink. There's some issues you're gonna deal with."

"Great, sending me to Mom's shrink now? I guess that means I'm crazy too?" I snapped.

Dad's words infuriated me. I felt an itchy sensation behind my forehead, and my vision blurred. My precious anger wanted out! When Dad slammed on the brakes and the car halted an inch away from the bumper ahead of us, everything went back to normal. We had just hit another traffic jam. Glorious driving life in California.

"Watch your tone. You're on probation." He paused. "I'm just making sure you're alright."

"Yeah, whose idea was it?" He missed my glare, browsing again through emails on his phone. "What does probation even mean? Like I'm going to jail if I mess up?"

"It doesn't matter whose idea it was," he replied. "Great, the deal won't go through because of this moron..." he mumbled, and dialed a number.

His job was obviously more important.

A shrink? I laughed at the idea. Who wanted to lie on some sofa and reminisce about childhood memories while some weirdo took notes? Or, better yet, doodled on his pad as he thought about what to buy with the ridiculous amount of money he made listening to people's senseless rants. Ugh, I didn't need a charlatan thrown in! I was fine. Perfectly fine on my own.

Stuck in the jam, I spaced out while Dad spoke with every possible employee at the studios. I wondered briefly if he would even notice if I left the car and walked down the freeway. Was it something I should attempt just to make sure? I was dying to try.

But that wouldn't make my whirlwind of emotions go away.

Wherever I went, I'd still feel lost.

Just like I did now. No sign of Evan.

The overbearing quiet made my head spin. Memories kept coming, reminding me of everything I had done, said and felt.

The Mighty Listener had decided I was worth a second chance.

"Hey, Evan, where are you?" I called out, and the sound of my voice traveled throughout the Cave; but I received no answer.

Was I stuck in a dream?

I rubbed my eyes and pinched myself, just to make sure.

This didn't feel like a dream.

19

My entire body couldn't stop trembling, and my teeth chattered so hard I thought they would shatter. Stunned by the cold of the icy water, I felt a hand probing my hair. Thick air bubbles escaped my mouth and nostrils.

Just for kicks, I fought some more—and then quit struggling. A deep sense of relief came over me as I sank, and the ache inside my chest dwindled.

Images of Kara's face flashed before my eyes.

Then I saw the beautiful beach in Oceanside. The sun was setting on the horizon. A wave licked my feet, and foam covered the top of my toes.

My best friend stood next to me, holding my hand. I noticed the light in her eyes. The eerie purple glow mirrored a dark pain I knew all too well.

"What's wrong?" I asked.

"You know what's wrong," she replied.

I shook my head. "Tell me."

"You're still ignoring the truth."

"You know I'm making an effort. I have an anger problem."

"You still won't accept what happened, will you?" She frowned and a small, sparkling tear appeared at the corner of her eye.

"What happened? I'm here. In the Underworld."

The purple glow intensified.

"You have to listen to me!" she said, grabbing my arm.

I tried to pull away. "Let me go!"

She maintained her solid grip.

"Remember what you did to me. Remember how much you hated me."

I stared at her face and screamed. Her skin was now covered in blood and dirt. The sky turned dark and the ocean stormed. She let go of my hand, and a wave caught me in its grip. I fell and swallowed water. I paddled back to solid ground with all the strength I had, but the ocean was too strong. I was carried away, submerged in the abyss. Lost in the silence, I heard the beating of my own heart that thumped more slowly and more softly as I sank deeper.

I awoke to a burning ache that left me gasping for air, before twisting to the side and coughing up water.

"Thank God!" Through blurry vision, I recognized Evan. His hands still lay on my chest, right above my heart.

"W-Where were you? I was looking for you," I said with a broken voice.

"I was here the whole time! I told you I'd never leave your side. You must have been sleepwalking. Dove right into the pool," he said. "Unless... Gosh, Julie, don't tell me you tried to kill yourself!"

My heart racing, I ran my fingers over my clothes. Blood throbbed inside my head and I felt groggy, hung over almost, although I didn't remember drinking.

Evan sat next to me and helped me move into an upright position, using the wall of the Cave as support for my back. I stared into his green, glowing eyes.

"You wanted to die, didn't you?" he asked.

I ran a parched tongue over my lips.

"So many nightmares..." As I swallowed a threatening sob, I noticed my throat felt like sandpaper. "I didn't do it on purpose."

"Your thoughts wandered for a long time in the darkness."

"I was looking for you," I replied. "I couldn't find you. And then she appeared. Gosh, it felt so real." I shivered. "I thought you had left me."

He smiled. "No, I didn't leave you. Everything we discussed must have made a profound impact on you. Your dreams spoke to you."

I nodded. "Good. I don't know what I would do if you left me."

A tear slowly rolled down my cheek.

"You shouldn't worry. You're simply starting to understand what you're made of," Evan said. "There's a lot of pain you need to deal with. It takes time. The healing process doesn't happen overnight."

"Yes. I should go back into the water and tame the ugly fish," I said.

"Um... How about we do something else before that?"

"Like what? Talk some more about my feelings? You're just like a shrink," I said.

"Well, a shrink would ask you to come back for another session after the hour was up."

I nodded. "Yeah, you're right. How can you be so nice to me?"

"What do you mean?"

"You're so kind all the time. Even when we met for the first time during that storm, you gave me a poncho. That was ugly, gosh, but at least I didn't get drenched."

He laughed softly. "Well, there's no reason for me to be mean to you."

"Kara's mean to me!"

"Kara is mean to you because you're hurting from the friendship you've lost. Once you learn to forgive yourself for the wrong you've caused, you'll see her in a different light."

I sighed. "I don't know if I'll ever be able to forgive her. My recollection of the night of the party is still so foggy. I know she was there, but I don't know exactly what she did. And I went crazy on her. I drove us off the road. I don't even know what happened to her after the accident. If she recovered. If she..." my voice trailed off.

"Died?" he asked.

I nodded.

"You'll see in due time. Right now, though, you need a distraction."

"What are you going to make me do?"

"We're going for a little walk. Outside."

My eyes widened. "What?"

"Don't you want to do something else? I understand we're living under strained circumstances, but I miss being outside, don't you?"

"But outside is so gloomy. And those horrible explosions."

"We could go to the greenhouse."

"Susan told me about it. Why do I want to go there?"

"You love watermelon. There's plenty of watermelon there."

"I don't know."

"Hey, we're not going for long. Come on, have you lost all sense of adventure?" He laughed.

"I don't know," I repeated.

"Listen." He locked eyes with me. "You just tried to kill yourself for crying out loud! Seriously, food is good. And eating good food will put you in a better mood. Am I wrong?"

I smiled. "Okay, okay. I guess... Maybe I could take another shower while we're at it, not in sewer water, and find different clothes?"

"Sure. We'll break into a house."

I smiled. "Okay."

"Do you think you're good to walk now?"

"Yeah, I'll be fine," I said.

He grabbed my hand. "Then let's go!"

Because my perception of events was flawed from the very beginning, I thought the Underworld was a made-up place created by my crazy imagination, while

I sat gosh knows where lamenting myself. The more I talked to Evan, the more I opened up to the idea that the Underworld was real. The monsters and memories inhabiting this place helped me dig through the crap I had ignored for years.

And the guilt lifted, little by little.

"So, will Kara tell me what really happened to her after the incident?" I asked Evan, as he walked in front of me through the tunnels.

"Yes, she will. If you let her," he replied.

"What do you mean?"

"You have to be ready to hear the truth," he said.

I shook my head. "I feel like I'm making progress, though."

"Oh you are. But the root of the problem hasn't been dealt with yet. Remember, we're trying to understand your mental obsession, and as a result tame your anger. This takes time."

"This means I will understand you, too?" I asked.

He stopped by a ladder affixed to the wall in front of us.

"You will understand everything," he said.

I stopped talking and focused on climbing.

After a short ascent, we landed inside a tiny glass room. The sky was still obstructed by the rain of ash that hadn't stopped falling since my arrival in the Underworld. Some windowpanes were broken, pieces of glasses scattered on the floor and cracking under my steps as I ventured further into the greenhouse.

My jaw dropped when I saw colorful green patches in a corner.

"Dude, this is cool!" I exclaimed.

"I knew you'd like it." Evan chuckled.

"How do watermelons grow here? Without sun and water?"

"This, my friend, is called a little bit of faith."

I stared at him with raised eyebrows.

"And a complex system of irrigation. Even in the roughest environment, beautiful things can blossom," he said.

"So, what, they also grow on sewer water?"

He nodded slightly. "Filtered sewer water, but yes."

"Gosh, you fed me fruit infested with germs?"

"Hey, hey, you're not gonna get sick. I don't know where this germaphobia is coming from."

"Really?" I rolled my eyes. "How do the watermelons grow without light?"

"Simple answer. We use our eyes. A few minutes a day suffice."

"Right." I grunted. "I still can't believe I'm swimming in and eating crap in this place, and no one seems to be bothered by it."

He raised an eyebrow. "Last time I checked you were buried in crap up to your neck."

I huffed. "Metaphorical crap. Not real crap."

"Are you mad at me?"

"No. No. Never mind. It's my punishment for being bad in the real world. I get it." I looked at the watermelons. "I don't have a shopping cart to carry them back to the Cave," I added.

He smiled.

"We only need a little bit," he said.

He picked a watermelon off the ground and handed it to me.

"Use the wall to break it open."

"Not sanitary," I answered. "Oh crap."

He laughed. "We can wait until we find a knife. Maybe in that house we wanted to break into?"

"Alright."

"Good. Let's scout the perfect location then."

"Well, I have an idea," I said.

"Yes?"

"Let's go to my house."

His eyes glowed stronger. "Excellent!"

I laughed. "Yeah, sometimes I come up with good plans."

He placed a hand on my shoulder. "You're doing great."

Standing before the door of my parents' former condo, I took a deep breath.

What would I find inside?

I pressed the button above the knob and pushed.

The door opened.

Aside from a broom I found in one of the closets, and the nails still protruding from the walls where pictures used to hang, the apartment was empty, just as it had been once the movers packed all our belongings into the truck.

My heart sank when we stepped into my bedroom.

"No change of clothes," I said, peeking into the closet. "Gosh, I'm going to live with this dirt and sewer stench forever."

"Maybe the shower still works," Evan replied.

I checked the bathroom and turned on the faucet. Nothing came out but a gurgling sound. I jumped when a spider emerged from the drain, slowly making its way up the side of the wall.

"Of course. Like I said. Sewer stench forever." I sighed.

"Well it was worth a try," Evan said.

"How is this supposed to help me?"

"Hey, don't get frustrated. The chance of finding anything here was very slim."

I scowled. "I hate this place."

"Allow yourself some breathing room. Why would you have left anything behind? You said it yourself, Oceanside was dead to you."

"Yeah, that means you won't find a knife to cut the sewer grown watermelon. So here, just throw it at the wall. I don't care about germs anymore."

"You hungry?" he asked with a smile.

"No, but what else is there to do here?"

"Maybe we could go elsewhere."

I raised my eyebrows. "Where?"

"Los Angeles," he replied.

"Right. I already went there, remember? And found this stupid note."

He stared at me.

"Fine. Why return to Los Angeles? I thought we were going to eat a watermelon."

"Well, it's very possible we'll find a knife. And I think you overlooked a few things last time. One stone, two birds," he said.

"How do we travel?"

"Wander into your thoughts. I'll come with you. Look at me."

"You're going to use your eye trick again."

"Uh huh."

The glow in his eyes intensified.

"Let's dig deeper," he said, and I felt my eyelids flutter.

"Don't forget the watermelon."

"I won't," he answered, and my eyes sealed shut.

20

This chair was very uncomfortable. Probably expensive, but a hefty price tag didn't equal lush support for my back and behind. Why did I have to come here again? Oh right, because Dad paid for the appointment.

The old man sitting across from me looked at least seventy years old. With his bald head and gray beard, there was a slight resemblance to Sean Connery which didn't make him unpleasant to stare at. I didn't like to stare at him though. Dr. Ronstein might have been a very kind man but, given the circumstances, and the fact Dad essentially forced me to be there, I hated him right off the bat.

"Let's talk about you," he started off the conversation, and I rolled my eyes.

"There's really nothing to talk about," I replied.

He smiled. "Are you sure?"

"Positive."

"Good, then you can leave."

"You serious?" I shook my head. "Nah, this is a trick. You're trying to be my friend, pretend it's okay for me not to talk if I don't feel like it."

"Julie, overanalyzing my words won't get you very far."

"Mom already tells you everything there is to know about me. What else is there for you to find out?"

"I'm held by secrecy when it comes to my patients. The same goes for your mother. Now give me something to think about. Or don't. The ball is in your court."

"What the heck are you talking about?"

He smiled again. "See, Julie, I don't need to ask you questions. You talk if you want to say something. Anything. And whatever you say will help you understand why you're sitting in this chair. Clear and simple."

"Talking about my feelings won't help me feel better," I replied with a flat tone.

"Trying to shush your feelings when they want to be heard can be a dangerous game."

I took a deep breath. "I know what to do to shush them for good. And it usually works. Except when I run out of booze."

Ronstein gave me a non-judgmental glance in return.

"And then feelings scream and bang louder, wanting your attention."

I nodded. "It's not easy to be me."

"I don't think being anyone is a piece of cake. But we all have to try our best; otherwise, what's the point?"

"I thought you didn't ask questions."

"That was a rhetorical one."

"Oh." I stayed silent for a few minutes. "I don't like my feelings so much."

"Who does, right?"

"Right. I don't think I'll ever find peace in my heart. I did some pretty stupid things I regret."

"You can't change the past, only the present," he replied.

"Yeah. If I shush my feelings with booze, I don't have to think of the past or the present."

"There must have been a point in your life when feelings didn't hurt so badly."

I shook my head. "I can't go back to that point."

"Why not?"

I exhaled slowly. "Because I'm addicted."

Ronstein nodded. "New form of slavery. The true journey starts when you stop running."

Tears welled in my eyes and I sniffled.

"I don't know when I'll stop running. I just want to go far away and start over."

He handed me a tissue.

"You'll find the strength to overcome this challenge. But you have to hit bottom first."

I rolled my eyes. "Bottom? I think I've already hit it hard."

"Doesn't look that way to me."

I huffed. "How would you know?"

He smiled. "We all have our cross to bear. You'll know when yours has become too heavy. Just keep coming."

"Coming where? Here?"

"Anywhere you'll feel safe."

I blew my nose. "I don't want to talk anymore."

"Okay."

"So that's it?"

He shrugged. "Appears so."

"I hate this game."

"What game?"

I threw my hands up in the air. "This whole charade! You really think talking about my feelings will help me feel better?"

Ronstein didn't respond.

"I hate this so much," I mumbled.

"Don't we all? And yet, it's the best exercise in the world."

I didn't understand what he meant, then. Since I began my journey in the Underworld, his words didn't sound so meaningless.

The hills of Los Angeles greeted me with their sunny sky, cute cookie-cutter houses, and deserted streets.

"Just like I left it," I said. "Empty of life."

"Well, you jumped into your car after punching Melissa and decided Los Angeles was dead to you too," Evan replied.

"That's harsh."

"Life will come at you with a rocket launcher, and it's your decision whether or not to let it blow you up. You merely exist, Julie. You don't live. And here is what your anger has done to your mind. You don't see anything past it. You don't acknowledge there are other human beings involved. All you care about is your own little self."

He juggled with the watermelon. "Care for a little refreshment?" he asked. "This one will be real sweet. You'd love it, if only you could only bring yourself to."

I glared at him. He sounded so mean right now.

"Why the sudden change of attitude? I thought you were here to help me."

"Oh, but helping you is all I've been doing since the beginning of this journey."

"I've made good progress!" I said, stomping my feet.

"You are barely grasping the reality of your condition, girlfriend," he replied in a flat tone.

"You want me to forgive, but I can't forgive!"

"See, you still don't get it. You think you're doing all this work to please me? It's all you, Julie. Your anger is striking back, using devious ways to make you believe you're better, but you aren't. If you were, your perception of me wouldn't change in the blink of an eye."

"Are we going to stay here or are we going somewhere?" I felt the frustration building up.

"Well, let's see. Is Dr. Ronstein in his home office right now? There's only one way to find out."

We followed a driveway which, after many turns and a steep incline, took us to Mom's shrink's mansion. Ronstein loved avant-garde architecture, and his three-story house, with its curvaceous shape, was one of a kind. It looked so odd from the outside, like a sandcastle half eaten away by the waves. The living room had a huge bay window that offered a breathtaking view of the mountains and the valley.

Evan pointed at the entrance.

I huffed. "Why am I back?"

"You've left something behind," he replied. "Ronstein should have a knife too. I'm hungry."

I struggled not to slap him with his watermelon. As I swallowed my irritation, we walked among lozenges of orange and yellow light, piercing the foliage of the huge cedar trees covering the property. Evan followed me, not saying a word.

"There's no one at home," I said, as we stopped by the massive, glass double-doors.

"Uh huh," Evan answered. "Perception is everything."

Huffing and puffing, I rang the bell.

"So what am I supposed to find?"

"More answers," he replied.

How ridiculous he looked with his watermelon tucked under his arm. "I really don't see the point."

"Why do you always have to debate everything?" he asked back.

I shrugged. "I don't know. That's just what I do."

He sighed. "Let's just be patient, okay?"

And, like an old and grumpy married couple, we waited.

"I'm going to make a fool of myself," I said under my breath.

"I understand why you would hide things from your mother and father, because you're angry with them just because they're your parents, and think they don't love you enough; but Ronstein isn't your mother or father. Like it or not, he's your shrink."

"Stop it. I saw him only once!" I protested.

"You're telling me to stop it?" He sighed. "After what happened with Melissa, don't you think you should meet with him again? You're scared crapless of facing another lawsuit. Gold can help you with your legal troubles, but not the mental ones. I told you that fear is the reason behind your anger. So now is the time to come clean and tell Ronstein what's really going on with you. Admit what you did wrong to someone else, instead of burying yourself under a mountain of guilt that will lead you nowhere. Just do it."

I cringed. "But this encounter and confession won't happen in the real world until I'm out of here. So why bother now?"

"Because you need to start making peace," he replied. "And Ronstein is the best person to talk to at this time."

I raised my hands in surrender. "Fine. Fine!"

The door opened and my jaw dropped.

"Well, to what do I owe the pleasure, Miss Jones?" Ronstein asked, a wide smile stretched across his wrinkly face.

I wasn't sure how to continue that awkward conversation. "You brought a friend?"

"I apologize, but would you have a knife by any chance?" My guide extended his hand. "I'm Evan."

Ronstein shook Evan's hand. "Well come in! And yes, I do have plenty of small and big knives you can use."

"Swell!"

I shook my head in disbelief as we entered the lobby.

"No worries. Nice to meet you, Evan. Should we go to my office? We'll be more comfortable there."

"I don't want to make a mess. Where's the kitchen?" Evan asked.

Ronstein pointed at a hallway behind him.

"Please, make yourself at home."

"Thanks, I won't be long. Where should I meet you?"

"We will be on the second floor. Last door to the right."

"Got it."

Evan vanished from sight.

"Well, Miss Jones, you look tired and in need of a shower," Ronstein said.

"Yeah, sewer water doesn't do the job, and last time I showered, I had no soap. You don't have soap in your goodies by any chance?"

"Um, well, I do," Ronstein replied. "Maybe you can enjoy some nice relaxing time after our conversation."

I nodded. "Great, because I didn't pack a travel kit."

Ronstein sat behind his desk and crossed his fingers. "So, this is a surprise. What brings you in?" he asked.

Evan had taken the small couch against the wall hostage and was munching on watermelon. I glanced at him, then back at Ronstein.

"Evan brought me here because my perception is screwed up, if that makes any sense to you."

Ronstein nodded. "The mind and heart often see things differently. The battle between instinct and reason never ends. I'm sure your friend had good intentions in bringing you to me."

"Yeah, I still wonder why."

Ronstein smiled. "Simple answer. You need someone you can talk freely to."

"I don't understand. I saw you only once."

"That's okay, you're safe here. Just say what you have to say," Evan piped up, with a mouth full. "Hungry yet?"

I huffed. "No! For crying out loud, what is this about?"

Ronstein took over. "Sometimes we ignore what's obvious. And the realization of certain truths makes us angry. That's normal."

"This is nuts!" I shook my head.

"The mind does weird things!" Evan exclaimed.

"I punched Melissa because Mark cheated on me. What else should we talk about? And the whole ordeal with Kara..." I stopped. The weight over my chest had become unbearable. I wanted to cry, hide in a hole in the wall and disappear.

"Admitting the truth can be liberating," Ronstein continued. "That day you came to see me, you began to talk about shushing your feelings because you couldn't deal with them, and how booze helped you numb your mind. You didn't say much then. Do you want to share more now?"

"I have no idea!" I replied.

"Well, let's start with the facts. Since you were young, you always craved the attention that no one seemed to give you. And you feared rejection. You were madly in love with Dan but, sadly, he didn't reciprocate. You let his best friend Mike play with you because you thought it was a smart way to get back at Dan—"

"He raped me!" I interjected.

"Okay. That's what you believe. Let's look at the course of events in a different light. You had consensual sex with Mike out of spite, and the experience was disastrous because you were drunk, and unable to control your emotions. Plus, you were still a virgin. You couldn't admit this truth to yourself, because you saw your behavior as a weakness. So... You made up this whole lie about being raped, and had a valid reason to be mad at the world and play the victim. And this wasn't your only attempt at bending the truth sideways. When we met, you were in the midst of a lawsuit involving a kid who you claimed groped you without your consent. But, in reality, you went to him first; and when he turned your down, you saw red. Rejection hurt more than you'd imagined. The same thing happened with your ex-boyfriend Mark, who you claimed cheated on you, when you had no proof of his infidelity! And as a response to this alleged behavior, you punched a girl and broke her nose. Have you ever thought about how twisted your perception is? You crave attention, Julie. It's a fact. When you don't get that attention, you act out so you can get that attention one way or another; and by doing this, your goal is to make the world see how strong and brave you are. But you aren't." Ronstein finally fell silent.

I was in shock.

"This is unbelievable! I-I can't... I can't even fathom the thought I made up the rape! Memories came back..."

"You make your memories tell you what transpired, but what really occurred? You went to that party, you drank—a lot—and lost sense of right and wrong," Ronstein continued. "Kara was your best friend and she dated the boy you were in love with. How could she betray you like this? How could she not walk away and make Dan love you in return? Oh, but you decided she had stabbed you in the back by not saving you from a guy who wanted to hurt you? She loved you. You, on the other hand, didn't love her as much as you believe you did. Or else you wouldn't have taken her into Dan's car and run her off the road!"

"I know, I—" I blurted.

"Your anger made you do terrible things, Julie Jones." Ronstein slowly shook his head.

"How do you know all of this?" I asked, while glancing at Evan, who was busy eating his watermelon.

"Because deep down you trust me," Ronstein replied. "And you trusted me enough the first time to admit you were an addict."

I exhaled loudly. "So Mark didn't cheat on me?"

"Mark broke up with you because you were an inconsiderate, selfish brat. That's the truth. Everything else you think happened, the girl's voice in the background, for example, your mind made up. It's you against the world, Julie. You destroyed the past and swept everything under the rug so you could be in control. But things didn't work out in your favor. You're not living life on life's term, but on your terms. And these terms failed you. These terms might land you in jail or a mental institution. I speak to you as a friend. And as your friend, I'm asking you to reassess everything. You put yourself in situations that make you hostile. It's all your doing. No one has intentionally tried to hurt you. You make up that alternate reality and live in it, thinking it's going to save you. It won't."

He paused. "I'm telling you right now, things won't improve until you break this pattern. Do you remember what you wrote on this note you found not so long ago? Because I have it right here in front of me:

Forget me not,
Wherever you go,
Memories are like daggers,
And your heart holds the truth within.

"Your heart has been telling you all along you were wrong, but your mind told you to keep lying to yourself."

Unable to contain my tears, I broke down. "I'm so sorry..." I sobbed.

21

ere I was crying again, while my whole existence crumbled beneath my feet, but I had to come to terms with what Ronstein said. Wiping tears from my face with a tissue he handed to me, I took a series of deep breaths before talking. Evan was absorbed by his watermelon and seemed unaffected by my distress.

"Okay," I said. "If I'm bending reality to suit my needs, how will I know what truly happened?"

"You keep a journal," Ronstein said.

"Yes, we found it in the high school library," Evan added.

"Well, then, you should go back there," Ronstein suggested.

"Wait," I interrupted. "How do I know what I wrote in the journal is true?"

"You can make up a whole new reality, but to do so you must keep track of the truth somewhere. The note I have here comes from your journal."

"That's it? I read my journal and get back to normal?"

"It's not that easy, but yeah, it's a good start."

"How am I going to see Oceanside? And Kara? What about The Mighty Listener and her chocolates? Will I even need them?"

Ronstein raised an eyebrow.

"I'm not sure why you're asking about them."

"Evan told me every memory had one they could give me in case I wanted a kick," I said.

"And do you want one now?"

I shrugged. "Evan gave me his already. I don't know if you will give me yours."

"What do you believe?" Ronstein asked. "If I give you mine, what do you think it will do to you? Heal you?"

I shook my head. "Never mind. It was a stupid thing to ask."

"No, if you ask, it means you're interested in the effect the piece of candy will have on your feelings. Have you asked yourself whether you could have defeated the goo monster with faith alone? By taking a chocolate, you only seek to control your fear. But do you really feel less afraid when you're high?"

"I'm still confused. I really believed I was raped. Evan showed me what I did..." I mumbled.

"Alright." Ronstein stood. "Let's see what happens if Evan vanishes from the picture, shall we?" He snapped his fingers and Evan disappeared from the room, as if he had never existed. "And what about this entire place?" He snapped his fingers again and the furniture and the office went. Then the house, the hill where it was located, and the entire deserted city of Los Angeles.

When my butt hit the ground, we were in the middle of a blank canvas.

"This is your fresh start, Julie. Everything has been wiped out. Evan, Kara, Susan, Mark, Melissa, your awful parents, all these folks are gone. It's only you and me. And this," Ronstein said.

He opened the palm of his hand and showed me a little dark ball.

"But what will this chocolate do to you? Tell me, since you're being offered a clean slate. Do you need to know what kind of life you've led until now? Is it important to you?"

I stared at him. "I'm ready to change!"

He moved closer to me, and I recoiled as his eyes ignited gold.

"Really, Julie, are you willing to go to any length to change?" he asked.

"Yes!" I replied, my body now shaking.

"Then why do you need this chocolate? Can't you just make the decision to change on your own and stick with it? Are you afraid you will fall back into your old ways?"

I choked on my words. "I-I thought, maybe, I'd feel strong again. Please, I-I didn't mean to—"

"What I believe is that you're still trying to lie to yourself. And eating this chocolate will make you feel as though everything is okay. Your feelings of insecurity are shushed, and your fear of change is under control. Am I wrong?"

I shook my head. "No, no. I'm sorry. It was stupid to ask."

"You know deep down that in the real world you will wake up somewhere unknown to you as yet, and have to deal with the consequences of your actions. You're on your own, Julie. And you must pay for what you did. You can pay by learning what it takes to grow up, or by perpetuating this deceitful behavior until something else really bad happens. That's the choice you have to make. No more stalling. No more trying to have someone else take the blame for you. No more hiding behind a mask."

I stared at him for a long time, not knowing how to respond. Honestly, there wasn't much to argue. I was fried like a chopped potato, ready to be served with a burger. And this truth didn't feel good. Oh no. This truth made me feel horrible.

"What do you decide?" he asked.

"I want to be a better person," I replied with a trembling voice.

"Are you willing to go to any length to change?"

My hands were shaking.

"Yes," I said.

"Do you know what this means?"

I nodded. "I'm terrified, but ready to face the truth and nothing but the truth."

"You believe this? You're not telling yourself a lie again?"

"No. No, I'm not. I can't go on like this."

"Okay. Do you still want to eat this chocolate?"

I broke down. "I just thought I could feel good for a little bit longer..."

He sighed. "I can't force you to choose the path of light if you still want to remain in the darkness. This mental obsession of yours is very powerful. You haven't admitted complete defeat yet, I'm afraid."

I stared at the chocolate still in his hand, and my mouth salivated.

He looked away. "No one will help you if you don't want to help yourself. Next time you ask for a chocolate, be assured this means you still have some work to do."

Sniffling, I nodded. "I know. I'm so powerless."

I snatched the chocolate from his hand and put it in my mouth before closing my eyes.

"One chocolate is too many, and one thousand are never enough," Ronstein said. "Good luck to you, Julie, until we meet again."

Lying on the floor of my old bedroom, I rolled to the side and sat with my legs crossed, leaning my back against the wall.

"Well," Evan said. "Those were exquisitely freely roaming thoughts you had. Until Ronstein kicked me out."

"Yeah," I said back.

"How are you feeling?"

I grunted. "My head hurts. And I didn't even take a shower."

He patted my arm.

"I think you know where we should go now."

"Yep, yep, back to the library."

He gave me a weird look.

"What?" I asked.

"You seem off. Are you alright?"

I nodded. "Yeah, just feeling groggy. This will pass. No need to use your eyes on me. I'm growing tired of these glowing things."

"Are you scared Kara will come?"

I shook my head. "No. And if she does, I'll handle her. Although I don't know how yet. We'll cross that bridge when we get there."

"Okay," he said. "Are you sure there isn't anything else bothering you?"

"Everything is bothering me here. But I have no choice but deal with the crap, huh? Like Ronstein said, choose the path of light, and I'm still stuck in the darkness. Blah di blah." I brushed my hand through my hair. "That chocolate he gave me didn't even get me high. Must have been a placebo or something. And I missed my opportunity to finally use soap and get rid of that awful pee stench."

He stared at me and his jaw dropped. "What did you do?"

"So what? I had one, big deal!"

He exhaled loudly. "I told you the chocolates wouldn't help you. Why did you take one?"

I frowned. "Yeah, I heard that. But I wanted one. End of story."

He paced across the room, avoiding looking at me. "This isn't fine."

"What's done is done," I huffed. "Can't change the past."

"No, you can't. What you can do is change the present. And you promised..." He brushed the thought away.

"Never mind. If you're feeling alright then let's get moving."

"Are you mad at me?"

He stood looking down at me.

"I thought you knew better."

"You didn't answer my question."

"I don't want to fight. We have better things to do."

"Oh yeah? Like wander in this dead town, and eat watermelons that grow with sewer water because there's no drinking water available?"

He clenched his jaw. "I don't like your tone."

I laughed. "Got any sewer watermelon left?"

He stepped closer. "I ate it all. You didn't want any, remember?"

I shrugged. "Well, when you offered me some I wasn't hungry."

"Right. And now you are?"

I shook my head. "Nah, the thought of eating that stuff makes me want to puke."

He grimaced. "No hope, no faith. Gosh, even what Ronstein told you didn't strike a chord."

"Why do you say that?"

"Because you chose to get high instead of finally facing the world with a clear mind."

I huffed again. "I needed a break."

"Excuses, excuses."

I stomped my feet. "He gave me one."

"You could have said no."

"I couldn't!" I shouted.

"Yes, you could. It's called willingness. The word 'no' is the main defense against using again. Deep down, you didn't want to stop. So let's cut to the chase. You want to stay stuck here forever?"

"No."

"You're welcome to, if that's what you truly want," he continued.

"No!"

"Okay."

We stared at each other in silence. After a few seconds, I stood.

"Fine. Let's go to the library then."

"Après-vous," Evan replied in a flat tone.

We exited my parents' condo and stepped onto the street. I looked at the sky. Some rays of light pierced through the rain of ash. I wasn't sure if this temporary change was any of my doing, given I felt far from happy, joyous and free right then.

"I'm not a bad person, you know," I said to Evan as we continued our walk. "Just effed up in so many ways. I can't even begin to make a list."

An explosion popped in the distance.

"I know that, Julie. What matters is that you believe it too," he replied.

"Yeah, yeah, I'm not going to make you say what I want to hear."

"It's okay. Every good thing comes to those who wait."

I nodded. "Yeah. Eating that chocolate was more an impulse than anything."

"Isn't any mental obsession just an impulse?"

"Probably. I don't know yet. Too much information and too little time to process," I replied. "What pisses me off the most is that I wasted the opportunity to finally clean myself."

"Oh that opportunity will come again, trust me," he said.

As we approached the high school gates my stomach tied into a knot. A little bird told me my next impulse would have to be secured behind bars if I wanted to make real progress and not upset Evan again.

We returned to the library's occult section.

"Alright, here it comes," Evan said.

I pulled down the journal and opened it at a random page.

"Gosh, what am I doing to myself?"

"Start on page one. Come on, let's have a seat and read."

I picked a chair by a table against the wall, and took a deep breath.

I've always felt an overpowering loneliness that no one else can understand, this darkness that sucks everything in its path like a black hole, and leaves nothing but more darkness behind. I have it, and don't want to live with it anymore.

Today, everything felt bleak and insignificant. I went to school, attended Spanish class with Mrs. Rodriguez, and thought to myself the whole time I'd rather be elsewhere.

This new girl came in for the first time, an exchange student from Kyoto, Japan. Her English was far from perfect, and she struggled to put two sentences together. If she can't speak English, how is she going to learn another foreign language? I shook my head when she introduced herself. Miko something Yama. The whole time she spoke, I thought of miso soup and sushi, chopsticks and a bowl of rice. What did this chick want in Oceanside? There were enough freaks around already. I guess one more won't hurt. If she could get used to this place, why couldn't I?

The truth of the matter is, I don't belong here.

My best friend Kara is perfect. She's popular. I'm not. She's pretty. I'm not. She loves to make new friends. I don't. And the fact that I feel this way will cause my downfall. I can't play games like everyone else. But no one will ever accept me for who I am.

So I've decided to spice things up a bit. Make people believe what they want to believe. I'll blend in like this Miko girl, and pretend to follow. And my life will become this story people read about in books. Full. Happy. Flawless.

I turned the page.

Dan Goldberg. Susan warned me about him, and I still fell for his cheap tricks. There's no denying it. Every time he asks me to do his homework, I give in. He doesn't consider me attractive. He thinks I'm his friend and helper, nothing more than that.

I know Kara likes him. I've noticed the way she looks at him. And I'm pretty sure he likes her too. It's because she's perfect and I'm not. But someday, I'll be perfect too.

I exhaled loudly, holding back tears. "This is horrible. It's like looking at a Dorian Gray portrait of myself."

"All the misery you've been harboring for too long is finally coming out. Just keep reading."

I nodded, sniffling. "Okay, okay."

I feel horrible, and the cherry on top of the icing of crap I have to eat with a smile on my face happened yesterday, after Dad came home from work. I found him in the kitchen, hugging and kissing Mom on the mouth—right in front of me—ugh, I hate public displays of affection! And here he was, bragging about how he got this job offer. I couldn't believe it.

He said we had to move. I'd go to a new school, and he'd make tons of money, and Mom jumped in the air, and kept clapping like she was at a show, and I couldn't stop thinking what the heck? What would I do without my surfing? Mom gave me a hug, told me everything would be alright, but I knew nothing would be fine. I was angry so I ran to my room, and started pounding my fists on the bed, screaming into a pillow so no one would hear me. But I could hear myself. I didn't care if Dad made more money. I didn't care about his career in the movie industry. Why was this mess happening to me? What had I done to deserve this crap? It was all a conspiracy.

I'd move from this town, and everyone in school would ask me why. Kara would be sad. She'd cry. I'd have to console her. Promise her we'd stay in touch. Bunch of dog crap. I got so mad over this I threw my electric toothbrush against the wall and broke it. Whatever! It was only a toothbrush. I could go to the drugstore and buy another one. But a heart, where would I find a new one? This mess was too much for me to take. And the darkness inside, it didn't want to shut up.

"I'm so bitter. It's horrible. I-I want to read about the rape," I said, my hands shaking.

He nodded. "Do what you gotta do. Let it out."

"I think I need a break first. I'm a mess."

"Okay, do you want me to go with you?"

"No, no, I'll be fine alone. Won't be long."

22

I stepped away, leaving the journal on the table. While strolling between rows of bookshelves, I cried. Tears fell like never before. My heart hurt as if stabbed a million times. The person who wrote in that journal was unhappy, and her unhappiness ate her alive. She changed. Became a monster.

There was one thing I knew, though. I didn't want to be that bitter and angry monster anymore.

Outside the library windows, more rays of light pierced the gloomy sky like swords. One day, Oceanside would look beautiful again. One day, I'd sit on the beach and watch the sun set and vanish behind the vast ocean. Listening to the sound of waves crashing on the shore, I'd close my eyes, and peace would settle inside my heart for good.

I heard something ruffle papers behind me.

Had Evan followed me?

I turned around but saw no one.

The ruffling happened again.

"Who's there?" I asked.

I heard laughter.

My skin crawled inwards. Kara.

"What do you want?"

The laughter echoed louder inside the library.

My stomach turned upside down, and my palms began to sweat as my breathing accelerated.

The laughter echoed again, like a deafening siren. I covered my ears.

She was near. She was around me. She floated inside the space, completely invisible, watching me.

"I'm not here to fight you," I said.

The laughter stopped.

"Why? Don't you think fighting is awesome?" Kara replied, without showing herself.

Her voice came from above but when I looked up, I saw nothing.

"No, Kara," I responded. "I don't believe I need to fight you anymore."

She laughed again. "Bullshit. You know you want to. You hate me. You hate me so much."

"No, I don't. I'm just trying to understand what I did and why I did it, so I don't repeat my horrible behavior in the future."

"Right. Whatever you do now won't fix the mistakes of the past," she shouted with her strident voice.

"I know that," I said. "I did stupid things. But I'm willing to change."

She snorted. "You know what I think of your resolutions? You can shove them up your butt and recycle them back up through your lying hole of a mouth—all you'll get is crap, because that's what you're made of. Crap. Crap. Crap. Crap. Crap..."

She kept going like a broken record, and I tried to block her voice by covering my ears.

"Crap. Crap. Crap. Crap. Crap. Crap. Crap..."

"Stop!" I begged, kneeling on the ground, wrapping my arms around my head to reduce the noise. No matter what I did, I could still hear her.

"Crap. Crap. Crap. Crap. Crap. Crap," she continued. "You're so full of crap, crap, crap, crap, crap, crap, crap, crap, crap..."

"STOP!" I screamed.

I felt a hand on my back and jumped.

"What, who, oh bejesus!"

"Are you okay?" Evan held his hands in front of his face, like he was ready to block an uppercut. Admittedly, I was ready to deliver one, given he had scared the crap out of me.

"Shizzle nizzle," I said. "I thought you were her."

Evan's eyes widened. "What happened? I heard you scream."

"Kara talked to me."

"Oh," he said.

"Yeah, fun, I know."

"But she didn't show herself?" he asked.

I shook my head.

"Good, good..."

"Why is that good?"

"Well, she's testing you. But you held on. If you had gotten angry, she'd have broken out of her shell and fought you harder," he explained.

"Yeah, well, I don't have bad intentions. I wasn't even pissed at her. Why does she hate me so much?"

He laughed. "I love your positivism, but getting rid of bad memories will take more than just good intentions."

"She's so insidious," I groaned. "Why? Why can't I just forgive her? Or myself? Why is it so gosh darn hard?"

He smiled. "Forgiveness must come from a place of love. And right now, you don't know where to find it. No offense."

"Yeah, I can see that. Sucks."

"Are you afraid?" he asked.

"I-I'm not." I paused and stared at the ground. "Yeah, yeah I am."

"Great that you didn't lie. It's hard to lie to me, though. Since I can read your thoughts." He laughed.

"Glorious," I said.

"You crack me up. You're a funny gal, you know?"

I chuckled. "Yeah. Yeah. I've been telling myself that a lot lately."

"Don't be sarcastic," he replied. "It doesn't do you any good."

I nodded. "Great words of encouragement. Thanks."

"Remember, you're not crazy."

I sighed. "I can try to convince myself all I want I'm not crazy. I sure feel like it."

"Cheer up. We have more reading to do. You up to it?"

"Yeah, I just wish you had some watermelon left," I said as we walked back to the occult section.

He patted me on the back. "Craving some sweet sewer deliciousness? We can get some on the way out, my dear."

"Okay." I picked up the journal. "Let's do this."

I watched Dan practice today. I snuck behind the bleachers while he ran around the field like a lion. I held my breath when he threw the ball. His stance, his speed, his perfect balance and coordination made me squirm with every heartbeat. Who cared if he wasn't smart enough?

I paused, glancing at Evan.

"I'm writing about this kid like he's a god," I said.

"Yeah, because you made him one," Evan replied.

"Love is blind."

"Not any type of love is blind. This wasn't love. This was teenage lust. Hormones wreaking havoc inside your mind and confusing your feelings." He winked. "Let me tell you about my other crush, Marcus."

"Oh, a war story?" I laughed.

"Yeah, well, Marcus was also a straight kid."

I tapped him on the arm. "Ha, you devious bastard, hunting outside your territory."

He chuckled. "I was in boarding school. We all experimented," he said. "But this kid Marcus had the same effect on me that Dan did on you. And I didn't really understand why. He had no interest in me, not the slightest, but I found him to be simply the most beautiful boy on the planet. Given I had been rejected once before by George, I did everything in my power to get Marcus's affection. Naturally, 'everything' meant do his homework, since he wasn't the nerdy type." He winked. "But I worked things out to the point where we became friends too, and he asked me for advice. He saw in me a confidant, and I saw in him my next boy-friend. Whenever he needed something, he'd come to me. I thought what he felt for me was love. I thought he trusted me and cared about me."

"So what happened?"

"He didn't love me the way I loved him, and that realization made me feel like a piece of crap. And that's okay, because I was willing to become that piece of crap. Only an insane mind repeats the same action, while expecting a different result. Why go after a straight kid again? Obviously, he broke my heart. I felt rejected once more, and got really mad. But I had set myself up for failure from the get go. I couldn't accept that fact, though. Once Marcus pushed me out, there was no turning back for me. I had to show him how much love I had for him. So I sent him a note, begging him to come see me after class, because I had something important to tell him."

"Like what? You wouldn't do his homework any-more?" I chuckled.

"Well, he knew that without me he wouldn't pass any of his classes. But I guess he showed up because we were friends. So he cared at least a little bit. And that's when he found me."

I raised an eyebrow. "Found you?"

"Yeah. In the bathroom, with my wrists slit open."

My jaw dropped. "What the fly? Are you serious?"

Evan nodded. "Dead serious. Now keep reading."

"O-Okay. That's pretty morbid," I said.

"Go on."

I shook my head. "That was a terrible war story."

"Yeah, yeah."

"You're a sick memory, you know that?"

"Uh huh."

I cleared my throat.

I wanted him so much I came up with this brilliant idea. What if I sent him a note and asked him to come talk to me? What if I told him I wouldn't do his homework anymore? He would freak. I knew he would. He counted on me to graduate. Without my help, he'd fail all his classes.

"Holy crapola," I said.

"Keep going."

He needed to find me at my most vulnerable. If he did, he'd love me. I knew he would.

"Shizzle," I whispered. "What the heck did I do?"

I checked my wrists for marks but didn't see anything, and sighed with relief.

"No, girl, you didn't cut yourself. Now what else could you have done? Think of some hopeless measure you thought would make him pay attention to you."

"I went to the party," I replied.

"Uh huh."

"And I drank. A lot."

"Yes."

"I gave myself to Mike..." I continued with a trembling voice.

"May I?" Evan grabbed the journal and flipped the pages until he found what he was looking for.

"Here." He put his finger on the page. "Read."

I've never been much of a drinker, but yesterday I couldn't stop. Mike came up to me at the party, completely out of his mind. He was a lovely host. He gave me beer. Lots of it. We did shots. I loved the high of the first drunk. I craved it. I felt powerful, in control. I could do anything. He was all touchy-feely. He complimented me on my outfit, said how good I looked. This was the first time a guy found me pretty. He got totally hammered and didn't stop touching me. I was ready to go further. When I made the first move to kiss him, he suggested we go to his bedroom. I nodded without a hint of hesitation.

"Jesus," I said under my breath.

"Keep going," Evan said.

We went upstairs, and I lay on the bed next to him. His hands went everywhere, touching me, but he was too drunk to know what he was doing. The alcohol helped me break out of my shell. I guided his hands to my breasts. Then to my crotch. Soon enough, though, he was snoring. How could he do this to me? I got so mad I started splashing booze on my clothes, ripped the corsage off my dress, and smeared makeup over my face. I pulled off my underwear and threw it on the floor next to the bed. Then I grabbed my cell phone and texted Dan that he needed to come right away. I positioned Mike's arm on top of me, moved my body under his as best as I could, and waited. The door finally opened, and Dan entered the room.

"What's going on, nerd?" he asked.

I was crying.

He stepped closer and noticed my ripped clothes. When his eyes spotted my underwear, he gasped. "Oh my God, Julie, what the heck happened?"

He sat on the bed, pulled me from under Mike, and gave me a comforting hug as I broke down on his shoulder and drowned in his embrace.

"Talk to me," he said, while brushing my hair with his fingers. He was so kind, so loving. So perfect.

I had him.

"He...he..." Tears flowed. "He attacked me," I said.

"Oh my gosh, are you alright?" Dan asked.

"No... No..."

I was holding onto him so hard, all I wanted was to tilt his head and kiss him.

As I prepared to make a move, I heard laughter.

"Hey, I've been looking for you..." Kara said upon entering the room, but when she saw us together, stopped cold.

"What the heck is going on?" she asked.

I looked at her. Then refocused my attention on Dan.

He was too slow to react, and I seized the opportunity.

I kissed him. Right in front of her.

How good it felt to finally make him mine!

She screamed.

"What the heck do you think you're doing?" She yanked me off Dan.

She was heartbroken, furious.

Her eyes went from Dan to me, and then she noticed Mike passed out on the bed. When she looked at my face again, saw my ripped clothes, and the underwear on the floor, she flipped out.

"WHAT DID YOU DO?" She slapped me.

Dan didn't know what to say. He wasn't smart enough to find a good explanation quickly. The alcohol didn't help.

I could have said a million things. Instead, I just laughed.

"WHAT DID YOU DO?" She grabbed me by the shoulders, shook me and pushed me down on the bed.

I kept laughing while she pressed herself against me, pinching the skin of my bare arms, thinking she was hurting me.

"WHAT DID YOU DO?" She pounded her fists on my chest, and I smelled her hot, alcoholic breath.

Her eyes filled with tears and she grunted, hitting me harder. I didn't move and simply stared back at her.

"I took what's mine," I answered.

She shrieked.

"What are you talking about? What the fuck did you do?"

"I told you." I grinned.

She looked at me, stunned.

"I can't believe this. Who are you?"

I pushed her off me by elbowing her in the ribs.

She cringed in pain and rolled to the floor.

"I told you already. ARE YOU DEAF?" I shouted.

I moved away from the bed, but she came after me and started punching me in the side.

Of course, I retaliated. I was done being nice at this point.

We fought like cats. She pulled on my clothes, ripped them some more, and then went for the hair, the nose, anything she could grab onto. But I was taller than her and held a serious advantage. I put her in a headlock. And my anger made me invincible.

Dan didn't even try to separate us. All he did was stare at us with his jaw wide open, like he was at the movies and expected his bucket of popcorn to appear on his lap at any second. What a dumbass.

I clocked her right in the jaw. She stared at me, her teary eyes now expressing only fear, and tried to run away; but of course I chased her throughout the entire house.

She found shelter in another room and cried for help. Everyone else was too high or drunk to even notice the fight. I went after her and dragged her outside.

In her jeans' front pocket I noticed a bulge. Dan's keys.

She escaped from my grip and ran to Dan's car, but I caught up to her.

I pushed her away from the driver's side and knocked her out by slamming her head against the frame of the door.

Once behind the wheel, I turned on the ignition and pressed hard on the gas pedal. Kara was out cold on the passenger seat in the back.

I laughed the whole time I drove. I was a sucky driver but didn't care.

This was all a game to me. A wonderful game I had won.

At some point I hit something, and the car flipped upside down.

I managed to get out. Pulled Kara out of the wreckage. I checked her pulse. She was still breathing.

"FUCK YOU!" I screamed at her.

I woke up in the ER with a bad headache, unable to remember what had happened after the accident.

Mom picked me up once the doctors said I was good to go.

She didn't speak to me much. Just asked whether I was okay.

Yeah, at that point I was golden.

I'm not sure what became of Kara. Mom tried to talk about it, but I kept repeating I was too tired.

My life in Oceanside was over. Everyone I knew was dead to me. Dead like I had burned them all in my wrath. No one paid attention to me. No one cared about me. They only used me. Played with me. Well, who had won the game now, bitches?

I had.

I stared at Evan, feeling so disgusted with myself I wanted to throw up.

23

"Lord have me struck by lightning," I said. "This is no joke."

He patted me on the back.

"You acted out, did something completely crazy and desperate under the influence of alcohol," he said.

I stared at him. "No shizzle. I don't remember being punished for this accident."

"Well, given the amount you drank, you blacked out. You were a few miles away from Mike's house when a drunk driver, who missed the stop at the intersection, hit you on the passenger side and sent you tumbling in a full three-sixty. Had Kara sat next to you, she would have died on the spot. Given she lay on the back seat, she didn't suffer grave injuries. Just a few bruises and broken ribs. The faulty drunk driver died upon impact," he explained. "You exited the vehicle and pulled Kara out of the wreckage before the car caught on fire. Despite your anger at her, you saved her life. You weren't found at the scene of the accident. You walked for a couple of miles until you passed out on the street. When cops asked who drove Dan's car, no one knew what had really happened. Not a single person at the party saw you take Kara hostage. Cops concluded Kara drove Dan's car, and got into this accident by herself. When you were found and taken to the hospital, nurses and doctors were more concerned about you being sexually assaulted than you totaling a car under the influence and hurting your best friend in the process."

I felt tears coming up. Again.

"But Kara could have said I was with her!"

Evan shook his head. "She didn't pip a word about what happened between you and her."

"Shizzlenit. Why?" I asked.

He shrugged. "I don't know. Remember, she was drunk too."

"But she got in trouble, and I didn't!"

"Yes, she did. And so did Dan and Mike."

"I hurt her! And she didn't say anything at all?" I huffed. "This is unbelievable!"

"Just because you're feeling vindictive doesn't mean others feel the same way. Kara had her reasons for not saying anything. I guess you'll ask her why once you see her again."

I cocked my head to the side and frowned. "Where? Here?"

He laughed. "No, dummy, in the real world."

"Yeah, right. At this rate, I'm not coming back out."

"You're Julie Jones. And you always will be," he said. "We all make mistakes."

"I put her life in jeopardy!" I shouted.

"Well, that's why you're here, isn't it?"

I sighed. "Yeah. I feel awful though."

"That's pretty understandable."

"I get why she hates me."

"Uh huh."

"So what now?" I closed the journal.

"Well, how about we digest this information, and then go back to working on improving yourself?"

I nodded.

"You can cry if you want to," he said.

I sniffled back my tears. "I've cried enough. I just want to get better." I replaced the journal on the shelf.

"Oh, trust me, you will." He smiled. "Still craving watermelon?"

After a quick stop at the greenhouse, we walked back through the tunnels. The sweet watermelon calmed my nerves, but didn't prevent my heart from feeling heavier after reading excerpts of my horrible journal. Evan was very supportive, though, and refrained from passing judgment.

"I was such a crappy friend. I didn't care about Kara, or anyone else for that matter. I didn't give a darn about you either," I said.

"Yeah. You didn't. And that's fine. We can't be friends with everyone. It would be way too much work."

"But we're friends, now, right?"

He smiled.

"Yeah. We are."

We reached the Cave, and the humidity in the air made me sneeze like crazy.

"Bless you," Evan said.

"Thanks." Given I had no tissues, I blew my nose on the sleeve of my jacket. Gross, I know.

We stopped by the pool.

"I suppose it's time for me to take an icy dip?" I asked. The sewer water would wash the snot off my jacket too. Double gross.

"Eager to tackle the ugly fish again, huh?"

I nodded. "Well, you said it yourself, that thing is supposed to teach me patience."

"Yes, it's supposed to help you let go of whatever control you think you have over people and things."

I stared at the dark mass of water and sighed. "Did I hurt Kara simply because I wanted to control her?"

He took a deep breath. "Julie, your anger is rooted in fear. Fear of losing your individuality, your friendship, your home. Once you've accepted you cannot control anyone else's behavior but your own, your pattern will change," he explained.

"Yeah, I guess," I said. "But to what level?"

"The sky's the limit."

"Gee, then I'm doomed. When will I learn to turn on my beams?"

He laughed. "You're obsessing about this, aren't you?"

"Yeah. Anyone should obsess about it. It's a pretty cool power to have!"

"Julie, all your life you've imposed your will and your way, and never cared about anyone but you. Am I impressed by you? Not at all. Am I impressed by how much progress you've made on this journey? Yes, of course. But you have the ability to destroy everything you've worked so hard to achieve just because you want to show off again, don't you?"

I looked at him, confused.

"You think I want to use my beams to destroy this town even more?"

"You"—he stepped closer to me and pointed his index at my forehead— "need to see the bigger picture."

I pushed his hand away.

"The beams are a tool, not a main objective," he continued.

I huffed. "Still. I'd like to have them."

"So earn them."

"By taming the fish?"

He smiled. "We should maybe work on some meditation techniques to help you get rid of this fear," he suggested.

"Lovely, we worked on my confidence, now we work on my fear! And with meditation!" I protested. "I feel like I'm being analyzed by Dr. Phil."

"Uh huh. That's right."

"This sucks. This truly sucks. I thought we could fight some monsters, and..."

"Eat some chocolates?"

"Right, yeah, I guess the chocolate part is overrated, although I enjoy eating these things, and—"

"Julie."

"What?"

"You know what I think about the chocolates. Let's not have that conversation again. Why don't we focus on the present task?"

I scoffed. "Meditating?"

"That's right."

I waved my hands in surrender.

"Fine, you're the boss and know what's best."

He chuckled. "At least you're not fighting me about it for hours now. You're doing great."

"I hate you," I mumbled.

He winked. "You're going to love it."

Meditation. What the heck was I going to do? Sit in the lotus position with my thumb and index fingers pressed together, while humming some weird mumbo-jumbo?

Evan sat across from me with his legs crossed. I did the same.

"Are you ready?" he asked.

"Yeah."

"Okay. Take a deep breath, and let go of all the tension crippling your mind. Focus on every muscle in your body. Starting with your forehead, eyelids, jaws, and going down... Your shoulders, back, and belly. You're with me?"

I nodded.

"Now close your eyes. Picture yourself as a very tiny being. An insect," he said.

"Like a cockroach?" I laughed.

"Be serious. No. Like a bee."

"Okay."

"You're flying from flower to flower, looking to harvest some pollen. You know you need to return to the hive once you've collected enough. Remember if you gather too much, it will weigh your body down and prevent you from flying from potential predators. After buzzing around, you find the perfect flower. What color is it?"

"Red," I said.

"Okay. Do you see the red flower before you? It's getting bigger as you fly closer. Each petal is ten times your size. The red color attracts you like a magnet. It's the only thing on your tiny mind. You need to land and start the harvesting process."

"Okay."

"Yet, you are so focused on your task that you don't notice the big black spider hiding under one of the petals. The spider has cast a web over the bud."

"Shizzle!"

"Stay with me. You only want one thing. And you're going to get it. When you're close, your little feet get stuck to the web. Very quickly, you are trapped."

"How is that supposed to help me calm down?" Cold beads of sweat trickled down my spine.

"Stay with me," he repeated.

I suppressed a shudder. "Okay."

"Now the flower has become your grave. You use your little wings to try to fly away, but all your efforts leave you even more trapped. Soon, your entire body is stuck to the web. And you can't escape from the big spider coming very fast toward you. The beast is hungry and determined to suck you dry. At this point, you're nothing but a victim. But you know you have a weapon. Your sting kills. Can you manage to kill the spider before it's too late?"

"Yes!"

"Remember, you're a prisoner and have no way out."

"I will... I will try to sting the spider as it approaches," I said, without much conviction.

"You're scared. The spider is powerful, ready to destroy you. It's moving fast towards you. Its legs are strong, causing the web to tremble as your tiny body fights against it. And now, as the spider is ready to prick you, you have no choice but to surrender to your fate." He paused. "The spider represents your darkness, and the web is your fear. The longer you remain afraid, the more the darkness will grow and eat you alive, turning you into a shell of yourself. So... How do you make the web disappear?" he asked.

"How do I get rid of my fear? What, fear is a feeling we all possess!" I reopened my eyes. He was staring at me.

"How do you make the web disappear?" he repeated.

I cast my hands in the air. "I got no clue, man!"

"Fighting your fear will only accelerate the process, and won't bring you anything good. Learn to surrender," he said. "The darkness eats you because you're full of fear."

"How the heck am I supposed to surrender to my own fear?"

"Well, you must accept your imperfections. A guilt-ridden journey won't take you anywhere but straight into a wall."

"But I can't help feeling guilty for what I did!"

"Pray with me." He smiled.

I recoiled. "What? I don't know... I've never been very religious."

"Just try," he said.

I exhaled deeply. "Fine. Fine."

He grabbed my hands. "Please, forgive me where I have been resentful. Help me to not keep anything to myself. Show me where I owe an apology and help me make it. Help me to be kind and loving. Remove worry and remorseful reflections. Help me find hope, even in the most hopeless situations. I am not alone and, as I grow, I give away the control and become open to living without fear."

I took a deep breath and repeated his words, trying to commit them to memory.

"Help me find hope even in the most hopeless situations. I am not alone," I said out loud. "Gosh, this is hard."

"There will come a time when you'll have to say these words to stay strong," Evan said.

My body tensed up. "Why? What will happen?"

He smiled. "Promise me you won't let fear rule your life anymore."

"I-I promise not to let fear rule my life," I replied.

"Do you believe these words?"

"Y-Yes."

"Do you trust me?"

"Yes," I answered.

"Good."

A small tear rolled down my cheek, and he caught it with his finger.

"Ronstein asked if you were willing to go to any length to change. Change starts with surrender. You have finally taken the first step toward becoming a better person."

"So is that it for the meditation?" I asked.

He nodded. "For now, it is. You've worked hard and deserve some rest. Why don't you get some sleep before we continue?"

"I-I don't feel tired."

"Look at me," he ordered.

"Why?"

"Just look at me."

As I stared into his glowing eyes, my eyelids felt heavier.

"Are you using your mind tricks again to make me fall asleep?" I asked.

"Shhhh."

"Seriously I don't..."

I slurred my last words and tiredness dropped me like a rock.

24

One hot summer afternoon I took a stroll by myself on the beach. Barely thirteen years old, I already felt very self-conscious of what I was. An anomaly. My mood had been fluctuating a lot lately. Hormones raged inside my tiny body, pushing me out of my child's state and into adulthood at a pace I wasn't ready to keep up. The physical aspect of my metamorphosis caused my chest to hurt, because breasts were growing inside me.

Yet, I didn't want to be a woman.

My feet dug into the sand and I stared straight ahead at the ocean, watching waves move toward me. Observing the cadence of their relentless journey to the shore, I wanted to become one of them, armed with a single purpose, finally rid of doubt, fear and all those existential questions that kept looping inside my head for days on end.

The water didn't look frightening, despite the cold, the abyss, and the unknown. I walked knee deep into the ocean and closed my eyes.

The waves brushed the skin of my legs in swift up and down motions, like the soft lick of a tongue on ice cream.

Engulfed in the salty air and the warm breeze, I felt one with the elements. The beach was my safe place.

I heard children's laughter in the distance, a dog barking, people chatting. Words of a conversation caught my attention for a split second. Then I redirected my focus on the waves moving up and down my legs, the water now feeling warmer on my skin. My toes dug deeper into the wet sand, until my feet were completely buried.

I stayed in this position for a long time and, breathing slowly, worked on releasing the tension that paralyzed my body. If only I could stay like this forever, I wouldn't have to worry about anything.

Fingers gripped my shoulder, startling me.

I opened my eyes and saw an old woman standing beside me, smiling. She wore a white linen blouse and black capri pants. Her wide, straw hat hid half of her face, but I noticed her eyes. Blue like the sky, bright and glowing. Strands of her long, white hair flew in rhythm with the wind.

Her smile soothed the turmoil creating havoc within my heart. Mom always warned me about talking to strangers. But I didn't think this old woman would do me any harm.

So I smiled back.

"Hi, little girl," the old woman said.

"Hi," I replied.

The woman looked at the ocean and then at me.

"Do you enjoy being here?" she asked.

The sunlight hit the bottom of her face, below the shadow of her broad straw hat, highlighting deep wrinkles around her mouth. How old was she? She could have easily been my grandmother. I had never known my grandparents. They lived too far away and died when I was just a baby. My world didn't revolve around many relatives. Mom and Dad were all I had.

I nodded.

"Why are you so angry, Julie?" the woman asked.

My heart jumped inside my chest.

"How do you know my name?"

She smiled again. "You're a bright little girl," she continued. "But deep inside you're in pain. So much pain."

I stared at her, frozen in place. The water hitting my calves seemed colder now.

"The world won't be nice to you," she continued. "But you don't have to take everything personally. Often people don't realize when they're hurtful. You need to let go of all that anger, or it will get the best of you."

"How do you know my name?" I asked again.

"I know what's inside your heart, Julie. You're made of darkness and light and, right now, darkness and light are fighting for control. Soon, darkness will become very powerful. You'll feel hatred. You'll feel alone and completely misunderstood. You'll have the choice to give in to your anger, or fight back and let the light in. This process will take some time. It won't be easy. You'll cry a lot. You'll ask yourself why you're here, and why you're the way you are. But you must not lose hope, even in the most hopeless situations. You are not alone."

Her eyes glowed like sapphires and I didn't feel afraid, just confused.

"Remember me, Julie. We'll meet again. Now please, close your eyes and empty your mind of all the worry and concern you feel today. Let your heart find peace."

I wasn't sure whether to comply. I was still processing what she'd told me. And in my thirteen-year-old mind, what she said didn't make much sense.

"Come on," she insisted.

So I closed my eyes and took a deep breath. I thought of surfing, the ocean, being one with nature. Taming the waves, toppling off my board, laughing with Kara while watching the sunset, lying on the sand and basking in the sunlight like a cat.

A smile creased my cheeks. Yes, that's what true happiness felt like to me.

When I reopened my eyes, the old lady was gone. I looked for her on the beach, but she was nowhere to be found. The image of her glowing eyes lingered in my mind for days after that strange encounter. And then I forgot all about them and the anger came back.

I wasn't good enough. And no one would convince me otherwise.

Mom and Dad did the best they could to raise me the right way. I still messed up. I hated them, and thought they were too self-absorbed with their lives to care about my silly problems. The boy I loved who didn't love me back, my friendship with Kara, school, schoolmates who didn't treat me the way I wanted to be treated, teachers who didn't understand my mind-set, and my own self, constantly dissatisfied with my appearance, the way I talked, walked, ate, breathed... I became a machine of self-contrivance. I contrived to fit in. I contrived to become someone I wasn't. Meanwhile, the acting-out escalated. The fear of losing control dominated.

The old lady who visited me on the beach that hot summer afternoon was the old lady who visited me outside the one-dollar store. The Mighty Listener. The one who pulled me into this world because my life had spiraled into absolute mayhem.

Evan shook me awake.

"Time to go," he said, as I opened my eyes.

"Where?" I blurted out, still lost in the fog of my thoughts.

"See the others." He smiled.

I jumped. "What?"

"You're ready return to the Dome."

I stared at him in disbelief. "Really? How?"

"You changed your state of mind."

"Because you saw my dreams?"

He nodded.

I hugged him. "OMG! This is great! This is amazing!"

He laughed. "Yeah, but don't get too excited. More challenges await."

"I know. I know. But I feel so good." I pointed at the pool. "What about taming the fish?"

"Oh, that thing will never be tamed. Have you looked at it? It's so ugly. Who would want to tame an ugly fish?"

I raised an eyebrow. "But you said if I tamed the—"

He cut me off. "The fish was part of an exercise. We could have gone down there a million times, it wouldn't have mattered. What matters is that you're ready and willing to take the next steps. You've opened your mind to change. The seed has been planted."

He patted me on the shoulder.

"Come on," he said.

After spending all that time with Evan as sole companion and guide, I felt nervous about seeing the others.

Evan led the way as usual, and I shuffled behind him. I tried to be tough, but inside I was a wreck. I feared the others would judge me, try to test me, see if I'd act out, so they could send me away again and be done with me.

We entered the Dome, moving from the darkness of the tunnel into the dimly lit area, and the whole notion of finding the light took on a new meaning for me. I had been stuck in a dark fog for too long. I felt I had been reborn, and was learning to crawl, and then walk. My anger didn't bother me so much now. But what would become of it once I was challenged again?

I had to keep hope, even in the most hopeless situation.

We found the others sitting around the table, and I could tell they were eager to speak with me. Sloan especially didn't stop staring, his eyes following my every move as I approached and took a seat next to Evan.

Susan smiled. "Hi, Julie," she said, and her tone was softer than usual.

Miko waved and Sky gave me a friendly nod.

I nodded. "Hi, Susan. Hi, guys."

I glanced at Evan. He looked very serious.

"Why this decorum?" I asked him. "I feel like I'm being judged for some crime."

He didn't glance back at me. "Well, today is the day you show this assembly you're willing to take action."

I jerked backward. "Isn't it enough to know I'm willing to better myself?"

He shook his head. "No. You gotta prove it now."

Oh Lordie. I exhaled deeply.

"Alright, how was your time with Julie?" Susan asked Evan.

"It was necessary and helpful. She made a lot of progress," he replied.

I focused on my fingers to avoid Sloan's persistent stare. He sat right next to Susan.

"How's the anger?" she continued with her questioning.

"It's better. More manageable," Evan replied.

She nodded. "Good, good."

"We haven't seen much progress above ground," Sloan said. "Still lots of explosions and ash."

His tone made my skin crawl. I didn't like his insinuations. I could feel deep within that something had changed. Couldn't he sense it?

Evan placed his hand on mine and pressed it slightly.

"Julie needs a lot of positive reinforcement," Evan continued. "But progress in Oceanside is visible."

Sloan raised his eyebrows. "Really? Where?"

"Everywhere," Evan replied. "It's slight, but there."

"Kara and her friends are dying to get a piece of us," Sloan snapped. "So why are you telling me there's been progress?"

"I haven't witnessed any major incidents," Evan said.

"What Sloan is trying to say is that Kara and her two vengeful friends are roaming outside, waiting for any opportunity to have the upper hand," Susan interjected. "You haven't seen what they can do because you were with Julie this whole time. But we had to contain them."

"I understand," Evan replied. "Julie went through a very tough process, remembering every single thing she did. These bad memories were part of that process. I believe, however, that she's ready to tackle them now. She's armed with tools. She is ready to move on and grow. I can assure you of that."

Sloan laughed. "Okay, fine. Julie, what do you have to say about this?"

I shrugged. "I'm ready to do whatever I need to do to get better."

"Are you willing to go to any length to get better?" Sloan continued.

"Yes, I'm willing to become a better person. I won't hurt another human being again, if that's what you're implying."

Sloan gritted his teeth.

"Good, because I wanna see you fight," he said, pounding his fist on the table.

Evan stood. "Is that necessary now?"

"Yes," Sloan answered. "I want to see it with my own eyes."

Blood rushed to my face. "W-What do I have to fight?"

Evan looked at me, then back at Sloan. "Okay. If watching her fight will make you happy, so be it."

I stared at Evan. "What? Is this a simulation we're talking about?" Panic crept into my insides, giving me cramps again.

Evan smiled. "Actually, yes, it's going to be a simulation."

"F-For real? You're not playing games?" I asked.

"Sloan has a different take on what simulations are supposed to look like," he added. "But no, we're not playing games."

I swallowed over the lump in my throat. "Lovely," I said. Sloan was smiling his butt off at my reaction.

Sky patted me on the shoulder, holding a platter of fried critters ready for me to devour. Except, I wasn't hungry.

He waved a rat in front of my face, and my first reaction was to retch and vomit all the watermelon I had gulped in the greenhouse moments ago.

"Darn, girl, now I gotta mop the floor again!" Sky exclaimed.

Miko came to my rescue and handed me a piece of cloth to wipe my mouth.

"Too much sewer watermelon make tummy hurt," she said.

I nodded. "Yeah, yeah. I stopped questioning the sanitary conditions of this place. Was this really necessary?"

"What?" Evan asked.

"This whole shebang of a reunion only to tell me I had to fight again," I said.

"Come on now, Julie, I'm sure you're dying to demonstrate your skills!" Sloan commented.

"It's for the best," Susan added.

"You are not helping me!" I said, handing the smeared piece of cloth back to Miko, who gave me a comforting smile. "How can I fight if I feel sick?"

Sloan grinned. "Oh, I know how."

25

My father always yelled at me to get a grip, and I never understood why he said such a thing, until now.

Evan squeezed my hand as we stood next to each other on my former high school football field. The sound of explosions could be heard in the distance, although not as loud and threatening as I remembered them from my early days in the Underworld. The field didn't look too bad either. Blades of grass poked through the dirt, and the ground wasn't drilled left and right with holes the size of craters anymore. All this change proved to me I was making progress, and Oceanside was reverting back to its lively state.

So why did I have to fight anything here? Was Sloan just being an inconsiderate jerk?

"Well... What's coming next, then?" I asked Evan.

Sky and Miko guarded the Dome while Susan and Sloan had tagged along to witness my warrior moves in the open. They stood a few feet away, and Sloan was eyeing me like he was dying to see my head on a stick.

"I can tell you're uncomfortable," Evan said. "Don't worry about what Sloan does. He just wants reassurance you're getting better."

I huffed. "Why? Can't they read my thoughts?"

"Remember, Sloan is the doubting part of your mind. You need to learn to accept others' wants and needs," he replied with a smile.

"Yeah, and isn't Susan supposed to be a mediator right now? Keep this homicidal maniac from disturbing my inner peace?"

"Patience, Julie. Sloan wants to see things with his own eyes. Is that too much for you to handle?"

"How is my fighting a want or need for Sloan? And didn't he mention Kara was after him too? Doesn't he realize I'm dealing with a lot of crap here?"

Evan laughed softly. "Listen to yourself. As you make progress on your journey, more challenges will come your way. You can't get all riled up just because Sloan wants to test you out."

"This is ridiculous. And after this business is done, I want to take another shower. I feel disgusting."

"Deal." He laughed. "When it's time to gear up, we either run or stand our ground. This is life in a nutshell."

"Why are you so calm?" I asked.

"Because"—he winked at me— "this challenge will prove whether you still want to run."

I huffed again.

"Okay, consider this football field your fighting ring," Sloan said, stepping closer to us.

"Gosh, this sucks," I replied.

"Come on, you gotta show us what you're made of, huh?" Sloan shook my arm.

I worked hard not to slap him.

"Isn't he a challenge in and of itself?" Evan whispered to me.

I clenched my teeth. "Right. He's a crappy challenge."

"So, Julie, as part of this exercise, I'll give you something to help you defeat the opponent I've chosen for you." Sloan handed me a small dark ball, another chocolate.

"Why are you giving me this?" I frowned and looked at Evan. "I'm not supposed to eat this anymore."

Sloan laughed. "You think you can do without it? I thought you suffered from awful stomach cramps. Fine, I'll take it back."

He went for my hand but I recoiled.

"No." I put the chocolate in my mouth. "I'm too nauseous to think clearly. If this thing can help, then—"

"You still want to run," Evan mumbled.

"W-What?" I asked. "No, no this isn't what you think..."

"Alright, this is going to be fun to watch!" Sloan said.

As Evan walked away I felt a surge of adrenaline course throughout my body, giving life once again to my psychedelic vision. I was wired, with all my senses on alert. The adrenaline rush made me want to fly like Superman and revolve the earth around its axis a few times.

Wow, why did I decide not to eat chocolates anymore? Oh, right, because Evan told me not to. I was very dumb to listen to him.

"How can you surrender to your fear when you're high?" Evan asked in my thoughts.

I let out one loud, visceral scream in response.

The ground shook.

The gray sky melted into a canvas of fire, and the air became hotter with every breath I took.

As the heat increased, I felt my body melt.

A loud hammering invaded my brain as if a construction crew had just settled in. My heartbeat increased and my muscles tensed. A slithering noise resonated in the distance, growing louder and louder.

Something broke through the ground.

Oh crapola. What the heck was this thing? I had to get out of there. Except, I couldn't. My body weighed a ton and my feet felt like two blocks of lead.

Pure terror paralyzed me from head to toe, as I watched the thing emerge and rise like a skyscraper into the burning sky. A long and thick snake-like body the size of a large sewer pipe, with disproportionate tiny buggy legs, was attached to a huge reptilian head. And despite being at least one hundred feet in height, the genetic anomaly made its way toward me as fast as a cheetah running after a frightened gazelle. I gasped when the creature bared fangs three times my size, and a pair of glowing red eyes stared right at me.

"How the heck am I going to defeat this thing?" I asked.

My body temperature reached an all-time high.

"Gosh, help me!" I shouted. I tried to move again, but my feet were anchored to the ground.

"Who's going to help you?" Evan said. "You've made your bed by eating this chocolate."

I had no idea what to do. Sloan was laughing his butt off.

Susan was just waiting for me to act.

And Evan, well... Evan was pissed at me.

The creature was coming, and I had to do something if I didn't want it to eat me in one big gulp.

Closing my eyes, I mumbled the prayer Evan taught me in the Cave.

"Please, I'm sorry I gave in again but I need help right now. Forgive me where I have been resentful. Help me to not keep anything to myself. Show me where I owe an apology and help me make it. Help me to be kind and loving. Remove worry or remorseful reflections. Help me find hope even in the most hopeless situations. I am not alone and, as I grow, I give away the control and become open to living without fear."

As I said these last few words, heat ignited in my eyes. Taking a deep breath, I reopened them and faced the creature. Fear left me like water flushed down a toilet bowl, and two powerful beams shot from my eyeballs.

The beast growled and snarled, baring its humongous fangs, trying to take a bite of me; but I let it all out, flame-thrower style.

While the fire spread and crackled through the beast's head and body, I repeated the same words, over and over again.

"I am not alone and, as I grow, I give away the control and become open to living without fear."

I watched the strange looking animal disintegrate on the field, turning into a hill of thick, black dust.

The rush of adrenaline faded and my body temperature decreased back to normal.

When it was all over, and my senses returned to their far-from-superhuman-awesome level, I looked at Sloan and Susan, then Evan.

Sloan clapped and wooed, Susan smiled and Evan, well... Evan made a grumpy face.

Sloan proceeded to give me a hug.

Well, if that wasn't completely unexpected.

"Man! That was fantastic!" Sloan pressed me against him.

I still felt completely off balance. But at least I wasn't stuck to the ground anymore.

"You did it. You fought like a champion. Oh, wow, that was beautiful," he continued.

Evan didn't say a thing. He refused to look at me.

Susan nodded and gave me both thumbs up.

"Oh wow, well..." I said.

"You've been victorious once again!" Sloan exclaimed. "Darn, Evan taught you the right things."

Surprised by his reaction, but happy to see he didn't really hate me, I laughed too.

"This is tremendous work. Tremendous!" Sloan continued.

"Thank you," I said. "So now I get to shower?"

"No. Thank you," he answered. "Sure. All the shower time in the world is yours, mighty warlord."

Despite my crushing victory, the knot in my stomach didn't disentangle as I watched Evan walk away without saying a word.

Seeing the town of my childhood come back to life made me feel good inside.

I couldn't hear those horrible explosions anymore. The sky still looked overcast, but at least the rain of ash had stopped. The thick layer of dust and debris covering the ground had been reduced to a thinner and lighter coat.

As the four of us walked through the street, a tug at my heart reminded me that the hardest challenge still awaited me. And Evan was upset with me, because I had eaten Sloan's chocolate.

Sloan wrapped his arm around my shoulders.

"Still worried about Kara, huh?" he asked.

I nodded.

"Look at what you've achieved today. You turned on your beams! I have no doubt you'll do great against her," he added.

"How can you be so sure about that?"

"You might not realize it yet, but you've acquired a new freedom," he said.

"Really? You truly mean that?"

He smiled. "Yes, and I'm honored to be a part of this wonderful process."

I smiled in return, to be polite, but Sloan didn't know what he was talking about. Evan had been the amazing guide and friend. At the beginning of our friendship, I felt so resentful, angry, and misunderstood. But his advice helped me break out of my shell. I embraced the way he made me feel. He gave me confidence, faith and hope. And I failed him, because I was a dumbass addicted to those stupid chocolates.

I felt so disappointed with myself.

"I need to speak with Evan alone, if you don't mind," I said to Sloan.

He smiled. "Of course."

I paced to catch up with Evan.

"Hey," I said.

He stared straight ahead without acknowledging me.

"I'm sorry," I continued. The awful knot made my stomach as hard as a rock. "I know I should have fought the monster without eating that choc—"

"Stop," Evan cut me off. "I know what you did. I was there too, remember?"

I sighed. "I couldn't help myself. Sloan gave it to me and bam, I ate it!"

He nodded. "Yeah, that you did. You didn't even give it a second thought. Despite all the work you've done. I guess it wasn't enough."

I gasped. "No! What are you talking about? I feel fine. I'm not even angry, I just wanted to—"

"Patch things up? Make sure I'd agree with your actions?" He jeered. "Well, I don't. You're still running, Julie, and I can't stop you from ruining your life. Only you can."

"I listened to you. The spider and the bee. And I embraced my fears, I really did!"

"No, Julie. What you achieved on the field isn't what I call surrendering. And you can repeat the words of the prayer I taught you all you want, but as long as you stay stuck in your old ways, you'll never make progress."

I huffed. "So what, we're going to be mad at each other now? After all we've been through?"

"You are in control of your feelings, Julie," he replied in a flat tone.

"No, come on..." I protested, but he accelerated his pace and walked away from me again.

"But I love you!" I mumbled as the distance between us stretched.

I felt terrible. The knot in my stomach forced me to bend forward, and I struggled not to vomit on the pavement. When I regained some control over my severe bodily reaction, Sloan gripped my arm, saying something I didn't fully grasp right away.

"We need to go back under," he repeated, his face looking very serious.

"Why?" I asked, still feeling sick.

He pointed at something on the street.

"This is why," he said.

26

I stared in that direction, expecting to face a demented, weird-looking beast again.

But what I saw was much, much worse.

Picture a scene pulled out of a western, with weeds tumbling across the pavement from left to right, dust twirling above the asphalt and doors squeaking off their hinges, while three, purple-eye-glowing bad memories stand a mere hundred feet from us, ready to fire their beams.

My breath caught inside my throat as I repressed the need to throw up again. My former best friend still wore her beloved confirmation gown—which did nothing to make her look holier—her long blonde hair loose on her shoulders. And she was staring at me, her face as stern as a rock. My gaze shifted to Dan. He looked angry as hell in his football uniform, his jaw clenched and his eyes focused, as if he was about to lunge and land a thick punch in my stomach.

Michael stood right next to his best friend, also in his football uniform, and looked equally mad.

Gulp. The lump now forming in my throat was the size of an apple. And that apple wouldn't vanish anytime soon. My stomach cramped up until I couldn't handle the pain anymore and vomited again.

"They won't even grant me the pleasure of a quick introduction, huh?" I wiped my mouth with the back of my hand, tucking my sweaty palms under my armpits.

"Seriously, Julie, focus," Sloan said.

Evan stood between them and us, perfectly still.

"Evan!" I shouted. "I'm sorry!"

He didn't turn around to look at me.

"How did she even show up? I wasn't angry back there." I pressed my hands on my stomach. "Just upset because Evan's mad at me..."

"We need to run," Sloan replied.

"Why?"

"Because we aren't ready for this kind of showdown."

"Wasn't I supposed to face Kara, Dan and Mike, and apologize to them?"

Dizziness hit me next, and I felt light headed.

"They hate you. All that resentment you held for years, it's theirs now. You gave them so much power," Sloan said.

"Right." I swallowed over the apple in my throat. "Shizzle, she looks so darn scary." I turned to Sloan again. "You know, anger is overrated."

Susan put her hand on my shoulder.

"I can take us out of here," she said, "but we need to go."

Sloan let a chuckle out. "Yes, anger is definitely overrated. Try to explain that to them."

I inhaled deeply.

Clusterflying load of monkey bananas. I was about to be crisped to crumbles.

Kara was smiling at us now, the familiar sneer of victory halving her face like a lopsided slit. She looked so friggin' terrifying! I wondered why I hadn't peed my pants yet. Probably because I was too busy trying not to cover myself in vomit.

"Okay, where to?" I asked Susan.

She started running in the opposite direction. "This way."

A quick, sideways glance showed that Evan was following us. But Kara and her pals were right behind him.

Despite my upset stomach, we sprinted up the street, and Susan took us down an alleyway leading to the back of a building. I noticed an open sewer entrance in the middle of the alleyway.

"Are we going back underground?" I panted like I was about to die from a heart attack.

"Yeah!" Susan replied in between heavy breaths.

I hated running.

The sewer entrance didn't seem too far away. My legs spun under me like wheels, yet I somehow lost balance, as if the street shifted, the horizontal plane becoming vertical, and my rapid run turned into a laborious ascension. Weird, because we weren't running uphill. I glanced again behind me, and saw Kara, Dan and Mike catching up to Evan.

They were moving fast, much faster than us. These motherflying bad memories could break records at that speed.

Of course, the street hadn't shifted—I had tripped.

"Ouch, darn it!"

Sloan came to my rescue and helped me up.

"Come on!" he said.

"Crap," I stood and winced. "Now my ankle hurts like hell. I'm falling apart here."

He gave me his arm for support.

"Let's go!"

"I'm doing the best I can!" I protested, fighting another heavy retching session.

I limped toward the sewer entrance. Susan had already made her way down.

I dropped into the opening in the ground. My shallow breath caught in my throat, striking the apple, as my fingers gripped the metal edge of the tunnel entrance. I felt something pop inside my shoulder. I cringed and grunted, but held on, while Susan helped me from below.

"I need to slow them down. I'll catch up to you!" I heard Evan shout in the distance.

"Are you sure?" Susan shouted back.

"Yeah. Take Julie to the Dome. She needs to be safe."

I didn't fully process this exchange until I was inside the sewer and Sloan climbed above me to slam the entrance shut.

"Hold on, what are you doing?" I shouted at Sloan.

"We need to get to Sky and Miko," he replied.

"But Evan?" I asked.

"He'll be fine."

Susan touched my injured shoulder, and I let out a painful scream. Boy oh boy, that friggin' hurt. On the verge of passing out, I pressed my shoulder against the wall and focused on my breathing. My ankle throbbed, and my stomach wanted to jump out through my mouth. I was a real mess.

"We need to keep going," Susan said.

I stood still in the darkness. I hadn't even fought Kara, and already felt weaker than if I had run a marathon.

My shoulder hurt like hell, sending waves of pain throughout my torso. I couldn't move further or even breathe properly. Lord, where would I find painkillers in this sewer system?

"We need to keep moving," Susan repeated.

"Are you serious? Do you see the state I'm in?"

"You need help with that?" Sloan asked.

"What, like you're an MD now?" I cringed.

He grabbed my arm.

"It will take only a second. Take a deep breath," he said.

Oh gosh, please make it stop. Make it stop, make it —

Shizzle. Argh! F--
-------!

My scream echoed throughout the sewer system.

"There, all better. Now move," he said.

"Crap." I cursed for a good thirty seconds, trying to regain control of my ragged breathing.

"Go," he ordered.

I complied reluctantly. My ankle hurt so badly. "W-What's going to happen to Evan?"

"Just walk." Sloan had reverted to being in jerk cold mode right now. Just as cold as this darn tunnel. What was up with the attitude, buddy?

"Could someone please tell me what's going to happen to him?" I asked again, nausea still hitting me hard. Where were Evan's healing eyes when I needed them?

"Listen," Sloan said, "can we talk about him once we're at the Dome?"

"Why?" I asked.

"Keep going," Susan interjected. "We're getting close."

"What happened to him?"

Susan stopped and looked at me. "You really want to know?" she asked, and I realized she was on the verge of crying.

Now I felt tears coming too.

"No," I said. "Don't tell me I'm not seeing him again. We weren't even on good terms when he left..."

Susan didn't respond. Instead, she turned and kept walking. Sloan patted me on the shoulder—the healthy one.

"Come on, Julie," he said.

I couldn't believe this. One minute, everything was fine, the next...

"It's your entire fault!" I shouted.

"What?" Sloan looked at me like I had lost my mind. Which arguably I had.

I pointed a finger at Susan and him.

"It's your fault. You wanted to see if I could overcome my anger, and insisted on taking us outside. But you knew these monsters of memories were roaming the streets and wanted to harm us. You did this to him!"

Sloan moved toward me, but I stepped back.

"You did this to him. I can't believe this. I can't!" I kept shouting.

"Julie, please," Susan begged. "Please don't do this now."

"I don't care!" I said. "This is bullcrap. This is just pure bullcrap!"

I choked on my tears. The pain inside my chest was unbearable, like someone had cut it wide open and was twisting the knife in my heart. I couldn't accept I'd never see Evan again. How could my memories do this to me?

They wanted to take away the only friend I had. They wanted to hurt me like I had hurt them.

"I need to fight them back," I said.

Susan shook her head.

"Not now, Julie. Not now."

She pulled me toward her for a hug and I broke down.

Susan, Sloan and I made it back to the Dome. I wasn't sure how I managed to follow them. Lost in a funk, I didn't feel like being friendly with anyone.

All I wanted was to be left alone.

The pain in my heart was just too fresh. I missed having Evan by my side, to help me cope with my feelings.

I asked Susan to take me to the Cave.

"Are you sure this is a good idea? We shouldn't leave you alone," she said.

"No, this is what I need to do. It's my safe haven. Take me there, please," I insisted.

We walked down the tunnel, and all I could think about was Evan, my guide, helper and friend. I was so grateful to have found him, and now so resentful to have lost him.

But I wouldn't let the anger win. Kara and her evil pals wouldn't take me back to square one. I wouldn't allow it.

"We're all hurting, you know," Susan said.

I didn't reply.

"Just promise you won't do anything stupid," she added.

"Yeah, I promise. I owe that to Evan."

She smiled.

We entered the Cave, and a wave of deeper sadness crashed over me.

"Alright, Julie, I'll return in a little bit to check on you."

"Alright."

Her expression made it clear she wasn't entirely sold that leaving me there unattended was the best idea.

"I'll be fine," I said.

"Okay."

She walked out, and I sat by the edge of the sewer pool.

I stayed in the dark for a long time, thinking about all the conversations Evan and I had had there. Tears fell, as my heart ached.

He had taught me so much. If only I hadn't eaten that chocolate...

Listening to the soft humming of the water, I mumbled a few words.

"Evan, we started off as strangers and became the closest friends. The love I have for you will never die. If you can hear me, and I know you can, I want you to know I'll do everything in my power to be who you want me to be."

I stood.

"No more chocolates. I promise to win without them." And I dove head first into the water.

27

"*M*iss Jones? Miss Jones!"
I woke up, face flat on my desk, all eyes in the classroom, including those of Mrs. Pots, the American history teacher at my new high school in Los Angeles, locked on me.

Drool rolled down my chin as I sat up straight, and soft laughter spread out like the plague. Shizzle. Glancing away from the crowd, I wiped away the drool.

"Silence!" Mrs. Pots ordered. She walked up to my desk and stared at me.

"I'm sorry," I mumbled. "Did I miss anything?"

"You did!" she replied. She didn't really intimidate me. I would suggest she had a makeover pronto, because her dress style and hairdo dated back to when Madonna was still relevant. "Miss Jones, next time you wish to take a nap during the class, I'll award you with an F. Have I made myself clear?"

I nodded without conviction, and yawned when she turned her back and walked to the front of the room.

"Good. Alright, class, next time we'll have a quiz, so read your material please."

Everyone stood and put away their stuff in their bag.

"Miss Jones, may I have a word?" Mrs. Pots asked, as I headed toward the door.

I sighed.

"What's happening with you?"

I shrugged. "Nothing, everything's fine. Why?"

"Why? Have you looked in a mirror lately?"

I raised an eyebrow. "What does this have to do with me sleeping in class?"

She laughed. "Oh, don't play with me, Miss Jones. I'm dead serious."

"So am I. Say what you want to say. As far as I'm concerned, I didn't do anything wrong."

"No?" she asked.

I shook my head. "Nope."

We stared at each other for a few seconds, before she spoke again.

"Your eyes are bloodshot. You look tired. Your skin is white like a sheet and your hands are shaking. Now, is there anything you'd like to tell me before I proceed further?"

I snorted. "Gosh, what is this, the Spanish Inquisition?"

"If I see the signs, I say something about it."

"The signs?" I scoffed. "Great. I don't need your scolding. I got parents for that."

She sighed and took a step closer to me.

"You know, I was like you once. Rebellious, adventurous. Ignorant is really the word I'm looking for. I hung out with the wrong crowd and did things I'm not proud of. I took a few unfortunate turns before finally getting a grip and admitting my life was a mess."

I looked at her before bursting into laughter. "Well, I'm not like you."

She didn't seem fazed by my attitude. "My door is open if you ever want to talk."

I huffed. "Okay. Won't change the fact you'll still give me an F."

"You don't know how an honest conversation might help."

"Alright. Is that all?"

She nodded. "Take care of yourself. I'll see you next week. Or maybe before that."

"Right." I walked out.

As I stepped into the ladies' room, I exhaled deeply. I stared at myself in the mirror. Mrs. Pots was right. I looked worse than usual.

Time for a fixer-upper to stop my hands from shaking uncontrollably. I disappeared into a stall and pulled a tiny flask out of my bag. Two long gulps later, I felt as good as new.

I flushed the toilet and returned to the sink to wash my hands and apply some makeup. The door opened and a kid who I knew only too well—and certainly didn't belong in the ladies' room—entered.

"What the fly, Tom?" I turned around to face him.

He smiled and leaned against the door.

"Thought I'd say hi."

Tom was very good looking. Roughly six feet tall, with a slender but fit body, flawless skin, symmetrical face, strong jaw, almond-shaped, blue-gray eyes and ashen hair, he had worked as a model since he was four-teen years old. And he was a friend of Mark.

"Now?" I asked.

"Why, did I interrupt you?"

I scowled. "I don't have time for this."

He briefly opened the door.

"We'll only be a minute," he said to someone outside.

I laughed. "Oh, you brought some backup?"

"Nah." He stepped closer. "Just making sure no one bothers us."

He grabbed my hand and pulled me to him.

"So, Miss Jones, I got you a little gift."

I rolled my eyes. "Really? And what would it be?"

He dug a small transparent plastic pouch out of his front jean pocket and waved it in front of me.

"What's that?" I asked. "Pills to help with the headaches?"

He laughed. "No, better. Pills to replace what you're using now."

I took a step back and leaned against the sink. "I'm fine. Did Mark send you?"

He placed the pouch next to the sink. "You don't look fine."

I stared away. When my hands began shaking again, I tucked them inside my pant pockets and sighed heavily.

"Someone must have noticed by now. If not the smell of your breath, your appearance shouts out, 'I'm a big mess.' Let me help, okay?"

I sniffled back tears. "I'm fine," I repeated.

"You didn't look fine when Mrs. Pots caught you sleeping on your desk."

"Right. I'll go to bed earlier tonight. I don't need a babysitter."

He held me by the shoulders and locked eyes with me.

"Hey, listen to me. I'm trying to help you here."

I glanced at the pouch of pills and looked back at him.

"What do they do?" I asked with a broken voice.

He smiled. "Try one now."

He opened the plastic pouch and dropped a pill into the palm of his hand.

"It won't bite," he said.

I stared at the little black pebble, and took a deep breath.

"Come on, you know you're dying to try it."

"Fine." I put the pill in my mouth.

"Good girl. Keep the rest. When you need more, I'll give you more."

I sniffled again and swallowed the pill.

"Who's taking care of the bill?" I asked.

"Don't worry about it. What matters is that you feel and look better."

He gently moved me to face the mirror.

"Can't let that beauty go to waste, you hear me?" he said.

I stared and nodded.

"Okay," I said.

He smiled. "Good."

He walked back to the door. "I'll see you later, alright?"

"Yeah, yeah. At Mark's house." I was still staring at my reflection.

The gated property had been built in the hills over-looking Los Angeles. It offered absolute privacy. Given the Wilsons' popularity, tabloids often sent crews of paparazzi in helicopters to take pictures, but the chances of snapping a shot of Mrs. Wilson sunbathing top-less in her backyard were as slim as catching Jack the Ripper without forensic science in nineteenth-century Whitechapel. The paparazzi still tried though, despite the security cameras installed every twenty feet on the driveway, and along the fenced perimeter of the property.

I reached the entrance gates and wound my window down. The security guard smiled at me.

"Miss Jones! How are you today?" he said with a wave of his hand.

Johnny. He was a bear. Six feet three, two hundred fifty pounds, loved fried chicken and, more generally, all sorts of greasy food. As long it was unhealthy, it worked for him. I had no idea why he hadn't died of a heart attack yet. He was always nice to me, handing me lol-lipops and candy every time I passed the gate.

"It's good to see you too." I smiled back.

"Still a fan of Jolly Ranchers? I got some extra green apple!" He laughed.

"Thanks, Johnny."

He handed me the candy with his huge paw.

"Here to see Mr. Wilson, I presume?"

I nodded as I unwrapped the paper and popped one candy in my mouth. The delicious atomic flavor of Jolly Ranchers hit my taste buds in all the right ways.

"Yep."

"Ah, love is in the air..." Johnny started singing.

I choked a little.

He winked. "Well you have a good day now!"

The gates opened with a light squeak.

"Thanks. You too." I drove forward to the Wilsons' mansion.

Mark's father had become extremely rich after writing and directing a science fiction trilogy in the late seventies/early eighties, which broke every record in the movie industry. Since then he lived off the royalties, but still took time to release a re-mastered version for die-hard fans every decade or so.

Mark would never have to job hunt. My dad was a big shot in the Hollywood world too, but we still stood far behind Mark's dad on the scale.

Mark waited for me on the front steps.

I parked the Bubble next to a Lamborghini and a Porsche, two of Mark's parents' prized possessions, and exited.

"Hey," Mark said, greeting me with a kiss.

"Hey," I replied back.

He smiled slightly, before heading inside the house. As I followed him through the gigantic lobby, I recognized another familiar face along the way.

"Hello, Carl," I said.

The butler smiled. "Well hello, Miss Jones!"

If Mark were Bruce Wayne—minus all the bat costume dress-up—Carl would be the perfect Alfred Pennyworth. I liked Carl. Just like Johnny, he was always kind to me.

"We'll be outside," Mark interjected.

"Sure. Refreshments will be served shortly," Carl said. "It's always a pleasure seeing you, Miss Jones. Hopefully not for the last time." He gently shook my hand before excusing himself.

Without further comment, Mark and I exited the lobby in the direction of the backyard. Not a typical backyard either. It came close to football field size. To prevent prying eyes from taking valuable shots from the sky, Mark's dad had paid a fortune to build a retractable roof over the entire space, just like in a stadium. When activated, the roof still let in natural light but, from the outside, it reflected the sunlight like a mirror, making it impossible for anyone to see inside. Brilliant, really. Big money could buy anything.

Mark's mother, originally from New York, had always dreamed of having her own miniature Central Park. Well, that garden came close. The architect who designed it had recreated some of the fountains and hills of the original. For those who missed New York, it made for a great ersatz. Of course, Mark's mother had also added a few of her own fantasies to make it more hers; that's why, as I strolled around, I landed on a Venus de Milo bearing her face.

Mark and I walked in silence to my favorite spot, the Alice in Wonderland statue.

"How are you feeling?" Mark stared at me. Did I involuntarily make a funny face?

I nodded. "Everything's great." I sat down on the bench near the statue and crossed my legs.

As he continued to look at me, a distinct pinch bloomed inside my chest. Sitting next to me, he pulled a pack of cigarettes from his jeans.

"Want one?"

"Nah. Not the best thing for hair and skin."

"Ah, yes, at seventeen years old, it's all about hair and skin." He lit the cigarette and blew a big cloud of smoke. The Chesterfield scent filled the air, and I closed my eyes for a second.

"Okay," he said, and exhaled smoke through his nostrils. Gosh, he was cute.

"So what Tom gave you worked, right?" he asked.

I laughed. "Yeah!"

He nodded.

"That's great, babe."

He pulled on the cigarette. "Something bothering you, huh?"

As he looked at me with his big hazel eyes, I melted inside.

"How do you know?" I blurted.

"You're dying to ask me what the pills are."

"Yeah, kinda. Although it doesn't make a huge difference."

He smiled. "You won't stop taking them?" He laughed. "You're cute. They're actually homemade. Tom has a lab. We worked on a recipe. You're our first customer."

"Oh. So you don't know what they do?"

"Oh no, we know. But the world doesn't. Only you, me and Tom." He smiled and patted my leg. "This is a new gem we're dying to sell. Tonight, we're handing out samples. I'm glad they make you feel good. These things are amazing. A new high, without any side effects."

"That you know of," I said.

"Right, that's why we need to explore the market."

He exhaled smoke and crushed the cigarette in a little ashtray next to him.

"I'm so excited you're part of this adventure. We're true pioneers! Ready to test the waters?"

I nodded. "Yeah, I don't feel tired anymore. I'm totally wired. In a good way."

"Good, good." He pulled up his cell phone. "Tom is on his way. He'll be here soon."

He wrapped his arm around my shoulders and leaned in for a kiss.

"I love you. You know that, right?" he asked.

I smiled. "Yes, I do. And I love you too."

"Good. We'll have fun. Like we always do."

His eyes caught a spark of light, and he handed me another pill.

"One for the road," he said.

Closing my eyes, I took a deep breath and swallowed.

Swimming slowly through the murk without any light source, I probed left and right, up and down, expecting to be shocked by the ugly fish at any moment.

Evan told me taming the fish was just an exercise. Yet I wasn't totally convinced. I had to try one more time. I owed it to him. Strike that. I owed it to myself to finally feel peace in my heart.

I stopped swimming and waited. Then an electrical shock travelled through my spine.

Sneaky bastard.

I resumed swimming, but was shocked again.

The fish followed my every move.

"Okay, you wanna play? We'll play," I said.

Focusing on my breathing, I worked on igniting my eyes so I could see where I was going.

"I'm not afraid of you. I came here to make peace."

The fish just didn't believe me.

"Stop teasing me! You have an unfair advantage!"

I exhaled deeply, trying to relax my muscles.

"Ouch! Come on now!"

Another deep breath.

"Oh, enough!"

I was pretty darn sure the fish was laughing its scales off at my expense.

"Alright, you win," I said. "You've demonstrated your electrifying skills. I should have listened to Evan and considered you a simple exercise, not a mission."

"Oh, but I'm so much more than an exercise," the fish replied.

My jaw dropped. "Hold on, you can speak?"

The electrical current greeted me again on the side of the leg.

"Why couldn't I speak?" the fish asked. "Because I'm ugly?"

I suppressed a grunt. "Okay, you got me there."

"I'm far from being a simulation, Julie. And taming me is a very important but difficult task. It has to do with more than my peculiar looks."

"Then why did Evan say you were only part of an exercise?"

"Because he knew you weren't ready."

"Well, I'm ready, if only you'd stop shocking me every two seconds."

"Are you, now?"

I nodded. "Yeah, I am. I came in peace."

The fish laughed. "Is that why you tried to ignite your light? So you could see me better?"

"That's exactly what I intended to do."

"Okay."

"I can tell you don't believe me."

The fish laughed again. "There is a way for you to ignite your light without destroying everything. Do you want to know how?"

"Sure, yeah."

"Good, then extend your hand."

"Where?"

"Anywhere."

"You're going to shock me again, aren't you?" I asked.

"Just do it."

I sighed. "Fine."

I slowly extended my arm in front of me. "Now what?"

"Close your eyes and empty your mind. Feel only love, no fear."

I complied. Whatever happened now was out of my control.

I pushed away all distracting thoughts and relaxed every part of my body, like Evan taught me during meditation.

The fish brushed the tips of my fingers and, this time, no electrical current ran through my hand. Instead, intense warmth spread throughout my core.

When I reopened my eyes, soft orange light poured out and wrapped the fish's body, making it glow like a bulb in the darkness.

"You know you didn't have to come back here," the fish said. "But you showed courage and determination. You've been hard on yourself, thought the worst about what you could and couldn't do. Look at you now. How the light loves you, embraces every inch of your soul, reflects the beauty of your true nature. Believe in yourself, Julie, and the world won't seem like such a bad place anymore."

I stared at the creature in front of me, and a wave of emotions crashed inside my tiny chest.

"I don't think Oceanside or Los Angeles are bad places," I replied. "I just wish Evan didn't go in such a horrible manner."

"Why do you think he's gone?"

"He was mad at me, and Kara took him."

"The darkness overcame the light, is that so?"

"I didn't listen to him. I gave in."

The fish's orange glow intensified for a few seconds as the heat in my eyeballs increased, then reverted to normal.

"Why do you think he's gone?" the creature asked again.

"I watched it happen," I answered. "Although... I don't know anymore."

"Acceptance only hides behind a wall of fear."

"I've tried to make things right, and I've failed."

The stronger glow repeated itself.

"You know he's with you, and he'll always be by your side. No matter where you are and how you feel, Evan is your companion," the fish affirmed.

"I rejected him!"

"No, you doubted yourself. You doubted you could be strong enough."

"Sloan wanted to see what I could do. He needed proof!" I replied.

"Did he really need proof?"

"I-I asked Evan why I had to fight again."

"And you weren't convinced you were strong enough without ingesting those chocolates."

"I ran, instead of standing my ground," I said.

The fish's body glowed brightly.

"Don't fool yourself with empty promises, Julie. The chocolates have much power over you, more power than you're willing to admit."

"All I need is to not eat them."

"Will you be able to resist the temptation?"

"I have to try to say no."

"Your heart holds the truth within. Go with confidence. You're on the right path."

"The words from my journal," I said. "Memories are like daggers..."

The glow decreased in intensity as the heat in my eyeballs faded away.

"You know what to do, Julie. Don't underestimate yourself," the fish said. "You don't need to feel hatred or fear to be powerful."

"Thank you for your help."

"You're welcome." The fish started pulling away.

"Wait. Will I ever be able to turn on my beams on my own?"

"Yes. When the time is right, you will. Until then, keep working on yourself."

The darkness returned and the fish disappeared from sight.

Sitting on the cold floor of the Cave, I practiced feeling love without fear, to ignite the fire in my eyes again. No matter how hard I tried, nothing happened.

When Susan returned for me, I forced a smile.

"Hey there," I said.

She gave me a hug.

"You look better."

"I feel better," I replied.

"Not so angry anymore?"

I shook my head. "Not for now."

"Did anything happen while you were on your own?" she asked.

"Like what?"

"You can talk to me."

I cleared my throat. "Well, I learned to turn on my beams peacefully."

A bright spark ignited in her eyes. "That's amazing!"

"Yes, except I can't do it again. The ugly fish helped me."

"Don't beat yourself up."

I sighed. "Yeah."

We walked back to the Dome and were welcomed by Sloan, Sky and Miko.

"How are you doing, warrior?" Sloan pumped my fist.

"I'm good."

"Ready to kick some butt?" Sky piped up.

I laughed. "Yeah, yeah, if butt-kicking is necessary. I'm grateful," I continued. "It's been a tough journey for me, and believe me when I say how amazed I am at my progress. Nothing made sense. Not a single word anyone said struck a chord. I was stubborn and stupid so many times, I've lost count. For that, I wanted to express how sorry I am."

Susan patted my back.

"And I need a shower. I feel disgusting."

Susan nodded. "Miko can go with you."

"Okay."

"You'll be great, warrior," Sloan said.

"And once you're fresh and clean like a newborn, you will dine on a fine meal prepared by yours truly," Sky added.

"Right." I chuckled. "Sewer watermelon and fried rats. Great food choice for a newborn."

"Faith and fortitude, my friend!" Sky replied with a wink.

☾

I remained silent while we walked to the shower room. Miko's light illuminated the way before us, and I shuffled behind, lost in my thoughts again.

"You will turn on beams," Miko said.

I jerked.

"How on earth?"

She turned around and smiled.

"Beams are your obsession. Let go. No need to worry now."

"I-I am not worried," I replied.

"I like Oceanside. It is my home."

"Yeah, it used to be my home too."

"I still live here. I never left," she continued.

"Okay, and why are you—"

"You remember when you wake up. I am here. And you can come see me."

I looked at her, confused.

"Whatever you do wrong in past life, don't matter. You change, you don't forget. And when you come back, we have talk."

"Okay," I said. "And what are we gonna talk about?"

"Anything you like."

"We weren't friends."

"That's okay. We friends now."

I shrugged. "So you want me to knock on your door, and say what? Hey, I'm the jerk who ignored you for years, and also made fun of your accent."

She chuckled. "Anything you like, yes."

"Well, that sounds promising."

We crossed the threshold of the shower room.

"Just promise you will come see me. And the others," she said.

"Okay, I promise."

She smiled. "Good."

Miko helped warm up the water and I stood under the shower until the skin of my fingers pruned.

When finally done, I grunted at the sight of my dirty clothes.

"What wrong?" Miko asked.

"I have no desire to wear these dirty duds again. And Evan told me last time I didn't plan a change of underwear. So irritating."

She laughed.

"What's so funny?"

"I have underwear for you."

I gasped. "What?"

"Come."

Still soaking wet from the shower, I followed her through the tunnels until we reached a room I hadn't been in before. Her glow illuminated the space. There was a bed in the corner and a small makeshift dresser next to it. Miko opened drawers and pulled out clothes, which she laid on the bed.

"Here. Underwear," she said.

"Wow, thanks."

I grabbed the clothes and, without thinking twice, took off my dirty undies and tossed them on the floor. The panties were too big and the bra too loose, but I tightened the elastic band and worked out some magic with the sweatpants and the hoodie Miko had found for me. And tada! I felt like a million bucks.

"Darn," I said. "How come these things weren't there last time?"

"Change mind, change environment," Miko replied.

I nodded. "Yeah. That's true."

I pulled up the hood of my sweater over my wet hair. "Alright, I'm ready to see the others."

Miko smiled. "Okay."

Back at the Dome, I waved hello to Susan and Sloan.

"How was the shower?" Susan asked.

"Beautiful."

"Ah, not complaining about the sewer water anymore?" Sloan winked.

I shook my head. "Nope. Especially because Miko let me stand there as long as I wanted. And she found me a change of clothes."

He smiled. "Nice job, Julie. Your mind is improving after all."

I nodded. "Yes. And what needs to be done now? You know. We all know."

Miko clapped her hands.

"Hungry?" Sky inquired.

"I need to tell you guys something first," I replied.

Sloan's eyes narrowed. "Like?"

"Evan told me The Mighty Listener gave you all a chocolate," I continued. "And you had the option to either keep it, or give it to me. After eating three of those, I know the power they hold is unpredictable. I don't know why I am addicted to them, but Evan made it clear I shouldn't use them anymore."

Sloan burst into laughter.

"What's up with that?" he asked. "Evan told you the chocolates were dangerous?"

I nodded. "Yeah, they alter my perception and don't do anything to help me."

"Gosh, you saw what you did when fighting the big scary monster on the football field! How much proof do you need?"

I shook my head. "I can go on and face Kara without them."

"Is that something you believe?" Susan asked.

"I-I know Evan was mad at me because I ate a chocolate before fighting that horrible thing on the field. And I feel guilty because we didn't patch things up before he..." I choked.

Sloan put his hand on my shoulder.

"You ignited your beams without feeling any anger, girlfriend. And Evan is a poopy pants, and hypocritical at that, because he was the first to give you his chocolate while the two of you hung out at the Cave. So why should you believe anything he says?"

I sighed. "Right, right, yeah but..."

"No but. You know these chocolates help you. You need them," he said.

"I-I thought you represented the doubt in my mind. Why are you working so hard to convince me the chocolates are good for me?"

He chuckled. "I'm not doing anything you don't want to do. Simply pointing out the fact you're craving them."

I took a deep breath. The ugly fish told me I should believe in myself more and not give in to doubt. Plus I made the promise not to eat chocolates anymore. But Sloan was right. Deep down, I was still craving them.

"Did Evan keep his promise to protect you?" Sky inquired.

I stared at him in disbelief. "Evan protected me, he helped me, and..."

"And he also abandoned you when you didn't do as he said. He's the controlling type, you know. You're better off without him," Sky added.

I looked at Susan. "What do you think?" I asked her.

She shrugged. "You've experienced it firsthand. Each chocolate is meant to help, not destroy. They are nothing more than a pass to freedom, understanding and acceptance. Now, if you don't intend to eat them, feel free not to. We're not twisting your arm here. But don't you want to go outside and face Kara in the most awesome way possible? We all represent parts of your past you decided to shut down because you were in denial. Today, the denial stops."

"Right, and I choose to embrace the good, the bad and the ugly. I'm just unsure..."

Sloan came to me, grinning like a newlywed, and gave me a hug.

"You know you had fun turning on your beams, and you're dying to do it again," he said.

"Yes, but the ugly fish taught me how to turn them on without these magic chocolates."

"And, can you turn them on without them?"

"I tried, and it didn't work. But that doesn't mean I have to use chocolates to do it, right?"

He ignored my question and turned to the others.

"I've already given her my chocolate, but there are a few more to spare!" he said. "Julie, you've proven not only that you could change, but that change meant improvement, not regression. And for the big finale, what you need is a little kick. So, everyone, let's do this!"

Everyone cheered. I actually felt awkward about the whole thing, but didn't have it in me to say no. The ugly fish told me to trust my instincts more. Sloan, Susan, Miko and Sky wanted the best for me. Sloan was right, Evan had left me, and gosh only knew what he was doing in the company of Kara, Dan and Mike. If he really had my back, he would have returned to the Dome already. I didn't see how those chocolates could be so dangerous when they helped me be stronger. If only I could talk to Evan one last time...

"Julie, your journey to the Underworld has been perilous," Susan began. "Many times you could have given up and returned to your old ways. I must confess I didn't believe you could change, and thought Oceanside would remain this pit of darkness and pain forever. Evan reached out and helped you, but now he's gone. We all have war stories to share. I remember seeing you in school, so lost in your world, so oblivious to the rest of us. Just like you, I didn't belong to any clique. It was too hard to fit in. I decided to stand my ground by rebelling. I picked my looks deliberately to push people away. Some people followed my lead because they saw me as an example. I pretended to be strong. But behind closed doors, I ate myself to sleep and developed an eating disorder. And my anger at the world increased, the more miserable I felt inside. To me, love didn't even exist. It took three suicide attempts to realize how my own selfishness almost brought me to the grave. And how did I learn my lesson? By staring at the teary faces of dear family members and close friends who visited me at the hospital. They all looked so heart-broken. They didn't want to see me go. But I hated myself too much to recognize this love. I belonged to the dark-ness, and wanted to stay there forever."

Tears welled in my eyes as I listened to her. The way she described her pain hit so close to home.

She grabbed my hand.

"You should have this chocolate," she said. "May its strength burn through you and give you solace in the most desperate times."

She closed my fingers over the little dark ball and smiled. I smiled back, and hugged her tightly.

"Thank you."

Miko was next.

"Julie," she said with her thick accent, "many made fun of me for being different. And I cried, and cried, and cried. Hated everyone. But here"—she placed her hand over her heart— "was broken. And it took a long, long time to understand what to do to fix it." She handed me her chocolate. "The light is everywhere."

I nodded and took the candy from her hand. "Thank you, Miko."

She stepped away, and Sky came up.

"Hi, Julie. You didn't care much about us hipsters." He glanced at Sloan. "The twin brothers who were more comfortable on a skateboard than on their own two feet. We've had our share of challenges, though, like anyone else. Standing out wasn't fun, but we pulled through. You never liked us outcasts because you thought you were better than us. Look at you now. You belong here. This is your home. Mocking stares and gossip affected you as much as they affected us. You sheltered behind lies, and drove straight into a wall of denial, which you realize now was only a wall of smoke. The true Julie finally gets the chance to experience life in a better way. Here." He took my hand. "If you want to succeed, then you should have this chocolate."

I looked at the three dark balls in the palm of my hand and couldn't wait to gulp them all at once. The argument with Evan seemed so far away.

"Alright." My heart filled with hope. "I guess we're going to have a heck of a showdown!" And everyone cheered.

28

I always had this dream, as a little girl, that someday I'd take the world by storm. But it so happened that I turned everyone against me and, ironically, became my own worst enemy.

Kara wasn't the only friend I hurt. So many had bitten the dust after her. I found it difficult to trust people, and those I did trust I did everything in my power to manipulate and use, to accomplish a specific task on my self-centered agenda. These friendships never lasted more than a few months. Compromising and working out differences weren't part of my repertoire. Once someone disappointed me, I discarded them like used tissues. Until there was no one left to discard but myself.

The meal the memories prepared in anticipation of the upcoming battle against Kara was the best I had had so far. I helped Sky and Miko clear the table and wash the plates and utensils, knowing Evan would have enjoyed being there with us. I missed him.

"He's in our hearts," Miko said, while I wiped the table with a wet cloth and emptied the jug of clean water into a nearby drain.

I nodded slightly.

"Yeah, I know. It's fine. I'm not upset with him anymore. He chose to walk away."

She punched me in the shoulder.

"Hey, what was that one for?" I scowled.

"You cannot show weakness so close to final challenge. I understand you nervous, but we all depend on you to win this. So, chin up, smile."

I sighed. "I'm well aware of the warrior protocol around here. I thought my upcoming glowing artillery would be enough to breathe confidence into everyone."

"Inside match outside. If you feel strong here"—she pointed at my heart— "then your light will burn brighter than ever."

"Okay, okay, I get it. More glam and glitz. Let's put on a show that everyone will remember."

She laughed.

"Thank you for helping me today," I said.

"No problem."

Susan came up to me.

"Are you ready?"

I nodded. "Yes."

"I like your confidence," she replied.

"Well, I feel good now. I don't know about later."

"Just imagine you're balancing on a tightrope. As long as you keep improving yourself, you won't fall. Once you decide to give up, you'll drop and reach a new bottom."

I choked. "Nice analogy."

She laughed. "I'm serious."

"I am royally fried!" I chuckled, grabbing my head between my hands.

Miko punched me in the shoulder again.

"Ouch!"

"Remember to look like winner," she said.

"Right!"

"If it makes you feel any better, we're as nervous as you," Sky piped up.

"Thanks."

"Plus you got the chocolates!" he added.

"Yeah. You aren't the one risking a bad acid reflux." The knot in my stomach made its comeback and I cringed.

"Are you okay?" Susan asked.

I nodded. "Yeah. Can't wait to be done battling my own mind."

"I understand your nervousness. Kara's rather unpredictable," Sloan put in.

"Just follow your gut!" Sky said. "Take her where it hurts. Make her go bananas, and then break her."

"Right," I replied. "Where will she be next?"

"The beach," Sloan replied.

"How can you be so sure?"

"That's where the two of you spent most of your time. She loves riding the waves. It's pretty stormy out there. You're gonna have to use your swimming master skills."

"You can fly, become invisible," Sky added. "Throw jets of fire at her, drown her to the abyss…"

My stomach tightened. "Yeah, before I pee my pants again."

"Well, at least you'll be in the water," Sky said.

I glared at him.

"Just saying..." his voice trailed off.

The memories stayed silent for a few seconds.

I took a deep breath. "Okay, are you coming with me?" I looked at each memory, ignoring the knot cramping my stomach.

Sloan nodded and grabbed my hand.

"We should pray. Everyone, let's form a circle."

Once we all held hands, I closed my eyes.

"Help me to be kind and loving. Remove worry or remorseful reflections. Help me to find hope even in the most hopeless situations. I am not alone and, as I grow, I give away the control and become open to living without fear." We prayed in unison.

I pushed open the lid of the sewer entrance and peeked outside. More rays of light pierced the cloudy sky.

The upcoming showdown with Kara brought me closer to my return to the real world. This didn't make me jump up and down with excitement, mostly because I kept thinking that I'd wake up in a prison cell on a hard steel bench. Unless I was elsewhere, like the hospital. Or stuffed in someone's car trunk. Not exactly a spa treatment weekend.

What was up with this mental moroseness?

Susan squeezed my arm as we set foot on the street.

"Stop projecting," she said.

I nodded. "Right, right. I'll brush off whatever... There, all gone."

I forced a smile she didn't reciprocate.

"Let's get moving," she ordered.

My heart was beating at one hundred miles per hour. I was resolved to show Kara this new side of myself. If I received a slap in the face, I'd do my best not to get angry. Obviously, I hoped she'd act more friendly—but knew she still bore a lot of hatred towards me. To contain my anxiety, I distracted myself by scanning every street and alleyway.

Oceanside kept improving. Now that the explosions had stopped and the rain of ash had disappeared, I could look at my city with a fresh pair of eyes. Buildings didn't look as beat up. Grass grew between the cracks of the sidewalk, and in the front yards of houses.

As I peeked through the pickets of a fence surrounding a private yard, Sky gripped my arm.

"Dude, watch this," he said.

He kicked an empty can off the sidewalk right into a garbage bin that lay sideways on the pavement.

"Score!"

"Great job," I said, ignoring him. The ocean profiled itself in the distance. "Here we go."

I patted the outside of my pants pocket where I kept the chocolates.

"I've changed my mind. Maybe I should go there on my own."

"What are you talking about?" Sloan fired.

"I'll be okay. You said so yourself. The sooner this ordeal ends, the quicker I get to deal with my other problems."

"You need us with you," Susan interjected.

"What do I risk if I confront her myself?"

"You risk losing everything you worked hard for," she answered.

"Yeah well... If I eat all the chocolates, I'll be powerful enough."

I stared at the line on the horizon where water met sky and smiled.

"I can do this," I said. "This moment is supposed to be my grand finale. I want to wake up and deal with my life like an adult."

"So you don't want our help." Susan's glow burned stronger.

I shook my head. "I need to fight her alone."

"She won't be alone, you know that, right? Let us at least deal with her watchdogs," Sky said.

"No. You've supported me long enough."

Miko came up to me. "Follow your heart."

I hugged her. "Thanks."

I looked at each one in turn.

"It's time for me to say goodbye."

Sloan threw himself at me and squeezed me tight.

"Good luck, then, if that's what you've decided." I lost my breath for a second.

"Thank you," I replied, once he broke his embrace.

Susan and Sky kept their distance.

"I don't think this is the right choice for you," Susan said.

I put my hand on her shoulder.

"I respect your opinion."

"And I respect your decision. We will stand nearby in case things go south," she added.

"I'm sorry I was a jerk to you in school and never got to be your friend. But I'll make sure to come visit you once I'm back on the other side."

She smiled.

"I was not someone lovable in high school. You would never have made friends with me. Now was our chance to finally cross that bridge. Everything happens for a reason. The Mighty Listener chose you because she believed in you and wanted to offer you a second chance. Don't waste it. Don't take anything for granted. I'll be in your thoughts and you'll be in mine. Good luck to you, Julie."

We hugged.

"Don't forget to pray," she added. "And never lose hope..."

"Even in the most hopeless situation," I finished her sentence.

"Sky, your cooking skills are unsurpassed," I said.

He laughed. "Yeah, that and other stuff. Be careful out there. You've come a long way. I'd be sad to see you fail so close to the exit."

I sighed. "Yeah, I'd be sad too."

"Hey, how about we go skateboarding later, huh?"

I smiled. "I'd love that."

We hugged. "I'll teach you tricks," he added.

"I can't wait."

We broke our embrace and I began walking away.

"I'll see you in the real world!" I shouted, and turned around to wave at them.

The memories waved back.

29

I planted my feet in the ashy sand and stared at the murky water before me. The beach looked nothing like the place of my childhood. No sun shining brightly in the sky. No children laughing and jumping in the waves. No dogs running after a ball.

"Just have faith," I mumbled to myself. "Your heart holds the truth within. Soon it will all be over."

The cold breeze blew in my face as I started walking parallel to the edge of the water.

"Just have faith," I repeated to calm my nerves. "There's nothing to be afraid of. Worse comes to worst, you have your chocolates."

I took a deep breath to release the tension inside my chest, and shook my legs and arms to relax my muscles.

"Here, all better, see? Nothing to worry about."

Time stretched as I waited for Kara to show up. Tired of standing, I lay on the sand and stared at the gray sky above.

The vibration of the ground beneath me made me sit up, and my eyes caught the familiar purple glow.

"Here we are," Kara said, her fingers playing with the little crucifix dangling from the chain around her neck. "Face to face. Alone."

I stood and stared at the ocean.

"Whatever your intentions are, I won't fight you."

She laughed. "So why are you here? Are you offering me a truce? You think you can patch things up with a mere 'I'm sorry'?"

I nodded. "That's exactly what I intend to do."

"Bullcrap." She spat on the ground. "An apology won't fix the damage you've done."

"I know I wasn't a good friend to you and did things I deeply regret. Why did you protect me? You don't hate me as much as you say you do."

She didn't move. Staring at me with her angry, purple eyes, she was still playing with the crucifix.

"Where are Dan and Mike?" I asked.

"The ones you used to make me your victim? They're waiting, ready to teach you the lesson you deserve."

"Good, then call them up. Why should I only speak to you?"

"Oh, really. That's how you intend to play it?" she asked in an angry tone.

"Don't you?"

She smiled. "Fine, let's go."

We started walking.

"So tell me, Julie, why don't you burn me with your light and get it over with?" Kara asked.

"Because there's a better way to defeat you," I answered.

"Don't you think I'm your darkness?"

I shook my head. "No, you're only a memory. I made you who you are. And as painful as it is to see how much hatred you have for me, I accept it."

She scoffed. "How did you become so stinky wise?"

I smiled and glanced at her. "I learned from my mistakes."

Her eyes glowed brighter. "You won't win, you know that, right?"

"I'm not here to win anything," I said. "I'm only here to make things right again."

"Is that so? The savior of Oceanside!" she exclaimed. She waved a finger at me. "Aren't you craving to get mad again? Crush people's feelings and break things, curse until you're out of breath? You love your anger so much, you must miss it."

"I'm teaching myself to deal with life in a different way," I replied.

She laughed. "So full of crap. I'm not impressed."

"You want to plant a seed of doubt inside my mind, but it won't work."

"Well, smartass, it's not like you didn't try before. And where did your newly found escape mechanisms take you? Nowhere!"

"I feel different," I said.

"Oh really! Is that why you keep these chocolates in your pocket? You always loved to listen to yourself talk, but your actions always proved otherwise. Let's count the seconds before your next relapse!"

I shook my head. "The memories only gave them to me in case I wanted them."

"Stop your nonsense, will you? You love eating those little magic, dark balls. And guess what? If you're kind enough, I might give you mine."

"I don't want it."

She laughed. "Oh, you say that now. Just wait. You'll change your mind in a heartbeat."

Dan and Mike stood not far from us, each bearing an all-tooth smile and looking tough, visibly expecting me.

Kara walked toward them while I kept my distance. Dan greeted her with a passionate French kiss that made me throw up a little in my mouth, and Mike stared at me. Pleasant few seconds.

I quieted my stubborn agitation by patting the inside of my pants pocket. Playing with the chocolates helped me keep my peace of mind. Kara's tricks to ignite my fuse wouldn't work if I remained serene.

The two lovebirds finally broke their embrace.

"Where should we begin?" Kara looked at me and grinned.

I shrugged. "Wherever you want. Like I said, I didn't come here to fight you."

She took a step toward me. "Oh, you say that now..."

She saw my hand move in my pocket.

"I sense hesitation, girlfriend."

I scoffed. "What, me?" I shook my head. "Nonsense."

"I know you want them."

"So what?"

"When would be a good time to eat your precious chocolates? How about now?" She laughed.

I clutched my fingers around the three little balls and exhaled deeply.

"Come on, nerd," Dan said. "Why don't you show us how strong you are?"

"Now, or we begin without you," Mike continued.

"Give us a nice spectacle," Dan added.

I needed a kick in order to turn on my beams. Without the chocolates my chances were slim, because no matter how hard I tried, I didn't feel much love toward Kara and her pals.

Evan would be mad at me for taking the easy way out. Except that he had deserted me when I needed him the most.

I clenched my teeth. "I didn't come here to fight."

"Are you for real?" Kara asked.

"Yes, yes I am."

Without hesitation, she came at me and pinned me to the ground.

"How do you feel now, tough cookie?"

She pressed my head deeper and I swallowed sand.

"Feeling good, yet?"

I started choking.

"Too easy!" Dan piped up. "Come on, we're giving you a chance to redeem yourself."

"Take it." Kara released her hold.

Pressure settled on my bladder. If I didn't act quickly I'd pee myself again. No way.

My hand went from my pocket directly into my mouth, and I swallowed the three dark balls with one gulp. Adrenaline immediately kicked me in the stomach and coursed throughout my body.

Kara, Dan and Mike laughed in unison. The sky turned pink and orange, and sunlight pierced the clouds, as the ocean shone silver and gold. All prior discomfort abandoned me, and heat flared in my eyeballs. My beams were ready to be fired.

I remained still while Kara and Dan held hands.

"Julie says she's sorry for what she did to me, and to us all," Kara said in a derisive tone. "And she came alone, thinking she could beat us all with her stupid apologies."

"Do you mean she has become a better person?" Dan snickered. "Unbelievable."

"Yeah, she's accepted her anger," Kara added. "I wonder what she feels like now."

"What, you won't use us to cover for your lies anymore, nerd?" Michael asked.

I looked at all of them, ready to blow them to pieces.

Don't forget to pray... Susan's words echoed in the back of my mind. *Find hope even in the most hopeless situation.*

Sadly, there was no hope in my heart. Only rage.

"Look at you, playing tough!" Dan shouted. "But you made us who we are! How will you change when you're so in love with your anger?"

Overhead a dark cloud bloomed in the sky. The air temperature dropped and I shivered.

A loud explosion popped a few feet away, and sand rained over us. I covered my eyes and ducked.

"Your mind is made of darkness, Julie, and you won't ever change that. Stop lying!" Kara said. "Oceanside isn't getting better. You fooled yourself. The hatred you carry inside your heart is way too strong."

"We'll prove to you you're still the same person," Dan continued. "You cannot grow healthy crops on a rotten soil."

The heat within me burned stronger, ready to be released.

"You won't win," Kara added. "No matter what you think."

"What do you have to say about that, nerd?" Dan asked.

I smiled. "I'm ready."

I spread my arms wide, despite another explosion blasting next to us.

"Listen to her!" Kara shouted. "She's a liar and a criminal. She should pay for what she did to me!"

"She should pay for what she did to us all!" Dan added.

"That's right, coward!" Mike cheered.

The black cloud looming above us had grown huge, covering the immensity of the sky and descending upon the ocean, wrapping us in absolute darkness.

"This is the end for you!"

Raising her fist, Kara let out a chilling scream and, along with her crew members, ran toward me, moving like a powerful wave ready to topple me off my board and smash me into the abyss.

The heat inside my core flared up to a dangerous high, and I acted upon it. But when I attempted to release my beams, the dark cloud engulfed every inch of me like a deadly virus, and the fire died instantly.

Because I couldn't cast my light, Kara, Dan and Mike proceeded to crush me. When my head hit the ground again and I swallowed more sand, I lost my breath, and my sense of where I was. The angry memories bashed me with their fists, burned with me their glow, and threw me left and right until I tumbled like a washcloth in a dryer. I couldn't regain control and fight back.

My heart barely struck a beat inside my aching chest.

The memories dragged me face down, and my skin peeled off. Dan and Mike tied me to a wooden beam lying on the beach and moved me upward so I could face the stormy ocean.

My muscles twitched and shook. My jaw hurt. I forced my swollen eyelids open to look at Kara, who was standing before me. As I drew a shallow breath, she slapped me.

"YOU DESERVE TO SUFFER FOR ETERNITY!" she screamed.

I bit my lower lip and blood coated my tongue.

She looked so proud of herself. The glowing in her eyes burned strong.

What had I done wrong?

"You must learn humility," Evan's voice popped up. "Your ego is your worst enemy. You never stopped running, Julie."

I cringed. Lifting my head, I caught the outline of his face in a blur. Kara and the others stood right next to him, grinning with satisfaction.

"Evan? What are you doing here? I-I thought you were gone," I slurred.

The laughter that erupted from him made my ears ring.

"Gone? I will always be by your side. Acceptance, remember?"

"You showed me how to be a better person," I replied in between slow breaths.

"And at the most crucial moment of your recovery, you decided to go back to your old habits."

"I couldn't turn on my beams without the chocolates." I sobbed.

"Yes you could. You were simply too afraid to do so."

Tears burned my eyes.

"You're still mad at me because of them. I-I knew it."

He seized my chin and stared straight into my eyes.

"Your mental obsession will never leave you alone until you quit completely."

My heart broke a bit more as he said that.

"I want to quit! I couldn't help myself."

"What will The Mighty Listener think of you, huh?" Evan fired back.

"I-I am sorry," I choked. "I-I need help."

I cried some more, despite the pain in my ribcage with every breath I took.

"Can I ever be saved?"

Evan grabbed my face between his hands.

"The question is: do you want to save yourself?" he asked.

30

When I woke up, every part of my body aching like hell, the moldy underground stench immediately attacked my nose, and the humidity in the air forced a painful sneeze before I had time to collect my thoughts.

If there were any remaining thoughts to collect.

My life had taken a turn I hadn't imagined in my wildest nightmares.

Susan's soft glow illuminated the little room, where I had been transported while unconscious. Wrapped in rudimentary bandages from head to toe, she gave me water and food that I reluctantly accepted.

"You said you had my back," I said to her as she tended to my wounds.

"We came to your rescue as soon as we could. Kara acted fast, and she showed no compassion," Susan replied.

When she touched the side of my face, I winced.

"Your nose is broken, and the skin of your face is badly hurt. Your body is covered in bruises, but no other bones were broken. You will need time to recover."

"I can't believe what happened."

She forced a smile. "We should have come with you."

"Would it have made a difference?"

She sighed and looked down. "I don't know."

"How's the town? Has everything reverted back to its original state?" I asked.

She nodded.

Tears stung my eyes.

"All this work for nothing," I said.

"It wasn't for nothing, Julie."

"Really?" I cringed. "Then tell me, where did I fail?"

"The anger was still powerful. Kara is your Achilles heel."

"Yeah, no shizzle." I grunted. "I don't know what to do now."

"You need to rest and heal. Miko and I will check on you often." She stood. "I have to ration the clean water, given our supply is very limited."

"Right, because hope is dead," I replied in a flat tone.

"You'll get back on your feet soon. Don't give up now."

"How do you want me to feel love for her?"

She looked at me and squeezed my fingers gently.

"Because the darkness can't win."

My sneer was cut short by the acute pain in my jaw. "Yeah, I gotta embrace the light."

"Exactly." She stepped away. "You should get some sleep. I'll see you soon."

Lying in the dark for hours, I cried relentlessly and, when tears failed, I prayed to die. But death never came.

On top of the unbearable physical pain, the past haunted every second I spent awake, while my inner voice cried for help. Overwhelmed with feelings of loneliness and helplessness, I was inconsolable.

Miko and Susan did their best to cheer me up. Sky cooked more rats than I could eat, and even popped by the room to crack a few jokes. I laughed a little in their presence, but once they left I reverted to my depressive state.

My inner voice never stopped in the background. The same words played on a loop inside my head. I refused to listen until it became impossible to ignore them.

A few days passed, and I could leave the bed and take short walks through the tunnels in the company of Miko. The message of love and acceptance became louder and louder as my physical condition improved.

Julie, that anger of yours will always win until you let go completely and accept yourself for who you are.

"I thought I did that when I faced Kara on the field..."

Did you let the light shine?

"Yes, yes, I did."

There was still too much resentment within your heart.

"I forgave her."

Did you forgive yourself?

"N-No."

Well, how do you expect to move on if you're unable to do that?

"I-I tried."

Forget me not, wherever you go, memories are like daggers, and your heart holds the truth within.

"Dr. Ronstein found that note in my journal. The ugly fish reminded me of these words too."

Don't you realize you never needed magic chocolates to feel powerful?

"I was looking for an escape, an easy way out."

Your anger only shows you're afraid, and you can stop the pain now. Turn it over. Give up the last remnant of pride you're clinging onto like dear life. Let go.

"I can't die here."

Death isn't the answer.

"Start anew."

Find peace by loving yourself first, Julie.

"Will it be that simple?" I asked.

Yes, it will be.

"Okay."

I had to stop the spider from eating me alive, and get out of the web I was imprisoned in.

Days turned into weeks before I felt strong enough to walk on my own. Bruises vanished and my nose healed. Miko handed me a broken mirror so I could look at my face. The multiple scars on my cheeks and forehead were the only reminders of my last encounter with Kara.

"You be pretty again," Miko said.

Her words of encouragement didn't prevent me from scowling at my reflection.

"Yeah." I put the mirror away. "Let's go to the Dome. I'd like to talk to everyone."

❧

My jaw dropped when I saw Evan.

He was chatting with Sloan and didn't notice me until I tapped him on the shoulder.

"Julie!" he said with a wide smile.

"What are you doing here?" My hands balled into tight fists as I stared at him.

Sloan stepped in between us.

"Hey, he didn't come here to fight you." He grabbed my hands. "Anger isn't the solution."

I pushed Sloan away.

"Why didn't you protect me from her?" I pointed a finger at Evan.

"There was nothing I could do. Don't you understand?"

"Really? So you let Kara and her friends beat me up?" I sobbed. "I thought you were gone!"

"Julie..." Evan took a step toward me, but I moved further away from him.

"No!" I shouted. "You left me!"

Susan walked up to me.

"Here, calm down," she said.

"How do you want me to calm down?" I buried my face in the sleeve of my sweatshirt.

"Don't cry." Miko wrapped her arms around my shoulders.

"You can't blame me for what happened," Evan said. "You thought you were strong enough to defeat her."

I wiped my tears and looked at him. "Yes. I know what to do."

"What?" he asked.

"I know what to do," I repeated.

He chuckled. "Okay. So what are you going to do?"

"I'm going to save myself, just like you told me."

He nodded. "Good. And?"

My heart slammed against the bones of my ribcage, dying to escape. I looked at each memory and took a deep breath.

"I know my mind is turning against me, because my mental obsession is too powerful. And these chocolates are the root of my problems."

"One part of them, yeah," Evan replied. "But there's also this ego of yours, wanting to control everything, especially your recovery. You find shortcuts, thinking you don't have to work on yourself first. What did I tell you? Acceptance is the key."

"I never needed them. But you gave me yours, and everything spiraled out of control."

He pointed his finger at me. "What you've got to understand is that once you got a taste for them, you became addicted. You thought these chocolates would give you your freedom back. And they didn't. What power do I have over your mind? I give you suggestions. Whether you choose to follow them is your own decision."

"I made you a friend, kicked you out, and then brought you back as a villain," I said.

"Yes, because you love to self-sabotage. When everything is going great, you can't leave it alone. You must break it."

I grunted. "The Mighty Listener brought me here..."

"You took her chocolate voluntarily, like you did with mine and everyone else's. No one held you at gunpoint and forced you to ingest them. Do you realize this?" he asked.

"So what? I'm doomed to fail?"

"Listen to yourself playing victim again! I taught you how to better yourself by letting go of the fear that was crippling your life. But you were so stuck in your old ways that the darkness consumed you completely until you couldn't take it anymore. And here you are, asking the same question I've answered a million times already. When are you going to stop torturing yourself?"

"I want to stop! I want to feel better now!" I shouted.

He shook his head. "Listen to yourself again. You want instant gratification with a magic chocolate that will heal all your wounds and make you feel like Superman."

"No, no, I—"

"Stop talking," he cut me off. "Listen. You have the answer, Julie. You had it all along."

"Yes, I do. I know I do. I just—"

"Stop making excuses," he continued. "This process is something bigger than you. Your ego has affected people's lives. You chose to go one direction because you wanted to satisfy your selfish needs. I am nothing but a voice in your mind. What you see, feel, and think are all you. Take responsibility, Julie."

"I'm taking responsibility!"

"Okay, then do what needs to be done, and you'll be out of here in no time," he said.

"Really?"

He rolled his eyes. "Seriously, Julie, quit debating your own thoughts and act."

"Okay, I'm going to quit using chocolates as a cop-out."

He smiled. "Okay."

I stared at him. "So that's it?"

He sighed. "Let's hope everything I've told you will have an effect on you at some point," he said. "I wish you the best."

"No, I get it." I swallowed back tears. "I'm a drug addict."

The memories looked at me in silence.

"I'm a drug addict," I repeated with a broken voice. "And the last time I said I was addicted was during my first and only session with Mom's shrink. But I didn't believe those words then. Now I do."

"Oh, honey." Susan pulled me toward her.

"This is the truth I was hiding from," I mumbled. "And no matter what any of you said, I never stopped chasing the next high. I hid behind this unbreakable ego-shield, but deep down knew how weak I was. So here. I'm not hiding anymore."

Evan wrapped his arms around me.

"I'm proud of you," he whispered in my ear.

"Even gone, you were still there with me," I replied. "I'm sorry for hating you. I'm my own problem... and you are my solution."

He pressed me against him, and the rest of the memories joined in for a group hug. As we shared this embrace, the pressure constricting my chest lifted, and peace finally settled in my heart.

☾

The time had come to leave the underground tunnels, and the memories walked by my side through the streets of Oceanside. The town had reverted back to its original condition, and explosions blasted full force again, startling me whenever they popped in the distance. The rain of ash showered over us, covering our hair, skin and clothes with a thick, black layer, and my lungs ached when I inhaled the toxic air. But I didn't ask Evan to use his glowing eyes to ease my discomfort.

Susan smiled when I looked at her.

"How are you feeling?" she asked.

"Better. Ready to dispose of this heavy baggage I've been carrying around for years."

She laughed. "Good."

I coughed. "Gosh, can't wait to see Oceanside pretty and clean."

Sky stopped in front of a house.

"Guys, will you wait for me?"

"What are you doing?" I asked.

"You need something. I won't be long," he answered, and ran to the front door.

He disappeared inside, and I cast a questioning stare at his brother.

"What's he looking for?"

Sloan shrugged. "Oh, probably a gismo to add to his collection."

"A gismo?"

"Yeah, he loves his PEZ dispensers," he said.

"What?"

"Eh, don't look at me like I have two heads. I don't know what he's looking for in there. Could be anything."

I chuckled. "Okay."

Minutes passed before Sky reappeared, carrying under his arm something much bigger than a PEZ dispenser.

I gasped. "A surfboard?"

Sky smiled. "Yeah, so you can enjoy yourself!"

He handed me the board.

"I haven't surfed in such a long time," I said.

"It's like riding a bike." He winked.

"Great thinking, pal, except the ocean is unsurfable at this time," Sloan piped up.

"The board can also be used for other purposes," Sky replied.

"Like?" Sloan asked.

"Great to carry stuff."

Sloan scoffed. "You crazy."

"Kara's dead body would fit nicely!"

"That's alright," I said. "It's the thought that counts. Thank you."

"No worries," Sky replied.

"Yeah, carrying that surfboard around is the best way to start fresh," Sloan added.

Sky glared at his brother.

"Guys, let's not argue over this," Susan intervened. "Are you ready to talk to Kara?"

"Yes, I am."

"Good." She looked at the others. "To the beach!"

Sky raised his hand.

"We're keeping the board, right?"

"Yes," Evan replied on my behalf.

He squeezed my hand and smiled at me.

"So close to the goal again," he said. "Don't quit before the miracle happens this time."

"I won't."

I smiled back and we resumed walking.

31

As we set foot on the ashy sand, my heart took a leap once more inside my chest.

"This is it, huh?"

"You're very brave, Julie," Susan said.

"Yeah, I don't feel so brave right now, but let's wait until Kara shows up."

Sky waved the board. "Hey, you need to relax, pal. How about some mindless fun?"

Sloan huffed. "At it again?"

Sky placed the board in front of him and laughed. "Try me!"

Sloan grunted and grabbed the board.

"Stop!" Miko fired.

With a swift motion, she snatched the board away from Sky and planted it in the ground.

The twins stared at her like she was the one who had grown two heads.

"How rude," Sky mumbled. "We were just playing!"

Sloan sighed and turned his back on his brother. "Now is definitely not the time."

"Fine!" Sky stomped his feet like a two-year-old.

"Enough you two!" I said. "What's up with all the bickering? Are we back in kindergarten?"

"Well, kindergarten can be fun sometimes."

I jumped. Kara surprised me every time.

"And you brought your friends. How thoughtful," she added. She was still manically rubbing her beloved crucifix pendant between her fingers, as if it gave her strength.

"Right," I replied. My neck felt awfully stiff. I moved my head left and right to loosen the joints, and Evan placed his hand over my arm to calm me down.

"I see everyone's happy to see me again. Oh, and what is this beauty?" She pointed at the board. "So nice of you to bring me a gift."

Sky clenched his teeth and balled his hands into fists. "This is not yours!"

Sloan punched him in the shoulder. "Idiot!"

Sky glared at his brother while rubbing the spot on his shoulder.

"You're an idiot," he mouthed back.

Kara laughed.

"You guys are pathetic." She turned to me. "Are they supposed to protect you or slow you down?"

Her purple eyes glowed brighter, and pressure settled on my bladder.

"We're here to put an end to this feud once and for all," Evan piped up.

She looked at him and laughed louder. "Oh yes, especially you." She took a step toward him. "Why, didn't you have fun with us? Oh, but I understand. This crowd of losers makes you feel so good about yourself, am I wrong? Accept your true nature, Julie,"—she locked eyes with me— "because you're not ready to change."

"We're done talking," Susan interjected. "And Evan is one of the good guys."

Kara recoiled and raised her hands in the air. "Oh, I'm so scared. Boooooooooohoooooo." She paused. "Like I said. I'm dealing with a bunch of losers. And that includes you." She pointed a finger at me.

"Where are your friends? The non-loser kind?" I asked.

She smiled. "They're right here."

Mike and Dan appeared in the distance.

"So..." she continued. "Are you excited?"

I stared at the stormy water behind her and her watchdogs.

"Excited about what?" I asked.

"Well," she chuckled, "you came here to do something, right?"

I nodded. "Right. I came here to see you."

She placed a hand over her heart. "Touching. No, I thought we could have fun. Let me rephrase that. I thought we could have some *real* fun."

"W-What fun?"

The purple glow in her eyes intensified. "You know what we loved to do when we were still friends? We spent lots of time there." She pointed at the water. "So how about we try that, huh?"

I glanced at Sky whose idea it was to bring the surfboard. But as the wind increased in strength, and waves reached dangerous heights, it felt more like embarking on a suicide mission.

"Well," I said, "I didn't prepare myself."

She smirked. "Really. So what's the board for? What, are you scared?"

I shook my head. "No. No fear. Just being cautious."

"Why bother?" She laughed. "Oh, I know you're scared, Julie, admit it."

I held up my hands in surrender. "Yeah, being scared is part of being human."

She scoffed. "Do you realize you've been afraid all your life?"

I lowered my hands. "And I'm working on getting rid of the fear. It's not a piece of cake, but I'm trying."

"Trying is a start, I guess. At least you've accepted you're not perfect."

"Exactly, I like your approach," I replied.

"Oh stop it!" she said. "You came because you can't move on without making peace with me."

I nodded. "It's a fact that I need to apologize to you."

"You know what I thought of your apologies last time we met. Why do you believe it's going to be any different between us now?"

"Because," I answered, "I'm aware of a few things I missed along the way."

Her eyes narrowed. "Like what?"

"Why are we still talking?" Susan asked.

"Ha, you're funny!" Kara said. "You weren't so brave in high school, Goth queen." She put two fingers in her mouth and made retching and vomiting sounds. "Your secret wasn't a secret by the way."

Susan's jaws clenched and I stepped forward. "Alright. Enough."

Kara took a step toward me. "Tell me, Julie Jones, why should I forgive you?"

"Here's the thing. You don't have to do anything."

Her jaw dropped. "Who will, then?"

I pointed a finger at myself. "I will."

"Really?" She cocked her head to the side. "Without expecting anything of me?"

I shook my head. "No. All I know is that I must let go. So... I'm letting go. I can't live in fear forever."

A salty gust of wind blew in my face and I sneezed.

"Bless you," Kara said. "Although, you were never religious."

"Right," I replied. "Well, you were."

"Uh huh, that's right."

"Is that why I remember you in this gown?"

She shook me by the arm. "Come on, grumpy face, why ask so many questions? If it was that easy to let go, wouldn't we be friends again?"

"Seriously?" I pulled away from her reach. "Is my mind tricking me again?"

She stared at me and smiled. "Can't bear to trust yourself a little bit, huh?"

"It's complicated."

"Don't you think it's a problem?"

"What?"

She brushed that aside. "Never mind. I guess you'll remain stuck here for a while." She grabbed my arm again. "Unless... Come on, let's play!"

"No!" Evan placed himself between her and me.

"Fine," she pouted. "Then let's fight. That's what you want, isn't it? You're all a bunch of hypocrites, pretending to be sorry when your true colors scream carnage!"

"Wait," I said. "I'm not that person anymore."

"Then prove it!" she replied.

Evan looked at me and shook his head. "I know what you're going to say, and I don't think it's a good idea."

"She seems willing to compromise." From the corner of my eye I caught Kara smiling. "And you'll take care of her buddies, right?"

"What he forgot to mention is that you're also responsible for taking care of them," Kara interjected. "That means you'll deal with me and them alone."

"I'm fine with that."

Evan grabbed me by the shoulders and pulled me away.

"You know she wants to drag you deeper into the darkness," he said.

I stared into his bright green eyes.

"No, I won't let her."

"Then why face her on your own when you have us? You know she's lying when she says you gotta take care of them alone."

"You've seen how she is," I replied.

"Yes, and have you?"

"I need to trust myself."

He sighed. "Don't push us out again."

"I won't repeat the same mistakes."

"You're bound to repeat them if you don't ask for help."

"Then that's what I'll do. You defended me against her so many times, and I thank you."

He frowned. "Don't stray, please."

I pinched his cheek. "Don't be grumpy."

"I'm not."

"Then don't be afraid."

He scoffed. "I'm not afraid. Just careful."

I smiled. "With the board Sky gave me, I might stand a chance against these waves if I don't drown first."

He smiled. "Come here." He pulled me in for a hug. "You can do this," he said.

"I know," I replied. "Just gotta remember how to ride a board."

"Are you two done?" Kara shouted.

I chuckled. "Yes!"

"Gosh, she's like a kid," I whispered to Evan, and walked toward Miko.

"I'm going to borrow this bad boy," I said, and grabbed the board from her.

"Sure?" she asked.

I nodded, and she let go.

"Embrace light."

"Thanks," I replied. "I could correct you and say 'embrace the storm,' but heck, no time for a debate."

I glanced at Susan, Sky and Sloan, and gave them the thumbs up. They didn't reciprocate, worrisome expressions on their faces, like I was about to walk into my grave.

The wind blew harder as I approached Kara, the board tucked under my arm.

"Ready?"

"Under different circumstances, I'd probably have chosen a different game plan; but yes, I'm ready," I said.

While the distance stretched between the good memories and me, a chill ran down my spine. I hadn't surfed in a really long time. Granted it was like riding a bike, but nervousness clenched my chest, preventing me from drawing proper breaths.

When I stood only a foot away from the water, I stopped cold and shook my head.

"You know what, this was a terrible idea," I said. "How about we do something else? Hungry for a milkshake or a double-double? Sky is a killer cook."

Kara looked at me. "No cold feet, girlfriend." She waved at Dan and Mike who ran to us.

I held the surfboard like a shield as they tried to push me forward.

"No, no, no, no, no," I protested. "Don't touch me!"

I dodged Mike's grip and struck Dan in the groin with one end of the board. But my struggle was in vain, as Mike managed to grab me by the waist and hold the board and me above ground like a bag of dirty laundry.

Kara looked amused by my kicking and screaming. Evan, Susan, Miko, Sky and Sloan came to my rescue, but Kara ignited her beams immediately and fired a few warning shots that forced them back.

"Let's not start another bloodbath!" she shouted at them. "This is the deal. Julie comes with me, and you all wait here."

"If you hurt her again..." Evan shouted back.

She nodded. "Yes, yes. Like you'll help!"

Evan's eyes ignited but he didn't release his beams. Nor did the other memories.

"I'll be fine, guys!" I shouted. "Just peachy!"

"Let's go, Julie. We've wasted enough time already. Your friends won't bother us anymore."

She shook her head at Mike. "Put her down. She'll go in."

I grunted as Mike put me back on the ground. "This wasn't necessary."

"And hitting me in the groin wasn't necessary either, nerd," Dan said.

"I was defending myself." Mike gave me the evil, purple-glowing eye.

"Let's all take a deep breath and calm down," Kara added. "You're scared. I get that. Maybe you want a little kick before we start playing?"

She opened her palm.

"No!" I recoiled. "I can't have a chocolate again!"

She shrugged and put the chocolate away. "Good, then let's go!"

She entered the stormy water like she was going in for a quick swim.

"Wait," I said. "What are we going to do exactly?"

She exploded in laughter as the waves reached the top of her thighs after walking two feet. "Use your imagination, Julie! Surf, swim, fly, drill a hole at the bottom of the ocean... Do whatever you feel like doing. Let's just have some girly fun!"

Crapola in an empty peanut butter jar. How would I accomplish any of those things without a chocolate?

Dan and Mike made a move toward me and I waved them off.

"I don't need babysitting."

I followed Kara and shuddered as the cold water brushed against my legs. Cringing, I moved further in, the waves now slamming against my torso. The ocean was roaring, waves coming at me like a million fists ready to bury me in the sand with one powerful blow.

My heart beat so fast it was about to rip my chest apart. Why did I think coming here would offer me any redemption?

I laid the board on the water and jumped on top. Waves smacked me in the face while I paddled further from the shore.

No way I'd be able to stand and keep my balance.

"Come on, Julie, show me your skills!" Kara's head popped in and out of the water as she slapped the board with one hand. "You came here to have fun, remember?"

"Right," I said, before closing my eyes and mouth when water washed over me. "Your definition of fun needs some serious revisions."

"Just do it already!"

"Oh shizzle."

I held onto the board and moved into a kneeling position. As water hit me relentlessly, I focused my attention on the next big wave coming my way. The countdown started in my head. Five... four... three... two... I shifted into the upward position and bent my knees as the mountain of liquid rushed in my direction. Spreading my arms to either side, I exhaled and the bumpy ride began.

Pure adrenaline coursed through my body and a thrill of excitement made its acclaimed return for a few precious seconds. I became one with the board and the ocean. I forgot all about my fears, and embraced the freedom I had longed to feel for all these years.

When the ride ended and I landed in the water, all I wanted was to jump on the board again and surf until the end of time.

"Woah! Did you see that?" I shouted.

But the current pushed the board back to the shore, and I had to swim fast to reach it. I looked around for Kara. She was nowhere to be seen.

As my fingers made contact with the board, I felt a pinch on my ankle.

"What the..."

Then a strong pull from below dragged me under the surface.

Water entered my nostrils and my mouth. The roar of the ocean decreased and I sank deeper into the abyss. I battled the current and the invisible force holding my ankle and tried to swim upward, but I wasn't strong enough.

Water filled my airways, numbing my senses, and I swallowed more salty liquid. My chest constricted and my lungs burned as I drifted further down.

With no air left, I prayed for the underwater breathing process to kick in. My body twitched and ached, but I maintained my effort.

Air bubbles escaped from my mouth and nose. I shook and convulsed, fighting to gain control, while my body remained unresponsive to my multiple attempts at survival. When the last bit of resistance dwindled inside me like a dying flame on a melted candle, the hold on my ankle released, and I landed like a rock at the bottom of the ocean.

32

I lay on the ground ready to part ways with my consciousness, but death didn't come. Instead, a ball of heat built inside my core. I opened and closed my eyes a few times, as a series of fiery sparks lit my limbs like the filament inside a bulb, and cast a bright orange glow against the muddy ocean bottom. The stronger my glow became, the more I burned within, feeling my insides melt.

"You are light," The Mighty Listener's voice echoed in my head. "Fight the darkness at last."

I wasn't sure how I'd be able to fight, given my body was paralyzed from head to toe.

"I've been watching you," she continued. "It's okay. Soon it will all be over. You only need time to adjust. Your light burns so bright, and yet you're still letting the darkness control you. How can this be?"

I closed my eyes and groaned as the heat increased.

"Here, here. Relax," The Mighty Listener said.

"What's happening to me?" I whispered.

"The light is fighting the darkness inside your mind. As I said, soon it will all be over."

My body had become an oven. How much longer could I endure this torture?

"I know you've been fighting with all the strength you were given. This is your chance to finally make peace. This is your chance to finally accept your true nature. You were born a fighter, Julie."

"I don't know," I slurred.

"If you truly want out, you will get out," she said. "Use your light."

"Kara likes to torture me. That's exactly what she did today, didn't she?"

"No, you like to torture yourself. This is all your doing. But your heart holds the truth within, doesn't it? Let me help you."

I opened my eyes for a second, and the old woman stood above me, surrounded by a halo of white light. She held something in her hand, something that cast a glow bright enough to blind me.

"Believe in yourself, Julie. Find your way out. Your heart holds the truth within," she repeated.

I screamed when she plunged her hand inside my chest, and the heat inside my body burst like a nuclear bomb. The light continued to spread, and the ground trembled as if an earthquake split the bottom of the ocean in half.

"W-What is happening to me?" My voice trailed off while the ground shook harder, until a great push from below propelled me like a rocket back to the surface.

Catching my breath while paddling to stay afloat, I ran a quick check over my body, to make sure everything was where it belonged.

"What the flying banana?"

A bright golden dot pulsed right above my heart, in rhythm with my heartbeat, growing in size with every breath I took. The bigger the pulse, the stronger I felt.

"Woah, this is cool..."

I paddled faster, my arms moving at an incredible speed, and my body barely brushed the surface of the ocean as I swam back to the shore.

When I made contact with the ground, Dan and Mike ran in my direction. I jumped to the side to avoid their tackling.

"Go back in there!" Dan shouted, missing me by inches.

"We'll get you, nerd!" Mike added.

They stared at me, their eyes glowing like crazy, but I didn't fret. The more they tried to catch me, the higher I jumped, and managed a leap that sent me ten feet above ground. I floated in the air like a cloud, and the golden dot in my chest pulsed more strongly, casting a halo of orange light around me. I looked down at Kara's watchdogs.

"What's so funny?" Dan asked. "You think you can beat us?"

They both jumped at me, but their unsuccessful attempts left them panting and whining.

"This is the end for you, nerd!" Mike shouted from below.

When they resorted to firing at me to force me down, my shield of light diffracted their beams into harmless particles.

"Just wait until you come back here. Then you'll learn your lesson!" Dan shouted.

I laughed at Dan and Mike. Then I scanned the rest of the beach and spotted the crew of good memories. Evan and Susan had run first in my direction, followed by Miko, Sloan and Sky. Sky clapped and cheered, while Evan and Susan gave me the thumbs up. Miko and Sloan waved at me.

I waved back. "I'm okay, guys!"

"Come back down!" Dan screamed. Oh, he was pissed.

All fear had abandoned me, to be replaced by serenity. Just for fun, I fired at him and was glad to see my beams worked. He shrieked like a little girl. I didn't need chocolates to be strong. What a relief.

"You want some too?" I released my light at Mike who immediately ran away.

"Now you know what it feels like to have your butt on fire," I said.

"Here you are!" Kara piped up.

She flew above the ocean surface, wrapped in a halo of purple light, cast by a similar dot pulsing above her own heart.

I frowned. "This is so not what I envisaged."

"What, you thought The Mighty Listener gave you an unfair advantage? At last, my friend, we spend this time together, bound by light."

As she spoke, her facial expression changed, the muscles twitching in all directions, rendering a distorted image that made her unrecognizable, as if her skin melted like wax.

"What are you doing?"

"I am showing you who I truly am."

I remained still, steadying my breathing. "I still want to make amends to you," I said. "Will you accept my apologies, now?"

"I already told you what I thought of your lame apologies."

Her purple light pulsed more strongly, and her face completed its transformation.

I gasped. Kara didn't look like her old self anymore. She was my fifteen-year-old me.

"Wait, Kara!" I shouted.

"No, my name is Julie Jones," she said. "And I'm a scared little girl."

"Impossible," I muttered. "Oh no. My mind is tricking me again. I won't let you do this to me!"

The golden dot above my heart grew bigger by the second.

"I want to show you the world as I see it," my fifteen-year-old self said. "Overcome with nightmares of that fateful night."

"I'm sorry for being such a jerk and for hurting you. I didn't know then I had a problem, but I am aware of it and am working to better myself."

"Cut the crap, Julie Jones."

"No, I'm done beating myself up. If I stay stuck in a world of pain with you as my only companion, I'll never move on. This is goodbye. I won't forget about you, and will always love you."

She laughed. "This is pathetic! And you're spoiling all the fun! Now shut up and watch!"

"No! W-What..."

The halo surrounding me intensified until it became a thick wall of light. First I couldn't see past my hands, then my elbows, until the light consumed me completely and my vision blurred.

When the fog lifted, I had been transported to the front step of our condo by the water in Oceanside. I stared at the door, my fingers fidgeting by the side of my leg, and worked up the courage to ring the doorbell.

"Do it," my fifteen-year-old self, who was standing next to me, ordered.

Without further ado, I pressed the button.

Seconds passed, increasing my nervousness. I wiped my sweaty palms against my pants and took a deep breath.

The door opened but I wasn't welcomed inside the house. Instead, there were white corridors, and people in scrubs, busying themselves around a gurney on which Kara lay, a breathing mask over her mouth and nose. Her face was bloodied, and smeared with black dirt.

My jaw dropped.

"Come with me," my fifteen-year-old self said. "Let me show you what it truly feels like to be powerless."

I followed the gurney and entered the examination room. A nurse proceeded to remove Kara's clothes, while a doctor used his flashlight to check her eyes, then inspected the rest of her body, before hooking her to an IV drip, and other equipment keeping track of her vitals.

I was shaking like a leaf. "What is this?"

"You need to see what you did to her."

"I already know what I did to her," I said. "My heart holds the truth within, and you're only working to bring me down. But I won't let you!"

"Your heart holds the truth within... What a joke! You don't need chocolates to embrace the darkness!"

"No, this isn't a joke!" I rushed out of the examination room. "I won't give in to my fear."

Pacing through the hospital hallways, I looked for the exit, pushing open doors I thought would lead me outside, but I found myself stuck inside the examination room again, watching people hover over Kara, who remained unconscious.

"MAKE IT STOP!" I shouted.

My fifteen-year-old self laughed. "Why? This is so much fun!"

"You're the darkness that's driving me bananas!" I buried my head inside my palms and huffed. "I drank too much that night and blacked out. Even after moving to Los Angeles, I continued using mind-altering substances because I couldn't live with myself. But I know now what I need to do to fix myself. And you won't haunt me anymore."

"I didn't punch Melissa. You did."

"Yes, yes, I did," I mumbled. "Because your anger guided me."

"Powerful, blinding rage that's still within you."

"Let me out!" I pushed a nurse out of the way and jumped onto the examination table. "I need help. I've been lying for too long and let you control my emotions. But this is the end, Julie!"

"Oh you're funny! It isn't so simple, darling."

"Yes, yes it is!"

"Stop this insanity. You don't even know what you're doing."

"I don't want to feel this pain anymore. And I know what to do. I know how to get out!"

"Really, how are you going to get rid of your fifteen-year-old self?"

"By doing this," I replied.

The golden dot over my heart pulsed more strongly and brighter.

"You're acting stupid. And now you're showing off!"

Heat built inside my eyeballs and I released my beams into the room. The nurses and doctor screamed and ducked onto the ground.

"No matter what happens next, I stop this charade now. You're keeping me in a place where I never belonged. The Underworld isn't my grave. It never was."

"What, by hurting these innocent people?"

"I'm not hurting anyone here."

"Believe your own lies, then," my fifteen-year-old self replied.

"This is not a lie. Not anymore. You used memories to torture me; but all this time I was really fighting you. Your time is up. I am made of darkness and light, and today I choose to be light. And I love you, Julie. From the bottom of my heart, I truly do."

I spread my arms wide and closed my eyes.

"NO. YOU CAN'T. STOP THIS!"

"Watch me," I said. "I surrender. I live without fear of failure, and without doubt in my mind. I am imperfect, and I accept this simple truth. No matter my past,

I'm not shutting the door on it, and I don't regret it. Please, forgive me where I have been resentful. Help me to not keep anything to myself. Show me where I owe an apology and help me make it. Help me to be kind and loving. Remove worry or remorseful reflections. Help me to find hope even in the most hopeless situations. I am not alone and, as I grow, I give away the control and become open to living without fear."

"Noooooooo! You belong here with me!"

"No, I don't. I never did, and I won't fight you anymore. This is over."

The fifteen-year-old Julie kept screaming while thoughts flooded my mind: my relationship with Mark and how angry I felt when I punched Melissa; my desperate escape from Los Angeles and my arrival here; my former hometown with the high school of my childhood and the beach where Kara taught me how to surf; my crush on Dan and my broken friendship; and all the lies I told to save face. The denial and the anger, cunning, baffling, powerful, because I dwelled on the past, harbored resentments, and never let go.

"YOU WON'T LEAVE THIS PLACE!" my fifteen-year-old self said. "NOT WITHOUT ME!"

The ruckus the old Julie made inside my mind became softer as I felt the heat of love spread throughout my body.

My life wouldn't end with mistakes. I knew that now. I would survive this ordeal and return home to make things right with Mom and Dad, Mark and Melissa, Dan, Mike, Kara, Evan, Susan, Miko, Sloan, Sky and all the others I'd selfishly hurt.

"This is not how we finish this!"

"I'm not listening to you anymore." I reopened my eyes, casting light from my heart inside the operating room, illuminating the entire space. The energy was so strong, it swallowed everything.

"What are you doing?" my fifteen-year-old self cried.

"My heart holds the truth within. And this truth isn't fear. It's unconditional love. I make peace today."

The hospital room holding Kara's body disappeared and I returned to my orange cloud of light, floating above the ocean.

"And now, I'm fixing this for good," I said.

The light continued to pulse, spreading across the sky, down to the water, onto the beach and further into Oceanside. Rays of light wiped away the darkness and the storm dissipated, as the safe haven of my childhood reverted back to its original state, the way I remembered it when I used to tame the waves, run barefoot on the wet sand and bask for hours in the sun.

"Noooooooooooooo!" the old Julie's voice faded into the background.

My light was bold, strong and beautiful, like the flames of the fire Evan had once lit in the Cave.

The silhouettes of Evan, Susan, Sky, Sloan and Miko were profiled on the beach, along with Kara, Dan and Mike.

I smiled and waved at them, and they waved back. They all looked so happy together.

I descended to the ground to be with them.

"You did it!" Evan cheered and ran toward me to give me a hug.

"Woooohoooo!" Sky and Sloan screamed in unison.

Susan and Miko joined the embrace, while Kara, Dan and Mike stared at us with grumpy faces, but without any angry glow burning in their eyes.

I looked at the ocean, so inviting, just the way I remembered it from my surfing days.

"Ready?" The Mighty Listener's voice popped into my head again.

I nodded. "Yes, the spider is finally dead, and I'm not stuck in its web anymore."

My return to reality brought me back behind the wheel of the Bubble, on the lot behind the one-dollar store. I patted myself down, just to make sure I wasn't stuck in an alternate universe.

"Shizzle," I exclaimed.

Inside my purse I found the items I had stolen.

"These I need to return pronto."

I checked myself in the rearview mirror. I looked tired, with eyes puffed out and my skin as white as a ghost. I reapplied some foundation, made myself presentable again, and exited the Bubble.

The clerk behind the checkout register stared at me in disbelief.

"You said you did what?" he asked.

"I took them without paying. And it was wrong. Awfully wrong. I'm sorry. I was a jerk, and here..." I handed him a twenty-dollar bill. "This will cover the damage caused."

"What damage?"

I shook my head. "You know, if you want to call the cops, that's fine with me too."

"I don't understand what you're saying..."

"Come on, take it!" I wiggled the bill in his face.

"Okay, but I will have to talk to my manager about it," he replied in a shaky tone.

"Do whatever needs to be done." I leaned against the counter and pulled my cell phone.

Blip blip.

"What can I do for you?" Didi asked with her computer-generated voice.

"Call Dad," I ordered.

A NEW BEGINNING

Downtown Los Angeles, 9 A.M. on a Saturday, one year later...

A group of approximately fifteen people gathered in a circle in a quiet church basement. Once everyone sat down, I looked at each member of the audience and smiled.

"Hi, my name's Julie, and I am an addict," I announced.

"Hi Julie!" everyone said.

I felt nervous. Speaking at meetings wasn't easy, but I knew I was safe there, and could freely open my heart without being judged. My sponsor, who sat next to me, gave me a nod of encouragement. All eyes were upon me, and I took a deep breath.

"Today I'm celebrating one year clean," I said.

"Whoo!" the crowd clapped and cheered.

"I couldn't believe I had a problem," I continued. "My addiction fought in the background for absolute control. I had developed over the years a mental obsession so powerful I lost track of who I was. As a result, my life became unmanageable. My destructive anger was a direct consequence of the darkness, following me like my own shadow everywhere I went." I paused and browsed the faces in the audience. "Because I was afraid to ask for help.

"I burned many bridges. Like many have shared before me, I never felt like I belonged, and couldn't maintain any sort of friendship or relationship. I was a solitary bird, uncomfortable in my own skin, and unable to understand my purpose on this planet. All I knew was hating and self-loathing. But I found my purpose by coming to meetings and telling my story."

My sponsor gave me a slight pat on the back as I exhaled.

"There were moments when I prayed to be gone, to fall asleep and never wake up the next morning. But every day the sun rose, and I set myself in motion. And every day felt like torture to me. Like a mouse trapped in a maze, I couldn't find the exit."

My eyes locked with one member of the audience, who nodded at me. Mrs. Potts. I smiled at her and she smiled back.

"I fell in love, didn't get loved in return, and hated the whole world because of it. I turned my back on my best friend. All this chaos, because I never felt good enough. I tried to prove to everyone I was the best, the smartest, the most adventurous. Mostly, I tried to prove to myself that I was great. But I never believed it. I always believed I was a piece of crap."

Tears welled in my eyes, and I choked on my words.

"I'm sorry. This is really emotional for me..."

"It's okay, take your time," my sponsor said.

I cleared my throat. "Okay. Alcohol and drugs gave me the relief I so desperately needed. For the first time in my life, I felt like I could conquer the world. I was whole at last. I had found my purpose." I chuckled. "It was all a lie. An illusion. My addiction grew and pushed me into a corner. I lied. I lied to myself and to everyone around me, and as a result I hurt people's feelings."

More tears flowed and my sponsor handed me a tissue.

"I got drunk for the first time at fifteen years old, but the mental obsession had already taken hold of me way before I touched my first drink. I was insatiable. I wanted more, always more, and the hole in my heart was never filled until I shushed my feelings with alcohol and drugs. My best friend was a victim of my reckless behavior. And I never forgave myself for hurting her."

I patted my eyes dry with the tissue.

"I thought the change of geographics would change me. I decided to become a new person, and buried bad memories very deep. Meanwhile, my addiction held my hand, and took me down an even more painful path.

"My anger issues worsened, and every time I got in trouble, I always ran away. After all, I was the only one who could fix the mess I created, and the best option was to sweep everything under the rug and start fresh someplace else.

"Little did I know I was striving to die as quickly as possible, despite pretending on the outside that everything was golden. When my ex-boyfriend broke up with me, he said I had issues. It felt pretty surreal, because we drank and did drugs together. I was his guinea pig when the time came to try out new stuff."

The audience laughed.

"According to him, I was doing too much. But I never felt like I was doing enough. I couldn't live without alcohol and drugs! My addiction told me everything would be okay. I'd be safe if I kept using. I believed for so long I was a victim and the world was out to get me. Not the other way around."

I sniffled.

"I got in trouble once more and ran away. Then, as a solution to my problems, I decided to get high. I passed out hard. While I was under, long forgotten memories haunted me. I traveled back in time and faced my demons, mostly my angry fifteen-year-old self. During that introspection, the drugs came in the form of magic chocolates supposed to give me superhuman powers. But these chocolates really gave me more pain. The truth was tough to swallow. I never thought I'd make it out. I prayed for redemption and begged for a second chance."

People in the audience nodded.

"After I came to, I dealt with my parents, cops, and rehab. Instead of going to jail, I made a deal with the judge to get clean. My counselor checks on me once a week, making sure I'm sticking to the program. And today, thanks to your help, I celebrate one year."

My sponsor gave me a gold coin and hugged me.

"I'm proud of you," she said.

"Thanks." I turned to the audience. "It took me a while to understand I had to change. I replaced my fears with love. I accepted I was an addict, and that my stubborn will would take me nowhere. When that moment of clarity everyone talks about came, it took only thirty-two seconds. No more, no less. Thirty-two seconds to turn my life over and surrender. Once I admitted complete defeat, I found freedom, and my life finally made sense. Thanks for listening."

After the meeting, my sponsor drove me to Oceanside, where I was supposed to meet with Kara to make amends. I hadn't seen her since the accident.

The whole drive was pure torture. I dreaded the moment I'd ring the doorbell and face Kara's mom, then Kara herself. Although I had prepared myself for this encounter, I couldn't shake off the anxiety that was crippling me from head to toe.

My sponsor looked at me as she put the car in park.

"You'll do great," she said. "Remember to breathe. And I'll be there if you need me."

I nodded.

The distance from me to the door stretched as I took steps toward the house. My sponsor walked behind me, offering this extra layer of comfort I so desperately needed.

My finger aimed at the bell. I took a series of deep breaths before pressing the button.

Seconds felt like hours, then the door finally opened. Kara's mom smiled at me.

"Darling, it's so good to see you." She pulled me to her in a hug I never thought would happen. I expected a slap in the face.

Kara waited in the living room on the couch. I was such a nervous wreck, I broke down.

"It's okay, Julie," she said. "Come here."

We hugged like we had never hugged before. I cried on her shoulder, repeating over and over how sorry I was for all the pain I had put her through.

"It should have been me," I blurted between sobs.

Kara held me tight. "It's not your fault," she said. "We were all drunk that night."

"Why didn't you say something?"

"What for? To punish you too?" She smiled. "I always loved you, even when you were mad at me. We grew up together. You were the little sister I never had. How could I stay mad at you because you did something stupid?"

"I-I could have killed you!" I cried.

"And you didn't. Despite all the blame you're casting upon yourself, you're not a bad person, Julie. I hope you know that."

I nodded, sniffling back tears.

"I didn't love you enough. I was selfish."

"Stop. You loved me. And you still care about me today, which to me is a sign of love. You weren't yourself, and the past cannot be changed. But today, you showed up, and guess what? I'm ecstatic to see you."

I hugged her again, crying on her shoulder.

"Acceptance is the key to forgiveness," she said.

I smiled at her.

I continued to make amends to all the people I had treated badly. Sky and Sloan welcomed my apologies, although they didn't feel I had caused them a ton of harm, because we weren't that close in high school.

Miko told me she had dreamt about me, and knew I would come to see her. To this day, I don't understand how she felt a connection to me, but our friendship has blossomed into something extraordinary. And her English has improved a million times too.

Susan gave me a hug that lasted an eternity. We reminisced about high school, and laughed about our shared infatuation for Dan. She is still a Goth freak.

After looking for Evan for months, I finally located him in New York City, where he goes to school studying fashion design. He invited me to spend a week with him, and we did all the touristy stuff. He acted so kind and loving. I couldn't believe it. When I asked him what color he'd choose for a rain poncho, he replied: orange because it's a conversation starter (and also because the rain isn't color racist).

My attorney Richard Gold gave me his usual pat on the shoulder, told me he was just doing his job, and was happy to see I was doing well.

Melissa didn't return my phone call.

Mark wished me good luck.

Michael never responded to my emails.

Dan accepted my apologies and asked me to keep in touch.

Mom and Dad didn't disown me, but restricted my cash flow. With them, "I'm sorry" didn't do the trick. I had to prove on a daily basis I could be trusted again.

Last, but not least, the most important person I made amends to was myself. As I stood in front of the mirror and stared at my reflection, I saw a girl who had a lot to live for. The shackles of the past didn't keep me prisoner anymore, and memories weren't daggers, but mere points of reference.

I strive to do the next right thing, and live a happy and healthy existence. Every day comes with its share of good and bad, but I choose to focus on the positive. Life is full of surprises. Now that I don't shush my feelings with drugs and alcohol, I can enjoy every minute I'm awake, and cherish simple moments with friends and family.

Most importantly, I don't hate myself anymore.

Every time I drive by a one-dollar store, I want to go inside and find the old lady who gave me the chocolate that put a serious dent in my roller coaster ride. But I know she'll find me if I ever need help again. She truly is my guardian angel.

As a one year anniversary gift to myself, I decided to get a tattoo of the number thirty-two, with the skyline of my hometown, Oceanside, and white roses to symbolize my new beginning. Mom wasn't too happy with my decision but she understood. I look at it every day, and remind myself I'm only thirty-two seconds away from destroying everything I worked so hard for.

Or I can continue the journey and keep improving, one day at a time.

POSTSCRIPT

Addiction comes in many shapes and forms. Always insidious, the mental obsession takes hold of the mind and drives addicts insane. Julie's tale is one of many, not worse or better than stories shared in rooms all over the world by recovering addicts who seek a new way of life, away from the pain and suffering they caused to others and, mostly, to themselves.

Julie would like to thank the author of this book for helping her write her story. She'd also like to thank the readers for taking a huge part in this strenuous but beautiful process that is her recovery. Last May, Julie graduated top of her class at UCLA and received her Bachelor of Arts. She is planning to go to law school in the Fall.

AUTHOR BIOGRAPHY

Johanna K. Pitcairn has dreamed of becoming a writer since childhood—authoring her first novel at the age of nine, and countless poems, stories, and screenplays by the age of seventeen. Later, rather than pursuing a career as a director and screenwriter, she decided to go to law school, driven by her father's opinion that "writing does not pay the bills."

Ten years later, she moved to New York City, which inspired her to go back to the excitement, wonder, and constant change of being a writer. Pitcairn is a huge fan of psychological-thriller novels and movies, and delves into her hopes, fears, friends, enemies, and everything in between in her own writing.